THE MOGUL: LEONARD

LOS ANGELES BILLIONAIRES SERIES
BOOK 4

ERIKA VANZIN

Edited by
STACI FRENES

Edited by
ANNALISA CORSI

ISBN: 978-1-958824-17-7 (Paperback)

ISBN: 978-1-958824-18-4 (Hardback)

For April, who taught me how to spank the mint.

1

LEONARD

I walk into the conference room, and every head turns toward the door I slam behind me.

"Aren't you a ray of sunshine this morning!" Patrisha, or Trish, as we all call her, jokes about my not-so-nice attitude.

"The air conditioning has been broken since Friday, and nobody has come to fix it!" I complain as I sit down at the table for the meeting.

Joel, the CTO of Walton Tech, Benjamin, the financial advisor, and Oliver, the head of the developers, are already comfortable in their chairs next to Trish, head of finance at my company.

"It's the weekend. What did you expect?" Benjamin chuckles.

"That someone does their job and comes to fix this

thing, so other people don't die coming to work." I open my laptop and start to go through the agenda for this meeting.

Trish rolls her eyes and smiles. If the people in this room weren't my most trusted friends and employees, I would have fired her on the spot for rolling her eyes at me. But every single one of them has been with me since I founded this company, and I wouldn't trade them for anything in the world.

"It's the weekend. They assume nobody is here to complain," she reasons, arching her perfectly manicured black eyebrow at me. She is always the one with no qualms about calling me out for my shitty attitude that sometimes slips through the mask of the emotionless tycoon.

Today, I'm not in the mood for any objections. "Well, they assume wrong. It's June first, and it's almost seventy-three degrees outside at nine in the morning. It will be hell in this room with the floor-to-ceiling windows facing south." Downtown Los Angeles is not known for being one of the coolest places on earth.

"Then let's get started and speed up this meeting so we don't cook in here all day!" Joel chimes in, and everyone except Oliver smiles.

I want this meeting to go smoothly, too, but I'm not sure about the short part. The truth is that the air conditioning has nothing to do with my mood. We are here today to discuss whether the acquisition of HD Security is a good thing for this company or not. Walton Tech is the worldwide leader in cybersecurity; HD Security is an up-and-coming startup that handles security hardware. We handle the software; they handle the hardware. It's as simple as that.

But nothing is simple when it comes to acquiring a company. First of all, they are a startup, and we need to be sure it's not just a fluke. Most of the time, they have a shiny facade, but if you dig deeper, you discover it's just that: a facade. Full of debts with no solid plan to grow into a reliable company.

Walton Tech is my most treasured jewel. It's the first company I founded when I dropped out of college and the one I love with all my heart. I have founded fifteen other companies since this one, but none compare with the work, effort, and sentimental value I put into this company.

"Are you sure you want to rush through something so important?" I arch an eyebrow toward him while my mouth curves into a smile.

I trust Joel with my life. I know he is as invested in this project as much as I am, and I know he is teasing me.

"I already told you. I'm on board with this acquisition. It's the best thing we've done since you funded this company two decades ago. There is nothing to discuss. We should just go for it!"

His enthusiasm is what made me choose him twenty years ago. He's never lost the optimistic attitude of the guy who's barely a couple of years older than me but has the vision of a seasoned CTO in this industry. We grew up with this company, and he knows the ins and outs of it as much as I do. If he's this attracted to this merger, it means he's already seen at least half a dozen new ways to grow Walton Tech to new heights.

Benjamin and Trish chuckle, used to his overexcitement, but Oliver is gloomier than usual. What got into his pants today?

"'Just go for it' is not exactly what I call a winning strategy for an acquisition," I chuckle, and most of my tension slips away.

I have the best people working with me. I need to keep my mind on these steps, and everything will be fine. As it always is. I started from nothing and built an empire with the help of these people. I shouldn't be nervous about what is coming next. We are a great team, and it shows.

Some people call me arrogant, but I'm not. I'm just aware of our potential, and I take advantage of every single skill we have.

"Think about all the new potential markets we can reach. They have impressive new technology they're developing. I was already looking into it because I believe this is where we're heading in the next few years, but I haven't seen anything this advanced," he explains.

"So why aren't any of our other competitors interested in it?" Oliver asks, annoyed.

His tone doesn't faze Joel but I give him a stern look, and he has the decency to look down. I don't know why he is so pissed off today, but he doesn't need to be rude. I'm a piece of work, I admit it, but he was plain mean, and I don't like it.

"Because they play it safe with the technology they have. They're making money from it and trying to milk the market the safest way they know how," Joel explains.

"Maybe because it isn't safe to change," Oliver scoffs.

"He's not completely wrong." I play the devil's advocate and support Oliver's concerns, even if I do want to throw him out of the room until he calms down a bit.

"Yes and no. HD Security has a new approach that fixes most of the issues other companies have with the new hard disks," Joel insists.

"Most of the issues are not *all* the issues," I point out.

Joel nods, but he doesn't lose his grin. "True, but they're minor inconveniences compared to the previous companies' results. They addressed the major concern about breaking down under high temperatures, and everything else basically just solved itself when they removed this issue."

It's a good start, I have to admit it. It's been a while since Joel started to talk about the new material used for hard disks that solves the problem of the size of the disk and the quantity of data you can store on it. It would allow us to build devices so small we can devise a new level of security cameras for use in the smallest spaces. And a lot more. That's just the tip of the iceberg this technology unlocks.

"What do you think?" I ask Benjamin, the financial advisor who has followed me since the first days of this adventure.

He was a bored forty-year-old working as a consultant for big companies and in search of new challenges. I stumbled into one of his conferences by mistake, and I found his ideas refreshing. I met him at the end of his session and blatantly laid out my idea for the company I was trying to build, adding that I didn't have money to pay him.

He laughed for a good five minutes over my lack of filters and then agreed to tutor me. In the beginning, he did it just out of curiosity. He thought I was a crazy dude who believed he would be the next Bill Gates. He stayed because I showed him I wasn't just a dreamer; I had a clear vision and a real path to follow.

"This company reached the pinnacle of success. You

can decide to stay on this level and work to keep competitors at bay, or you can decide to take a step forward and expand, reaching a new pinnacle." He never gives me a solution; he guides me toward an informed decision.

"The plan is to expand. I don't want this to become a stagnant company that becomes obsolete in a few years." The resoluteness of my tone doesn't leave room for arguments.

Benjamin nods and smiles. He agrees with me. I glance toward Oliver, and he is scowling at our financial advisor. My heart sinks a bit.

Oliver is not just the head of the developers' team. He is the co-founder of the company. We attended the same college, and while I dropped out, he got his degree. We stayed friends and shared the same dream about what we wanted to achieve. It was a natural progression to founding Walton Tech. He never wanted a political role in the company; he just wanted to develop the product. This is why only my last name is on the sign on the front door.

"Oliver, what are your concerns?" I go straight to the heart of the problem.

He scoffs for the second time this morning, and I have to bite my tongue not to point it out.

"You are going to put a perfectly healthy company at risk to buy a startup that's playing with new technologies nobody trusts just because you're bored?" He blurts it out like he was trying really hard not to tell the truth but failed.

We all stare at him dumbfounded. Where is this coming from? I can understand being careful, but this is just plain obstruction. I struggle to find the words to not cuss him out, and Benjamin comes to my rescue.

"There are ways to keep the two companies separate, so if one goes down, it doesn't drag the other with it. You don't have to worry about losing this company," he explains.

We all look at Oliver, trying to figure out why he is so against this acquisition.

"Yeah, sure. In the meantime, we're going to adapt the software to a new technology we don't know will work in five years because nobody has tested it for that long. And if it fails, then what? I put all the team efforts into something we have to trash?" he bites out.

"We are not going to change our existing product to sell the new one. We're buying a research team to build something new, not to replace the product we have," Joel blurts out like he is explaining it to a five-year-old.

Oliver is not stupid; he knows what our plans are, and this is why his fight is a bit concerning. It doesn't make sense.

"Yes, but my team has to write the software around that hardware," he counters.

"Are you worried about the workload you'll have to add to your team? We're going to give you new engineers. You don't have to worry about that." I point out the obvious.

He knows perfectly well this kind of job requires double the people we have right now and that I won't leave him stranded with double the work. I've never denied him new people when he needed them.

"Yes, whatever. You've already decided," he mutters under his breath.

Joel looks at me in disbelief. Trish, who stayed out of this part of the discussion, stares at Oliver with a raised judging eyebrow, while Benjamin looks at me with a worried expression.

I shake my head slightly, trying to tell him I will deal with Oliver in private and convince him.

"Let's take a step back. We're talking about problems before we've actually bought the startup. Can we just figure out now if it's a good investment first?" I try to bring this meeting back to a more civil tone.

I sigh in relief when Joel starts to ask Oliver some technical questions, and he answers in a civil manner. I glance at Benjamin, who gives me a small, reassuring smile.

This will be a headache for later.

After what seemed like an eternity, we are finally

ready to leave this room with a clearer plan as to what our next steps are.

"May I talk to you for a few minutes?" Trish asks me when the others have left the room.

I turn toward her. She is wearing a bright pink shirt that makes her dark skin stand out beautifully.

"Yes, sure. What's up?" I nod, leaning against the solid wooden table of the conference room.

"What's going on with Oliver?" she asks, curious.

I sigh. "I don't know, but I mean to find out. He was a pain in the ass this morning," I admit.

She chuckles. "You better do it fast because we're going ahead with this acquisition, and he needs to be on board."

I rub a hand over my face and sigh. "I know. Just another headache I need to deal with. What do you want to talk to me about?"

"I was going ahead with work for this acquisition, and looking deep into our finances," she starts to explain.

I smile. This is why I chose her. She is always a step ahead of everyone. She actually solves my problems before they reach me, and she comes to my office only when she has a solution, or she needs my help with a clear plan she has in mind.

"I can't find where fourteen hundred seventy-six dollars went. I swear I looked into it and tried to figure out why it's missing from the bank account and where it went, but I can't give you answers. Not with my technical skills. I need one of your tech guys to help me out with this," she admits and I know it cost her a lot. She is not a person used to failing at whatever task she has on her hands.

"It's a peculiar amount. Did you find the money missing? When did it happen?" I ask, more curious than worried about the ridiculous sum.

She shakes her head. "This is where it becomes funny. It's not just the entire sum. It's small amounts, never the same, during the span of a year. It's why we haven't noticed it before. If more than one thousand dollars goes out, we would notice. Fifty-six dollars in a month? That can be overlooked."

This is more worrisome. A chunk of money "lost" somewhere can be a bank error. It's rare, but it can happen, and it can be easily rectified. Many small amounts? It's probably someone taking advantage of Walton Tech.

"Do you suspect someone is stealing from the company?" I frown.

She shakes her head. "I'm not sure yet. That's why I need your guy. I want to check if there is something I'm missing." She smiles, reassuring me.

"If you want, I can take a look while we're here," I suggest, grabbing my computer, but I stop when she laughs.

"No, Leonard. Because of this meeting, I already stole Sunday morning time from my family. I'm not giving you my afternoon, too, " she points out.

I feel guilty. I never consider that they have families to return to, while I have no one waiting for me at home. They always say yes to my requests because they know I'm busy, but sometimes I would like them to tell me no, instead of agreeing to everything I suggest. I'm not doing it on purpose, I just forget.

"This is why I don't have a family. They require too much of my time," I half-joke. With my life, finding someone willing to spend long hours at home waiting for me is impossible.

She chuckles. "God, did she cheat on you with the pool guy to make you so cynical?" She's joking, not knowing how close that hits to home.

"My driver." I smile back, and her jaw drops.

"Are you kidding? I was joking!" She seems embarrassed by her lack of tact, but it's not her fault.

"They're now happily married with five kids. I'm not angry with them. But it opened my eyes to the reality of my life. If your significant other doesn't demand quality time with you, it probably means they're getting it from someone else," I explain.

She frowns. "This makes sense, and at the same time, it's the most depressing thing that could happen to a person."

"It's not sad. I'm perfectly fine with what I have."

"What? Your companies and more money than you could spend in a lifetime? That's not a life, Leonard. It's surviving." She smiles, but she seems sad.

"Go home to your family." I push her out of the conference room before this conversation becomes uncomfortable.

"Go home, Leonard. Go out with your friends, watch TV, do something. Don't focus on those numbers. They were missing twelve months ago; they can wait another day," she pleads.

I nod and smile to reassure her.

The truth is, without those numbers, I don't know what else I would do with my life.

2

ROXANNE

"**I** swear to God, if you don't stop jumping on my bed, I will kill you," I growl, hiding my head under the pillow.

My brain pounds from lack of sleep, and my eyes burn from staying up all night looking at my laptop. I need a little more rest.

"It's almost noon, it's sunny, and it's Sunday. We *have* to go out for lunch!" Spike cheerfully suggests sitting on my bed.

At least he is not making me throw up by shaking the mattress. Sometimes I really hate my roommate, but I can't afford to live alone.

"I went to sleep five hours ago, you dumbass!" I throw the pillow at him.

"Come on, Roxy. It's June. You should be baking in the sun on the beach, not hiding here like a vampire."

I open my eyes and glare at him. "First of all, my name is Roxanne, not Roxy or whatever your stupid brain comes up with. Second, I worked all night. I wasn't here playing video games with you idiots."

Spike rolls his eyes, and I want to throw the lamp at him. Sometimes I love him, but sometimes he is just insufferable. Lately, I lean toward the latter more often.

"Whatever. You know you can work during the day and not spend the night on your computer, right?" he says, even though he knows I hate it when he sticks his nose in how I handle my job.

"I work when the internet connection isn't shitty because you jerks play video games online," I spit out a bit too bitterly, but he seems not to care about my grumpy attitude. After all, he's used to my less-than-sunshiny demeanor when he wakes me up at ungodly hours.

"NASA could launch a space rocket with our internet connection, and you wouldn't know the difference," he points out. "But you like working nights because you enjoy playing the part of the badass hacker that kicks bad guys' asses."

I don't answer his accusation because, in part, he is right. I enjoy working during the night, but not because most of my activities are illegal, and I play hacker. I do it because it's the only time I get a bit of a break from the people coming and going through this house. I can't concentrate if people are shouting from the other room.

"Just go away, Spike. I'll take a shower and put on some clothes." I finally give up. I'm too awake to fall asleep again after this conversation.

He jumps out of bed with a grin on his sun-kissed face and pushes a lock of his blond curls behind his ear. His surfer body and killer smile are what get him all the girls. The blue eyes complete the panty-dropping picture.

I stroll to the closet and grab some shorts and a tank top to change into then head to the bathroom. I turn on the hot water and wait for it to warm up, but after a few minutes, it's still freezing.

The boiler broke down again, and we definitely don't have money to fix it. We can barely pay the rent and the bills, and the landlord is a lazy bastard who won't come out anytime soon.

"Fuck!" I scream, stepping into the cold shower.

"ARE WE DRIVING YOUR CAR?" SPIKE ASKS AS HE STEPS out of our apartment in Venice Beach.

We may be broke, but at least we have a great view. I share my apartment with four other people, and I'm lucky enough to have my own room like the only other girl, Candy. Spike has to share his with the other two guys, and the smell coming out of that room is unbearable. But at least we can see the ocean when we look out the windows.

"Do you have money for gas?" I raise an inquisitive eyebrow at him.

He stares at me like I've grown another head. "Do I look like someone with money to throw away on gas?" he points out.

"So, bus it is!" I singsong.

He huffs and pouts. "What's the point of having a car if you don't use it?"

I scoff as I step onto the strip of asphalt on the boardwalk. "Coming from someone who doesn't even own a car, that's rich."

"I barely survive paying the rent. I can't afford a car." He states the obvious, and I feel like a loser.

How did I end up at twenty-five, sharing an apartment with a bunch of other people who can't keep a job for more than a few weeks? Spike is twenty-six, stoned half the time, late for ninety percent of his shifts at the bar, and ends up getting fired twice a month. At least I have a job that I like. I don't get a lot of money out of it, but I'm able to save something every month for my retirement.

I keep quiet, not wanting to point out the fact that he shouldn't complain about not using my car. I'm relieved when we arrive at the bus stop, and we hop on the first bus heading downtown. The ride to the Grand Central Market is mostly silent. Spike knows that when he wakes me up like he did an hour ago, he needs to give me time to fully wake up or I'll rip his head off.

The Grand Central Market is bustling with tourists and some locals. The best part of this place is that food vendors do anything to attract customers to their stands, which translates into free samples to pick from the counter.

Spike and I come here almost once a week when we're low on food at home and don't have money for groceries. We walk from stall to stall and taste the goods without buying anything.

"Come on, guys. You're not even believable anymore," the guy behind the counter of our favorite Mexican place complains.

I stuff my mouth with a burrito sample and smile at him. "What do you mean?" I ask with a grin when I swallow.

He puts his hands on his hips and stares at me with a raised eyebrow. "Don't be a smart ass with me. You know exactly what I'm talking about."

"We're just two tourists deciding what we want to eat!" The smirk on Spike's face is irksome. Jesus! Could he be any more arrogant?

"Is that right? Considering I've seen you here several

times in the last year, that's a very long vacation you've got going on," the guy points out, and the tourists start to stare at us during the conversation.

Spike puts an arm around my shoulder. "Aren't we two lucky bastards?" His tone drips with annoying arrogance.

I roll his hand off of my shoulder and walk away from the stall.

"What are you doing? We could have snatched a few more samples," he complains, walking beside me.

"I'm not hungry anymore," I growl, and his smile disappears.

"Well, I am, and you ruined it," he spits.

"You should have thought about that before you acted so cocky. They're working their asses off to provide for their families. You shouldn't be so disrespectful!" I counter with more venom than I wanted to.

A glimpse of hurt crosses Spike's eyes, and I immediately regret being so harsh with him.

"Sorry, I just got a message from my mom this morning asking if I wanted to go back to their place until I find a decent job," I confess.

Spike stops dead in his tracks. "Are you seriously considering going back to the Pacific Northwest?"

Am I? I moved to Los Angeles to be near my sister, whom I found again after years apart. But she's married to a senator, always busy with something important, and I don't see her as much as I want to.

"I don't know. I barely make ends meet, and going back would mean saving some money," I reason.

His face drops, and he sits remarkably close to me on the bench beside me—uncomfortably close. It's way too intimate for two people who are just friends.

"If you need money, I can pick up a few more shifts at the café and help you out with rent," he suggests, nudging my knee with his.

I turn toward him and see equal parts hope and hurt in his eyes. I don't know how to react. I know his feelings for me are stronger than just a roommate's, even if he's never said it out loud, but he really is just a friend to me, and I have no idea how to make him understand I'm not interested without hurting his feelings.

"Spike, how long have you been working there?" I raise a questioning brow.

He looks a bit ashamed. "Three days."

"And how many times have you asked to switch shifts because you had other things to do?"

"Twice," he murmurs, knowing exactly what my point is.

"Shouldn't you work your regular shift before asking for more?" I point out the obvious, but sometimes he needs to hear these things out loud to understand the whole point of our conversation.

He lowers his head and says nothing.

"I haven't decided, Spike. I don't want to go back, but sometimes I feel it's the most reasonable choice."

He nods and smiles sadly. "I would miss you."

"I know, but I haven't packed yet. Don't ruin your day because of a text from my mom." I try to cut this conversation short before it makes us both uncomfortable.

"Okay, yeah. But I'm still starving, and you ruined my chance of getting another bite from that stand," he complains with a grin.

I roll my eyes at his dramatics. "Do you want to share a burrito? My treat."

His grin widens even more as he stands up and puts his hands in his pockets. "If you insist, who am I to deny you a meal?"

. I shake my head as I follow him through the stands and return to the Mexican one, this time to buy a meal.

When we finally get home again, I dread the moment we will open the door. I can hear from the landing of our apartment the shooting sounds from the video games on TV and the loud voices of the guys in front of it. A lot of them, if the noise is any indication.

Spike grins. I clench my jaw in frustration.

Every day is the same. A bunch of people I don't know invade our living room, play games, eat food, and drink beer. Four years ago, when I was twenty-one, it was fun, at least initially. Then it became old fast, and the fact that I can't kick them out drives me nuts.

I open the door and am greeted by at least ten guys I don't know. The stench of weed is overwhelming, and I make an effort not to yell at them.

Spike runs to the couch and slips between the two who are playing. They curse at him for distracting them and punch him in the shoulder. He grabs the joint they are passing around and takes a drag. In the corner of the room, I spot Candy's hurt face. Her smile dropped as soon as she saw Spike coming in with me. He has a crush on me and she has a crush on him, basically the triangle of unrequited love. Everyone is unhappy, and living together amplifies the feeling.

"You could at least bring some food since you're always here," I point out to no one in particular, but the disappointment dripping from each word is obvious to anyone listening.

One of the new guys grabs a bag of chips and waves it in my direction without even looking at me.

"Thanks," I murmur while I walk toward my bedroom.

I debate whether to stop by Candy and cheer her up. She is a sweet, shy girl in love with a jerk. I know it's not my fault that Spike likes me, but sometimes I feel guilty about the situation. She is staring at him with love-sick eyes, and I decide to leave her to it. I don't have the patience right now to deal with those two.

I close the door behind my back and lean on it. Shouts and laughs come from the other side, and I can feel the annoyance gripping my stomach.

Going back to my parents is not such a bad idea, after all.

3

LEONARD

"You have got to be kidding me," I whisper as I check the numbers for the billionth time.

Since Trish gave me the news about the missing money last week, I've spent every single free minute I've had digging into it. It vanished. Just like that, this random sum slipped out of our bank account and went nowhere.

I rerun the code I wrote to recheck our systems, but the results are always the same—no trace of the money.

I'm beyond pissed.

The problem is not the amount of money, which is ridiculously minor for a billion-dollar company, but the fact that we can't trace where it went is troublesome.

The fact that *I* can't find it is even more concerning. I created an empire in cybersecurity, for Pete's sake!

There is no way someone stole from me, and I didn't notice.

I stand up from my desk and walk to the floor-to-ceiling window facing downtown. There is something relaxing about watching the cars slowly moving around in the traffic without hearing the noise. I love this city, but the chaos is sometimes too overwhelming, even for someone like me who grew up in the chaos.

I turn back toward the desk and stare at the computer. Maybe it's time to admit defeat and ask for help from one of my employees. The idea of being unable to crack this problem is enough to lose sleep over. I'm the best in this field, and I have shown it time and time again. This is just bullshit.

"You look like you ate a sour lemon," the booming voice from the door diverts my attention from my computer.

Jack's imposing figure takes up the entire doorframe. He's the security guard I hired a lifetime ago.

"A lemon would probably be better than this headache." I smile at him.

He chuckles and I gesture for him to sit on the chair across from me. He hesitates for a second, then takes three long strides and sits down. We've had this conversation a million times before. He always points out that he shouldn't sit down and chit-chat during his shift, and I counter that I'm his boss and asked him to do it.

It took a long time to make him understand that it's fine for him to sit here with me for ten minutes.

"How's it going?" I ask, and watch his face light up with a smile that takes up his whole face.

"My little one is going to college this year." He beams like the proud father he is.

"Wait, what? Is she old enough for college?" How did she grow up so fast?

Jack chuckles. "Yeah, she's a smart one. She won't marry someone rich. She'll make her own money."

I'm glad to hear that. I'm not a fan of women financially depending on men. If a woman doesn't have a job to support herself, she'll never escape a loveless, abusive relationship. And men are such cowards that they count on that when they have nothing else to offer.

"I know she's a smart girl, but she was like five just a week ago." The last time I saw her, she was barely out of her diapers.

Jack's booming laugh fills the room. "You spend way too much time in this office, and you don't even realize that time is slipping through your fingers." He studies me intently with that fatherly gaze I'm accustomed to seeing from him.

I hired Jack when I started this company. He was fired in front of my eyes from the company that was remodeling this place. It wasn't his fault if the marble slab fell and broke, but it was easier to fire the Black guy who didn't go to college than the owner's son fresh out of his pristine education for rich white guys.

I tried to defend him to no avail, so I hired him on the spot and have never regretted my decision since.

"No! It's your kids that grew up way too fast."

He shakes his head. "When was the last time you took a Sunday for yourself?"

I think about it, but honestly, I don't remember. A few months ago, maybe? I'm sure I did it at some point this year.

"I have more pressing things to do." I smile, pointing at the computer, but I feel like a kid in the principal's office.

"Are you going to solve all your problems today?" He raises a scolding eyebrow.

"Probably not," I admit.

"Will they be there tomorrow?" he presses.

I look at my hands and smile. I know he's trying to make me understand that I don't have a life. But I'm okay with it most of the time.

"Yes, but if I solve some today, I have less to do tomorrow." I feel the need to find an excuse because, no matter what, his opinion matters.

He smiles sweetly. "Like you don't always have your hands full. You founded fifteen companies, for Pete's sake! You don't even know what it means to rest," he points out.

He's right. I always need something to do or feel like I'm wasting my time. It's why I don't have an active social life. I can't maintain a good relationship with my work schedule. My friends know they can see me only if they plan months in advance and if there aren't any major disasters when we have an appointment. On the other hand, if one of them is in trouble and needs my help, I will drop everything and run to them. I'm someone my friends can count on when they need me.

"Okay, you have a point, but tell me more about your kid. Where is she going?" I successfully divert the topic that was becoming suffocating and study the proud smile coming back to his face.

"Stanford. She got an early acceptance to Stanford. Can you believe it? It's an Ivy League college. She's so smart. She got it from her mother." He almost trips over his words, incapable of containing his excitement.

"I can believe that. I'm so proud of her." And I really am. I love his family like it's my own.

"Now she's waiting to find out if she has a full scholarship or if she'll have to pick up a loan. But all her brothers had it, so she's pretty confident that she won't have a problem with that." He seems a bit worried about it even though the smile never disappears from his face.

I make a mental note to look into it and step in if she can't get the full ride to her dream college.

"I'm sure she'll be fine," I agree with him and I can see his shoulders relax a bit.

Jack nods and looks at his watch. "Better go do my rounds. It's always a pleasure to chat with you. And go home, enjoy this sunny Sunday." He winks at me before standing up and disappearing behind the door.

I will leave my office but not go home. There is someone else I need to talk about this money thing. He won't be able to help me, but he will put my mind at rest. I text my driver to let him know to pick me up.

THE HELICOPTER RUFFLES THE PERFECT GRASS AS IT lands on his spot on the hill. I watch out the window, and I smile at the view of Raphael with his arms spread as if to say, "What the hell are you doing?" Right behind him, Silver is laughing and grabbing her dress to avoid flashing her underwear.

When the engine turns off and the blades slow down, I remove my headphones and step off the chopper. I walk to the backyard, where Raphael is shaking his head.

"You know I have a permit to land on this hill just because of my job, right? It's for emergencies, not for you to avoid the traffic," he complains.

"This is definitely an emergency." I grin at him.

He raises an eyebrow, scolding me, but I can see a

hint of amusement in his eyes. His wife, Silver, is not even hiding her amusement.

"What? Is someone threatening the life of the most handsome senator in the entire United States?" He drags me into a quick hug.

"Humble too!" Silver mocks him, rolling her eyes.

We walk to the patio near the swimming pool where they were having a relaxing time reading books, from what I can see. A grip squeezes my chest. Until five years ago, we spent Sundays discussing work and solutions to our problems next to this same swimming pool, but now he has a family, and I can't compete with that. Not that I feel the need to compete with Silver for my friend's attention, but it was nice to spend time with someone who could understand my massive problems instead of mulling them over alone in my office.

"No, someone is stealing from my company." This gets their full attention.

They turn around to look at me without a hint of a smile on their faces.

I motion for them to sit down in the lounge area so I can explain.

"This is confidential, so I count on your discretion," I say, even though I know they won't breathe a word about what I say here.

Raphael smiles. "You know so many secrets about

me you could drag me into the mud for ages if I spill the beans."

I chuckle. It's true. He has a couple of massive skeletons hidden in his closet that could cost him his career.

"Out with it. You're making me anxious," Silver presses me.

I take a long breath. It is difficult trying to summarize this mess without sounding crazy. "I'm trying to acquire a company to merge with Walton Tech."

Raphael's eyes widen, knowing what a big deal this is for me, but he says nothing, so I continue with my explanation. "We are looking into our finances to be sure everything is on track, and Trish noticed that some money is missing. It's been going out of our bank account during the last year."

"Are you serious? How much are we talking about? How haven't you notice it before?" Raphael fires with concern.

I look up into the clear sky and sigh. "One thousand four hundred seventy-six dollars."

They both stare at me with their mouth hanging open.

"That's it? Not even two thousand dollars? And you're making a fuss about *that*?" Raphael looks baffled.

"It's not the amount, per se, it's the fact that there's no trace of it. It leaves the account, and that's it." I can hear the defensive tone of my voice, but the way they're looking at me is unsettling. Like I'm crazy, and they don't know how to tell me.

Am I? Crazy about cracking a mystery and I don't even know if it will change anything in the company.

"What do you mean 'that's it'? It's not like money just disappears." Raphael frowns.

"That's exactly what happened. Not the entire sum, but small amounts from time to time. It got overlooked in the big scheme." It comes out like an exasperated groan.

"That's weird." The frown on Raphael's face deepens.

"Can it be something bank-related? You know, like a glitch or something," Silver suggests.

I shake my head. "I've looked into it, but I came up empty-handed. Jesus, it's driving me crazy."

"Why? It's just a small amount," Silver points out, and I understand her point. The first thing that comes to your mind is that it's a ridiculous sum for someone like me. I spend way more than that on coffee during the year. But this is deeper than just the amount.

"Because Walton Tech is the leader in cybersecurity, and the fact that someone is stealing under their noses is beyond concerning. Especially if nobody can come up with an explanation, it's a breach in security in their own systems." Raphael sums up the situation for me.

Hearing it out loud from someone else is almost terrifying.

"I see." Silvers seems concerned too.

Watching their faces darken with worry feels like a bucket of cold water getting dumped on my head. I haven't had the guts to admit how serious this situation is until I talked to them. I rub a hand over my face and try to calm down and be reasonable about it.

"It's so fucked up," I whisper, and Silver puts a comforting hand over mine.

"Who's working on it?" Raphael puts on his problem-solving pants and looks me dead in the eye.

"I'm handling it."

His brows shoot up in surprise. "And even you can't find a solution?"

I nod, knowing how much I failed this week.

"Have you tried asking Oliver for his opinion? He's a smart guy too."

I thought about it, but I don't know if I want to put this burden on him too. He's already reluctant about the acquisition. I don't want to worry him about this mess.

"He already has his hands full with the merger. He doesn't have time to look into this."

"You should ask Roxanne if she can help. She's a tech genius," Silver suggests, and I feel an uncomfortable sensation sneaking into my stomach.

Tech genius is an understatement. She is known in the industry as one of the best hackers in this country, if not the entire world. The problem is, I don't want to work with her.

"I can't give this job to a kid. It's a delicate matter. If anyone gets a whisper of it, I'm done," I say firmly.

Silver tilts her head and studies me. "She is twenty-five, far from a kid. And she's damn good at her job."

"She has pink hair. She acts like a kid," I point out.

"Just the tips," she counters.

"She does illegal things. I wouldn't count that as a 'job.'"

"She uses unconventional methods to obtain results, so what?"

"You talk like a lawyer."

"I am. Sort of." She grins.

I can't stop smiling. She is good at it, and it's a shame she can't work as a lawyer. She's one of the few people I know who had a really messed-up life before meeting Raphael.

"You know, Silver is right. When was the last time you saw Roxanne? Four years ago at our wedding? She's not the same kid. God only knows, I'm trying to keep the FBI away from her. They want to recruit her because they can't catch her." He sounds almost exasperated.

I chuckle in spite of what they're trying to do. There are a lot of reasons why I should stay away from Roxanne, and her being all grown up is only the tip of the iceberg.

"The answer is no, no matter what how hard you try to convince me." I stubbornly defend my position.

"Why? She's good and can help you!" Silver doesn't give up.

"Because I don't want to mix family and business." I come up with an excuse.

"Technically, she isn't family. Not yours, at least." Raphael raises an eyebrow, challenging me.

I would put that on the 'cons' list, but I can't tell him that.

"The answer is still no." My tone is so adamant they give up trying.

My life is already complicated as it is. I can't add a sexy sister-in-law to my never-ending list of problems.

4

ROXANNE

"Jesus, what are you wearing?" I ask my sister when I meet her in front of the fountain at *The Grove*.

I take in her pastel pencil skirt paired with a silky white shirt. This is definitely not the woman I remember when I was fourteen years old. But after eight years of not seeing her and another four trying to catch up, I realize we are two different people. Thirteen years ago, Silver and Roxanne didn't even have the same names. We *are* two different people in the same skin.

"What are *you* wearing?" she hugs me with a huge grin plastered on her flawless face.

I look down at my cut-offs and tank top. "What? You don't like my 'I don't give a fuck' print?"

"I was talking about the sparkly pink Converse, but

that tank top is also a concern. I'll have to explain to my husband's campaign manager why you're wearing that in my presence." She laughs, and I do it too, but inside I cringe about it.

It didn't occur to me that this could be a problem for her because she and her husband are public figures, and voters don't like insolent brats.

"If you want, I can turn it inside out," I suggest, but she waves off my concerns with a smile.

"Not necessary. The old bigots will get over it." She winks at me, and I see her bodyguard trying to fight a smile.

I'm still not used to her having security following her everywhere. I can't reconcile that my sweet big sister is a senator's wife. It's a wild twist in our life I would have never imagined.

"So, what do you want to eat?" she asks after the silence between us starts to become awkward.

Having your life on hold for eight years, far away from your sister, and then reconnecting as an adult isn't easy. Sometimes there are these long awkward moments that still remain after four years.

"I'm craving a Philly steak sandwich!" I say, but the truth is that I'm just plain starving. I haven't eaten since noon yesterday.

She studies me with worried eyes. "Are you eating enough? You look thinner than the last time I saw you."

"Jesus, you sound like Mom. Yes, I'm eating enough," I lie, knowing she will try to give me money like she has in the past.

"Well, get used to it because the next time you see her, she'll ask the same question," she states matter-of-factly as she walks toward the food court.

The place is bustling with tourists and we draw some attention from some of them. They may wonder what we're doing together, considering we are polar opposites. Or they're just curious about the bodyguard. That one is a huge attraction too.

We sit at the counter of the stand, and the guy at the grill double-takes when he sees us. He frowns and then goes back to his food, shaking his head.

"So, why are we here?" I ask after we order.

She frowns, glancing in my direction. "What do you mean? Can't I invite my little sister to lunch?"

"Not two weeks in a row. You never do that," I point out, and she seems genuinely confused.

"I didn't know I had a timeframe to consider before inviting you out."

"Don't be so dramatic. I find it strange that you can spend so much time with me. I know your life is a bit hectic."

Hectic doesn't even scratch the surface of the number of appointments she has. She was always someone who wanted to do something to help others, but this is ridiculous. Those who say politicians do nothing during the day have no idea what they're talking about. I'm surprised she has time to sleep.

"But, since you're asking, there is something I want to tell you." She smiles shyly.

"Here we go. I knew it!" I laugh.

"Stop it! It's not like I'm asking much of you." She gets defensive.

"I know, I know. I was joking."

She smiles at the girl behind the counter who is delivering our orders, and then waits for her to walk to the next customer before speaking again. I guess she is used to paying attention to her surroundings to avoid someone eavesdropping on her conversation. I can't even imagine living like that my entire life, scared that someone might use what I say to harm my family.

"We're going shopping for a party Raphael is hosting," she spits out in a rush. She knows I'm not too fond of those kind of events.

"No, we are not," I state resolutely.

"Please. Do it for me? Mom and Dad will be there, and they would love to spend time with you. I know you hate parties, but it would mean a lot if you come with me," she pleads, and I can see the doubt in her eyes.

She thinks I'll say no, and it hurts that she sees me like that. I know I'm not the easiest person to get along with, that I'm stubborn and always do what I want, but I have a heart too. She's family, and I would never let her down just because I feel itchy at the thought of putting on a fancy dress and high heels to spend my evening with a bunch of disgustingly rich old men who think they have the world at their feet.

"Okay, but I have the final say on the dress," I grumble.

She grins, and I can't stop my lips from tugging at the corners. She is so happy it's contagious.

"Thank you! I mean it. I owe you this one." She's sincerely grateful for something so small.

I know she still feels guilty for disrupting our lives and leaving our family in shambles so many years ago, but I never blamed her for what happened. On the contrary, I was proud of her bravery in doing the right thing, no matter what.

"We're going shopping, but you owe me a dessert," I say when we leave the food court and walk through the mall.

"That's why we're here," she says, waving at the Cheesecake Factory on the other side of the walkway next to the movie theatre.

"No Rodeo Drive today?" I raise a suspicious eyebrow.

She is used to fancy shops and luxury brands, while I'm the poor one who can't afford them.

"I thought you'd be more comfortable at Nordstrom

than those stuffy high-end shops." She frowns like she's wondering if she made a mistake.

I smile. "It's perfect."

She nods but says nothing. Sometimes we tiptoe around each other. We both grew up second-guessing our decisions because the cost of making mistakes was high. Being in the witness protection program for eight long years changes your behavior. And when you get out of it because the universe cuts you some slack, it's challenging to go back to being carefree. And it shows in how we behave around each other.

"So, do we have a theme for this party?" I ask, breaking an uncomfortable silence.

"It's Starry Night. We'll be dancing under the stars at the observatory." She beams like this one was her idea.

"Wow, fancy. I'll have to find something that lives up to the hype."

"I'm sure you'll be fine. You're gorgeous even in that ugly tank top." She chuckles, and I look down at my chest, pretending to be offended.

"What is wrong with it? It's hands down my best one!" It's not true, but seeing her face scrunch up in disgust is funny.

"Jesus. Your taste is worse than I remember," she teases.

I laugh out loud as the guard at the front door looks amused. Then he lands eyes on my sister and her bodyguard and almost trips to open the door for us. It's so strange to witness this behavior when I'm with her that sometimes I almost feel like I'm in a movie.

"Let's go get this dress and not talk about the fact that you probably sleep in your fancy businesswoman clothes," I mock, and she rolls her eyes.

It's not a very senator-wife reaction, but I like it when she loosens up a bit when we go out. She reminds me of my old sister.

IT IS ALMOST ANOTHER THREE HOURS BEFORE I RETURN to my apartment, but when I enter, I'm so exhausted I don't even have the energy to get angry at the usual players on the couch.

"I have cheesecake for everyone," I announce, putting the box on the table.

They all drop everything and run to the food.

"Jesus, are you people starving? Don't you have a home with food to go back to?" I mutter, feeling a bit of that disappointment sneaking in that I push down into my gut every time I come home.

Candy approaches with paper plates for everyone.

"Thank you." I smile at her, but she says nothing. She is always so shy that sometimes I just want to shake her to get a reaction.

"So, what's the occasion?" Spike asks while handing out slices to the other five guys who have been playing until five minutes ago.

I know he noticed the fancy bag with my dress inside it. He laid eyes on it as soon as I entered the room. Some suspicion and maybe a bit of concern crossed his eyes. He is not a fan of Raphael, my sister's husband, and he is slightly unsettled when I spend time with her. He says Raphael will find a way to drag me into a business that will land me in jail. I'm aware that Raphael's father is far from honest, and Spike knows it, too, but Raphael is a good guy. He is more than okay, or I wouldn't have let my sister marry him. I checked, and I found nothing wrong with him.

"I have to attend a fancy party, and I needed a dress. This is my sister trying to bribe me to go shopping."

The guys thank my sister with their mouths full of cheesecake, but Spike stops mid-bite and frowns. "And you agreed to go?" His voice has a shade of anger.

We've had this ongoing discussion ever since he discovered who my brother-in-law is, and it's becoming a bit uncomfortable.

"Of course, I'm going! She is my sister, and my parents will be there." The statement sounds a bit more frustrated than I intended.

The guys glance back and forth between us, and Candy lowers her gaze to her shoes, unsure what to do.

"You know you can always tell your sister you don't want to, right? She can't force you to go. You don't even like those events," he scoffs.

"Well, believe it or not, I want to go. I want to be there for her."

As soon as those words roll off of my lips, I realize they're true. I may not like that kind of event, but I love Silver and can't wait to spend the evening in her company.

"I'll come with you," he states like it's already decided.

My skin crawls at the idea. I don't want him there. He would ruin the night for everyone. He would make snarky, rude comments, maybe even make a scene, and I don't want that to happen. I can feel the embarrassment of showing up with him and it's so strong I almost feel guilty. I don't want to be like those stuck-up rich people who think they're better than everyone else and whom I despise, but I can't stop my heart from leaning that way.

"No, you are not."

"Why?" he challenges me.

"Because you're not invited, and I'm going alone." My answer is final, and he finally shuts up.

I grab a piece of cheesecake, the dress bag, and walk away before saying something I will regret.

It's time for me to find another place to live, even if I don't know how I'll afford it.

5

LEONARD

The limo line is endless. It seems everybody is here for Raphael's party, and maybe that's true. When the Senator asks you to attend a charity event, you cancel all your appointments and come in your best attire.

I study the parking lot from behind the tinted window. Leaving these comfortable leather seats and the refreshing air conditioning will take me a while. Mid-June weather will make us sweat in these tuxedoes, even with a pleasant breeze outside.

A loud bang from the left side of the car startles my driver, making him lose his usual poker face. I hired him ten years ago, and I haven't seen him smile once. Sometimes I wonder if he even has the muscles on his face to curve his lips upward.

I turn toward the noise and see a familiar rusty yellow Beetle parking beside the catering service truck.

"Jesus, is that thing still running?" I murmur to myself.

I notice the driver's eyes briefly meet mine in the rearview mirror. *Yeah, I know. I'm surprised too.* The last time I saw that car was four years ago at Raphael and Silver's wedding, and the most annoying girl was driving it.

As if I summoned her, Roxanne steps out of the car. First, her long, toned legs peek out of the slit in the fabric, her small feet wrapped in golden sandals. The rest of the lean figure follows, wrapped in a dress of the same color. She looks like a present ready to be unwrapped. Sexy as sin and with a regal bearing very few can pull off so naturally. It's like she owns the world, and she probably does. It's a shame that package comes with the most annoying attitude.

I watch her strut toward the entrance, her chin high, her strides long, and her long legs making more than a few heads turn.

By the time I finally step out of the car, she is already inside the garden, rocking the crowd next to her sister, Silver. She seems a bit detached, but the smile never leaves her face. These events can be very tiring, but they are also an excellent opportunity to revive those connections that are so useful in this environment.

I don't know what *she* thinks about them, though. She is not exactly a billionaire willing to open their wallet for a donation while discussing the most crucial work-related topics. She is probably here because her sister asked her to be, and is bored out of her mind. She probably already illegally obtained all the information she needs about the people here at this event. I'm surprised the FBI is not here to arrest her.

A small smile curves my lips at the idea of something like this happening tonight. Raphael is so deeply connected with the FBI that I doubt anyone will risk his wrath to get their hands on the little sister-in-law and famous white-hat hacker.

"Why are you smiling?" Harrison's voice penetrates my thoughts.

"I was thinking, how funny is it for Raphael to have a sister-in-law who can make his life a living hell?" I grin turning my head toward Harrison and his partner, Sienna.

"Who is she?" Sienna asks.

"The one in the golden dress next to Silver." I point at Roxanne.

"*That's* her? Jesus, she's grown up a lot since Raphael's wedding." Harrison's mouth is hanging open in surprise.

"Look at those pigs drooling all over her," Sienna points out with disgust.

I look past the two of them and see at least ten old

farts undressing Roxanne with their eyes. They could be her grandfathers, for Pete's sake! My gut clenches in an uncomfortable grip. She doesn't deserve those filthy eyes on her. Nobody deserves to be treated like a piece of meat ready to be devoured.

"You look like you want to murder someone."

I turn my gaze from the disgusting show toward Harrison, who has an amused grin on his face.

"Are you okay with the way they're looking at her? She's not a piece of cake to stuff into their filthy mouths," I point out.

My friend frowns. "No, I'm not okay with that, but I don't really want to smash someone's face in just for looking at her," he points out.

His statement unsettles me. I would do it because I know what thoughts are going through their minds at this exact moment. They're the same thoughts that have crossed my mind time and time again, and I feel guilty about them. She is a guilty pleasure a forty-year-old shouldn't indulge in.

"Well, I'll kick their asses if they try anything funny," I grumble.

"Who are we fighting?" Aaron joins us with Dakota at his side.

He is a famous producer in Hollywood, and his fiancé is one of the most promising actresses of our generation. He definitely gets what we are talking about.

A lot of men hit on his woman without any restraint, and he is doing a damn good job at staying out of jail.

"The pigs that are fucking Roxanne with their eyes," I point out, nodding toward the crowd.

"Jesus! She grew up," Aaron blurts out.

"She is gorgeous in that dress," Dakota adds, admiring her lean figure.

"Nobody is concerned about how they're looking at her?" I ask, frustrated.

All eyes turn toward me, and I feel suddenly exposed. Why am I so upset about it? I mean, I saw her once four years ago. *Just saw her?* My conscience reminds me of my faults.

"Yes, but it's not like we can cause a scene or gauge their eyes out," Sienna points out, and my friends look at me with curiosity in their eyes.

I look like a fool. "Okay, whatever," I grumble for the second time in a few minutes.

It's going to be a very long night. I usually try to enjoy these events, but I'm not doing well right now. Every time I'm in the same room with that girl, I become a mess.

"I'm going to drink something at the bar," I say stalking away without waiting for them.

I need to vanish for a few moments, before saying or doing something I'll deeply regret. I make my way towards the bar, but my path is abruptly intercepted by

Philip Sullivan. My mind, consumed with thoughts of Roxanne, had failed to register my surroundings. Now, it's too late to evade him.

"Leonard Walton! You're exactly the person I wanted to talk to tonight." He chuckles and extends his hand.

His handshake is unyielding, a reflection of his unflinching demeanor. Philip is a tycoon with an iron grip on the most lucrative oil-related companies in the United States, and he's a man of mystery. Speculations about his rise to power swirl wildly, but one thing is certain: crossing swords with him in a negotiation is a surefire way to end up on the losing side. He's a master at reducing opponents to tears, always getting what he wants.

This is precisely why I should steer clear of him, especially when my mind is preoccupied with a certain blondie sporting pink-tipped hair. The last thing I need is to be drawn into a business discussion with him.

"How come? Are you thinking about changing businesses? Am I in trouble?" I smirk at him.

Whenever we meet, we always engage in a playful dance, carefully balancing between teasing and delving into the heart of our conversation. We never reveal our intentions too soon, as no one wants to be at a disadvantage to the other.

"Why? Is there anything interesting I should know?

Are you branching out into my business…or, you know, some other area?" He raises a knowing brow.

He knows about HD Security. How the hell did he get this information? We kept everything under tight wraps. We haven't even discussed proceeding with the acquisition because we're still in the preliminary stage.

"I'm not going to involve myself in the oil business. Trust me, I don't want to have to negotiate contracts with you." I may have dodged the question, but I know he is not convinced.

His sharp gaze remains fixed on my face. The intensity of his scrutiny makes me feel uneasy, but I make sure to keep a smile on my face. Showing any signs of fear in front of him could be fatal.

Finally, a shark smile crosses his face. "I'm happy you chose not to cross paths with me. It would be a shame to squash your business. But don't worry, with anything else you'll be fine, as usual," he says and I don't miss the implication in his words.

My non-reply is confirmation for him. HD Security will be hearing from me as soon as I leave this place. I don't care if it's the middle of the night. We agreed not to utter a word about it. We signed a contract, and they breached it. I know my people didn't do it. I trust them with my life, so the information had to come from someone else.

Philip puts a hand on my shoulder and squeezes,

maybe for reassurance or maybe to let me know I don't fool him, but I'm happy when he excuses himself and leaves.

When I finally reach the bar, I'm more nervous than before—the Philip debacle has made me more upset than Roxanne's admirers.

"They let anyone come to these parties. I should tell my sister to be more selective with her guest list." Roxanne's voice brings me back to reality.

I turn toward her, leaning against the bar counter. She is even more gorgeous up close. She has a slight smile on her face, and I can't tell if the cutting remark is a serious jab or if she is teasing me.

"Yes, people with pink hair shouldn't be allowed in a grown-up place. Or the grown-ups should get a babysitter if they can't leave their kids at home." I grin, hoping she understands I'm joking and she doesn't get offended.

She rolls her eyes and smiles. "At least I'm a bit colorful. You're all dressed the same with freaking sticks up your butts. Do you all meet up somewhere to buy your identical tuxedoes?" she fires back.

She is a piece of work. I forgot how irritatingly teasing she can be.

"Right, and you're the one matching your hair with the car you drive. How can you even think about coming to an event like this in your own car?" I point out.

I'm not too keen on people trying to be unconventional just to rock the boat. You can have your own ideas and be an individual but show some respect for the ones putting their hearts into organizing these kinds of things —her sister, in this case.

"Of course, I should pay for my limo with the money I make enslaving my employees in shitty jobs that barely pay enough to support their families while I become a billionaire. Wait, that's you, not me. I don't have that kind of money, but I do have my dignity."

I feel the unease growing in my gut. How dare she judge me without even knowing me? She has no idea how I treat my employees, or she wouldn't say those things. She's just a kid playing hacker, thinking she's better than anyone here because she drives a shitty car.

"I can see you're still a brat." Gone is my playful politeness.

"Last I checked, you were the one being rude to me," she snaps, leaving all pretenses behind.

"And the last time I met you, *you* were the one acting like a spoiled teenager," I reply.

She scoffs, clearly offended by my statement.

"Sorry to interrupt this lovely conversation, but they're serving dinner."

Raphael's voice is like a cold shower. I suddenly realize I've lost my composure in a place full of people who know me and can tear me apart if I do something stupid, like fight with this girl.

It takes all my strength to get myself back in check and follow my friend to our table. Next to me, Roxanne struts with her chin high and long strides to keep up with us. God forbid she comes in second to someone.

When I look at the assigned places at our table, I lose my cool again. "Come on. Seriously? Next to her?" I ask Raphael, noticing Roxanne's name next to mine.

My traitor friend chuckles. "You're the only two singles. Do you want me to split up a couple?"

"I swear, any table but this," I murmur, but Silver can hear me.

"Don't be melodramatic. It's just a dinner, and, by the way, she's the only one here who even understands what you talk about. You're such a nerd, you could be from another planet. None of us understands when you start in with your commentary," she points out, not totally wrong.

Sometimes, when I start to rant about my job, I feel like a fish out of water. My friends lose interest after the first few sentences. Although they try to understand and ask me questions, it feels more like I'm teaching them instead of having a constructive conversation. Roxanne is probably the only one who can challenge me in that sense. When I glance toward her, I can see that she is trying to hide a slight smirk.

"Fine!" I give up and sit with Roxanne on my left and Silver on my right.

"And you can also talk to her about the problem you're having with your company," Silver drops with a wink in my direction.

I want to kill her. She did it on purpose. She suggested her sister a few weeks ago and didn't take no for an answer. I glare at her while Raphael clears his voice to hide a laugh.

"You have a problem with your company? What a shame you can't solve it yourself. Aren't you the big tech guru?" On my other side, Roxanne beams at my troubles.

Of course, she is enjoying every single moment of this conversation. She hates me; why shouldn't she be happy if I fail at something?

"I don't have a problem, and I certainly don't need your help," I spit rudely.

Her smile fades.

"Did you get to the bottom of it?" Raphael frowns, interested in knowing if there is some development I didn't tell him about.

I give him a scolding glance, hoping he drops the subject. But he doesn't and I feel obliged to give him an answer. "No, I didn't, but that's not the point."

"So, what is the point? Enlighten me!" Roxanne challenges me with venom in her voice.

I turn toward her and look her straight in the eye. "I

don't want to give a delicate job that could sink my company to a kid with pink hair who plays at being a hacker," I spit, and all the chit-chat dies around the table.

The fury that inflames her face almost knocks me out of my chair. A flash of hurt crosses her eyes before she can hide it behind her stony face. I feel like a complete jerk because I could have let her down with an easy lie, but nothing is easy when it comes to her. She makes me want to challenge and fight her every step of the way. My reasoning goes out of the window when it comes to interacting with her.

"Well, don't worry. I don't work for shitheads like you, so you don't have to ask me," she spits out before excusing herself to go to the bathroom.

And maybe that's the main reason I don't want to ask her. The fear of being rejected makes me a coward.

6

ROXANNE

"He's a jerk," I mutter after ordering a Cosmo at the bar.

The dinner was an awkward sequence of clipped sentences and long silences between Leonard and me. After his outburst, the tension at the table was palpable, and no one was up for a cheerful conversation. Luckily, that torture ended half an hour ago. Now, I must survive the rest of the evening, but at least I can avoid killing Mr. Jerk altogether.

"It must be pretty boring company if you're at the bar alone talking to yourself." A warm voice distracts me from my murderous thoughts.

As I turn towards the man, my gaze meets two stunning blue eyes. Taking my time to assess him, a smile slowly spreads across my face. He's handsome, with curly blonde hair and a couple of dimples on his tanned face. Though he's wearing a black tie, he's not in a tuxedo, which is a breath of fresh air. He exudes a surfer vibe that I find appealing. Maybe tonight won't be a complete waste after all, and I can let loose and have some fun.

"Worse, he's a pain in my ass," I admit.

His smile becomes almost shy, like he is embarrassed to be here with me.

"So, there is a *he*. Not my lucky night." His bravado fades a bit, making him almost cute.

"It's not what you think. I'm not linked to this guy in any way, but that doesn't mean he's pleasant company," I explain.

His smile comes back in full force. "So, can I offer you a drink?"

"I already have a Cosmo, but you can keep me company."

He orders a club soda from the barman, who brings my order. He leans on the counter, closing the distance between us a bit. He smells good too—something woodsy with an undertone of the saltiness of the beach.

"So, besides the asshole, are you enjoying the evening?" he asks.

"It's becoming more interesting by the minute." I nod, and his grin widens.

He sips at his soda and studies me. "So, what do you do here in Los Angeles? Are you an actress?"

"What gave you that idea?" I chuckle. I'm many things, but I'm sure as hell not able to act for a living.

He seems taken aback. "Sorry if I assumed that. You're very attractive, and I thought you were trying that route."

"Well, that's a bit sexist, don't you think? But thank you for calling me attractive, I guess."

He rubs a hand behind his neck and looks sheepishly my way. "It came out wrong. I didn't mean that an attractive girl has to be an actress. But I live in Los Angeles and all the good-looking girls I know are aspiring actresses," he tries to explain and somehow I get his point. Most of the waitresses I know in this city are drop-dead gorgeous and, as he said, aspiring actresses. I can't be mad at him for assuming it.

I also don't have to marry this guy. I want to have fun tonight, and I don't have to go home with him for that.

"I get it, don't worry. But to answer your question, I work with computers." I always use vague terms to describe my job.

Most people are content with my answer, and if they express further interest, I delve deeper into the technical-ities. However, often people lose interest in my explana-tions. But, when I come across someone who can match my knowledge and engage in a stimulating conversation,

I truly enjoy myself. Unfortunately, the person I am currently talking to is not one of those individuals. Despite my attempts to give him the opportunity to carry the conversation further, he smiles and nods without asking any more questions.

"What about you? What do you do for a living?" I try to keep the banter going, hoping to spark more interest.

"I work for my father's firm."

I wait for a further explanation that doesn't come. I guess neither of us wants to dig deeper into our personal life.

"Do you want to dance?" he asks when the song switches to a slower one, and the silence between us becomes awkward.

I suppose it's better than avoiding a conversation that didn't take off. I don't particularly feel the need to learn more about him. I'm not even bothered that he didn't ask for my name or offer his own. Plus, I can feel Leonard staring at me from the other side of this dimly lit, crowded place. Sulking like I was the one offending him somehow and not the other way around. Fuck Leonard, I'm having fun tonight.

"Yes, sure!" I smile and guide him to the middle of the dance floor.

The crowd is entirely different from the one you would find in a club. Nobody is sensually grinding against each other. The soft jazz sound is perfect for a slow dance.

The surfer boy wastes no time and pulls me close to his chest, placing a hand on my lower back, where my exposed skin is more sensitive. He holds me tightly, and I struggle to keep my distance and avoid getting stuck to his chest.

We sway to the rhythm of the orchestra, and I look around at the crowd surrounding us. The older couples keep a respectful distance from each other, and I feel self-conscious about how we appear to prying eyes—all over each other.

I push my hands against his chest and force a few inches of space between our bodies. It doesn't last long. In fact, his head lowers on my shoulder, and his hot breath hits the exposed skin. While I usually appreciate this closeness with a hot guy, this feels more creepy than intimate. The last straw is his hand making its way onto my ass, squeezing lightly.

I push him firmly and look at him dead in the eyes. "What the hell are you doing?" I murmur to avoid attracting attention.

He smirks. "Come on, don't play hard to get. I don't like that game."

Anger fills my chest, and it takes all my strength not to slap him. "I'm not playing anything. I don't want your hands on me. I agreed to one dance, not being groped in the middle of a crowd."

He chuckles, disbelief covering his face. "You don't dress like that and not want to be fucked. You're begging for it."

I scoff. "Are you serious right now?"

"You're a tease, you know that?" He sounds annoyed.

At this point, we are not even dancing anymore. He dropped the nice mask, and now he's just plain disappointed I'm not on my knee sucking him off. What a prick. He doesn't even deserve my time. I step back to turn around and walk away from him, but he grabs my wrist and forcefully drags me to his chest.

"Don't be stupid. Do you want to ruin your sister's party?" he snaps.

So he knows who I am. Was that his plan all along? To fuck Raphael's sister-in-law to get close to him? Or to get revenge for something?

I don't have time to ask him because Leonard's deep voice interrupts our conversation. "Let her go now, or I'll break every single finger in your hand before I start on the other bones."

I turn around, and Leonard's serene face starkly contrasts with the menacing tone of his words.

The guy scoffs. "Do you know who I am?"

Leonard's lips tip up on a corner. It's the closest I've seen to him smiling.

"I know exactly who you are, and I'm not sure your daddy will be fine with you pissing off his best client." He tilts his head toward a white-haired man with a scowl. "You fucked and dumped his daughter, am I correct? He'll be happy to run to your father and tell him you're groping a woman against her will. The senator's sister-in-law, no less."

The surfer boy pales, and his mouth scrunches in a grimace. He turns around and walks away without a word or a glance in my direction.

I sigh in relief. "Thank you for helping me out. I'll stick close to the bar from now on," I tell Leonard, peeking up at his eyes.

He is worried. He doesn't show it through his relaxed posture and hands in his pockets, but his eyes are loud and clear.

"Or you can dance with me," he suggests.

His proposal floors me. As of an hour ago, he couldn't stand my presence.

"Why should I?" I frown.

"Because right now, people are noticing that something's going on. We could dance, and it would seem like I'm taking over, wanting to dance with you. Or you could storm off, and people will be speculating about what happened and stirring up drama at your sister's party."

I look around and see what he means. Other guests are starting stare at us.

"Fine." I give up.

He extends his hand towards me, and I hesitantly take it. His hand is large and rough to the touch. I had always assumed he prioritizes his appearance, but feeling his calloused hand surprises me. He doesn't spend money on something as frivolous as a manicure.

The other hand reaches behind my back, placing its warm imprint at a respectful distance from my butt. He keeps a safe few inches between us, but I can feel the heat radiating from his body and the manly scent of his cologne. There is something powerful and protective in the way he is holding me. I feel small and safe in his arms.

He guides me, swaying to the music and giving me the impression he knows exactly what he is doing. How many women has he held like this at parties? And why is the thought of his hands on another woman's body bugging me?

My free hand travels up his firm arm and stops at his wide shoulder. Every movement enhances his toned body. I've never seen him without clothes, but I can make out the shape of his pecs through the tight shirt hugging his body. *I should stop staring at his chest.*

I look up, and I realize I made a mistake. His grey eyes roam over my face, hungry and desperate to go lower, so much lower on my body. His lips are set in a thin line, his brow furrowed in what seems like concentration, but it's the tick in his jaw that gives him away. He is trying to restrain himself, but from what? Barking at me? Running away from this dance floor? Kissing me? Every one of those is a possibility because his expression is so hard to read.

He lowers his head and our eyes meet. Am I standing on my toes? Perhaps to see the storm brewing in his beautiful eyes. He is so close I can feel his minty breath on my face. His toned chest is pressed against mine while my other arm has slipped up his shoulder, and now I'm cupping his neck, his short hair tickling my fingertips.

Since when do we get this close? I think as he places his other hand on the bare skin of my back. It's both infuriatingly protective and perfect, leaving me almost breathless. Leonard is someone I shouldn't have strong feelings for, but right now, I can't imagine being anywhere else. His embrace makes me feel like the most precious piece of art in the world. It's as if the world could fall apart around us, and we'd be perfectly fine.

We are still dancing for the sake of my sister's party, but I'm not sure what's going on between us. It's like when we touched, we altered the chemistry in our bodies, making it impossible to pull apart.

"Sorry to interrupt, but I need Roxanne to come with me." Raphael's voice is like a slap in the face.

Leonard tightens the grip on my body for a second longer before diverting his intense gaze from me to his best friend. When reality hits him he takes a step back and nods. I'm not the only one that got lost in the moment.

When I finally dare to look at Raphael, his expression is a bit suspicious. Did he notice the tension between us? I don't even know what it was, and I definitely don't want to give him an explanation about why I was all over his friend. Then a smile appears on his face, and his eyes soften, as they always do when he looks at me.

"Thank you for saving her from that prick. I was ready to make a scene if he didn't let her go," he says to Leonard, thanking him for his intervention.

I guess I don't have to explain myself after all.

"You should really check who you invite to these parties." I grin at him, but I glance sideways at Leonard. His lips curve in a small smile at my remark about what I told him just before dinner.

"It's nothing; I would have done it for anyone in that situation," he minimizes, and my heart sinks.

If I felt special in his arms, even for a moment, that feeling sure as hell goes down the drain with that comment.

I smile and nod in his direction without saying a word before following Raphael toward my sister.

"Come on, please, don't give up now," I murmur, leaning my head on the steering wheel and turning the key in the ignition for the tenth time.

I'm starting to regret turning down my sister's offer for a limo. Betty is the best car in the world but sometimes she dies at the most inconvenient times. Like now, at two in the morning, when I'm miles from home and wearing a fancy dress with heels that are killing my feet.

The parking lot is almost empty; just a few limos still linger, waiting for those who decided to stay longer than usual.

"Please, I don't have the money for an Uber!" I plead.

"Do you need help?"

I squeal like a little girl, startled by Leonard, who snuck up from behind without me noticing. "Jesus Christ, you scared the shit out of me," I say, turning around and facing his scowl.

Does he ever look at someone without that judging face? He doesn't even acknowledge my outburst but looks at me, waiting for an answer.

"No, I don't need your help," I grumble while trying again—and failing—to start my car.

He raises his judging eyebrow. "Are you sure about that?"

His condescending tone is even more infuriating than his face. But he has a point. Betty won't start anytime soon.

"Can you give me a jump start with your limo? The battery is dead." I glimpse past him to his driver, dutifully waiting beside the car.

"No, but I can give you a ride," he says.

"I don't want a ride. I want to go home with my car."

"Why? Are you worried someone will steal it? You'll find this piece of crap here tomorrow when you come back with a new battery." He is annoyed.

"Don't talk like that about Betty!" I scold him, and he fights a smile.

I get out of the car, tired and without any strength left to fight with him.

"Fine!" I accept his help for the second time tonight.

He puts a hand on my back to guide me to the limo, and the feelings from our dance try to resurface in my stomach. I squash them down as fast as they come up.

The drive to my apartment is silent and tense. Neither

of us wants to acknowledge what happened tonight on that dance floor. He was affected as much as I was, I saw it in how he was startled by Raphael's interruption. It seems I'm not the only one who avoids talking about their feelings. Things between us are complicated, to say the least, and maybe the solution is to stay as far as possible from each other.

"Thank you for the ride," I mutter, grabbing the door handle and trying to get out of the car. He stops me, grabbing my wrist, and I can't stop comparing his firm but delicate grip to that of the surfer boy.

He looks out of the tinted window, taking in the homeless population in this area.

"I'll come with you. It's not safe," he states in a way that won't take a no for an answer.

I roll my eyes but avoid fighting back. I step out of the car and walk toward my front door.

"Hi, Sam. How are you doing tonight?" I ask the homeless man sleeping on the concrete next to the entrance.

"Hey, gorgeous! You look stunning tonight." He winks at me with his head leaning on the rags I think are his spare clothes.

I chuckle. "Thanks! Have a good night."

He eyes Leonard behind me and grins, showing his yellow teeth. "You too!"

I look back toward my escort and study his frown. He

is not completely convinced I'm safer here than among the fancy people at the party.

He walks me to the door, and stands still until I find my keys in my purse.

"Do you think I'm safe now, or do you want to come in to check if there's someone who wants to kill me?" I joke, but I don't even want to contemplate the idea of having him in my apartment.

"No, I think you're safe. Nobody would dare to interact with a pain in the ass like you, not even to kill you," he fires back.

I open the door, and when I finally close it behind me without looking back, I sigh in relief.

"So this is why you didn't want me at the party? Because you were going with that asshole? Are you fucking him?"

I was so focused on getting rid of Leonard that I didn't even notice Spike waiting for me in the dimly lit living room.

Annoyance rises in my chest. "You know what, Spike? Who I fuck or don't fuck is none of your business. You should spend more time fighting for someone actually interested in you as more than a friend than my personal life."

I leave him there, confused by my suggestion, and walk to my room, more confused than him by the turn this evening took.

The most unsettling part is that I don't know if I'm angrier at the fact that I shared an intimate moment with Leonard or the fact that I actually liked it.

7

LEONARD

"Please, tell me you found a solution," I plead with Oliver as soon as he enters my office.

His scowl tells me he is not in a good mood, and when he sits in front of my desk huffing, I know it won't be a pleasant conversation.

"I looked at the file you gave me, and, as you already know, the money disappeared." He confirms but doesn't answer my request—or at least, his non-answer is confirmation enough.

"I didn't tell you to look at the files. I told you to dig deep into them and dissect them if necessary." I answer with the same annoyance I got from him.

As his scowl deepens, I'm met with an aggression in his eyes that catches me off guard. I find myself struggling to communicate with him lately, and I fear this could start to impact our relationship. We've been friends since college, but this is the first time I've felt at a loss as to how to approach him.

"It's barely over a thousand dollars, and you want me to spend my time on it. You're a billionaire. Do you really need that fucking money?" he spits, and I lean back in my chair, studying him.

"It's not that, and you know it," I say calmly despite the frustration boiling inside me.

"Yes, yes. I know. They're stealing from you and blah blah blah. The point is that they didn't do anything else. You lost that money. So what? Maybe they just wanted to demonstrate they were able to steal from the genius Leonard Walton. Big deal," he minimizes, and I'm baffled.

"It *is* a big deal! Someone managed to steal from me. I run a cybersecurity empire, and they were able to hack into my system. Can you imagine the consequences if this news gets out? We'll go down quicker than a shooting star," I exclaim vehemently.

It's his turn to study me with a small, irking smile curving his lips.

"What if your empire does crumble? You have your billions; we all do. Is it the end of the world if you shut down everything?" His question is a mixture of challenge and something else I can't pinpoint.

"Yes, it is. Because you know that it was never about

the money. I'm not doing it to amass even more wealth," I respond.

"Is that true? It seems like you're expanding your existing business. You never seem to be satisfied," he replies.

I find this hard to believe. We've discussed this acquisition countless times, and I thought he had a good understanding of the deal. It's frustrating to keep having this conversation again and again.

I don't have time to answer because someone knocks at the door and I welcome the interruption. I'm having a hard time going back to fight him on something that everybody in this company is happy about. It's like he made it his mission to make me pay for something I don't even know I did.

"Come on in." I can't hide the frustration in my voice.

Trish peeks her head into my office, and a frown appears when she spots the scowl on Oliver's face. "Is it a bad time?" she asks before stepping inside.

"No, come on in." I smile at her, hoping she gets that I would rather rip my nails off with a pair of pliers than continue my conversation with him.

She hesitates a moment before a grin appears on her face, and she struts into my office with a magazine in her hands. She puts it on the desk before me and crosses her arms over her chest.

"Raphael's little sister-in-law?" she asks in a singsong voice.

I frown. "What are you talking about?"

She points a finger at the article in the magazine, and it takes me a few seconds to realize what it is.

"You have got to be kidding me," I blurt out when I see the pictures covering the pages.

There are three of them, all from the party. Roxanne and I are dancing, and we look like we are seconds away from ripping each other clothes off. My hands are on her back, and hers are on my neck, but the gaze we are exchanging is so full of lust and sexual tension that I have a hard time denying I was flirting with her.

"I swear we were just dancing," I answer firmly.

She chuckles and sits on the free chair across from my desk, smugly smiling. She is always trying to set me up with a woman because she doesn't want me to die alone. Her words, not mine. She's having a field day with this article. The bold yellow title across the page says, *New Flame for Leonard Walton!*

"Yes, I know you didn't fuck her on the dance floor, but is it serious?" She pokes me for details.

"Nothing. Nothing is going on!" I almost shout. I don't want her to get any crazy ideas about what is happening in those pictures.

"Come on, Leonard! You can't convince me you

don't share a history with her. The way you look at each other is not something you can hide."

The history we share is not exactly the one she wants to hear and not one I'm proud of.

"Are you telling me that the 'sources near the couple' are wrong and you didn't leave together?" She raises a challenging eyebrow.

I scroll through the article and find the part where they describe her entering my limo but omit the part where her car didn't start.

"Her car broke down, and I couldn't leave her there in the middle of the night. She lives in an unsafe neighborhood. I couldn't tell Silver they murdered her little sister because I didn't give her a ride home." My explanation is far more detailed that I intended, and it's having the opposite effect on Trish.

Her grin widens. "And the dance?" she challenges.

I sigh. This will sound like an excuse. "A guy was groping her in the middle of the dance floor, and she couldn't get rid of him, so I intervened." I hate myself for sounding so insecure.

"Saved two times in one night? What an eventful party!" she teases.

"I know it sounds like an excuse. I swear it's not." I hope to be firm enough to shut down her ideas.

She laughs. "I'm joking, Leonard. Who you flirt with is none of my business, but I wanted you to know about those pictures in case you need to release a statement or something. I know you don't read those kinds of magazines."

I smile at her. "And why do you read them?"

"Because someone needs to tell you who your latest flirt is. You have to keep up to date." She shrugs and stands up. "Now, I'll leave you to your meeting," she adds, glancing at Oliver, who is still scowling.

For a few minutes, I forgot the discussion we were having, and now that I'm back to reality I don't know if I want to return to that argument. Trish walks out the door and hesitates a few moments before closing it. She looks between Oliver and me like she doesn't know whether to intervene in our fight or let it go. It's clear there is tension in this room, considering Oliver didn't even acknowledge her presence.

"Thank you for letting me know about those photos. I'll take care of it." I smile at her before she is gone.

As soon as the door closes behind her, I move my gaze to Oliver.

"A hacker? Seriously? Do you really want to associate yourself with such scum? You're the one who pointed out five minutes ago we're a cybersecurity company. How do you think they're going to take this? You're a pain in my ass for a few dollars, and then you fuck *her*?" he spits venomously.

I let him finish before letting loose with my frustration. "First, you're talking about my best friend's sister-in-law. I would choose my words very carefully if I were you. Second, as I told Trish before, I'm not fucking her. Not that it's even your business," I hiss.

"Fuck whoever you want, but remember that she's still a hacker, and she is the enemy here."

"She's a white hat, for fuck's sake!" I shout.

My tone gets his attention. He straightens his spine and tightens his jaw.

"So what? Are you hiring her now? Maybe she's the one stealing from you. Have you ever considered that?" He seems to get more and more angry about those fucking pictures and their meaning.

Yes. I have considered it, but I had my answer at the party: I'm not even worthy of her time at a social event, let alone being hacked by her. And I'm her brother-in-law's best friend; she would never mess with her family.

"She's not. Don't even insinuate something like that!" I spit angrily.

Oliver stands up and walks to the door. I look at him, baffled because this argument is far from over.

"Until you stop thinking with your dick, I'm done talking to you," he says, walking out of the office and slamming the door behind him.

"What the fuck just happened?" I breathe out.

I talked to him countless times without really under-standing what was going on. It might be time to talk to people close to him to see if they have a clue about what's bothering him. I'm not particularly eager to go behind his back, but at this point, his behavior is affecting our personal and professional relationship.

My eyes land on the magazine pages, where my face is clearly visible in all its lusty glory. How did I lose my composure like that? In front of Raphael, no less.

I need to stop this mess before it spirals out of control.

"I need your help," I blurt out when my lawyer answers the phone.

"Jesus, what happened? Not even a hello?" he chuckles.

I don't even have an excuse for my rudeness. Being angry with Oliver doesn't justify my shitty attitude with someone else. "I'm sorry, just having a bad day, but I shouldn't take out my frustrations on you," I murmur.

He sighs and softens his voice. "What happened? You seem agitated. Did you kill someone? Should we have this conversation in person?"

I can hear the smile in his tone but also the worried suspicion typical of a lawyer doing his job.

"No, nothing so serious. I need you to call a magazine and help me take down some pictures of a woman and me," I summarize.

The silence on the other side is long enough to make me nervous.

"Are they compromising? Are you or her naked or caught in a sex act?" He is definitely worried.

"Fuck, no! I'm not into public sex or anything like that. We were just dancing at a party," I explain.

The silence returns, and my worries skyrocket.

"That's it? What's the problem then?"

"We both look like we're seconds away from ripping each other's clothes off," I murmur, ashamed.

"Did you?"

"No, but that's not the point. She's Raphael's little sister-in-law. I want them gone!" I spit out.

"Is she an adult? Or are we talking about a minor?" This time I can almost feel his concern on my skin.

"Sweet Jesus, no! She is twenty-five. Who do you think I am?"

"Just asking, you never know. But if you're just dancing, don't worry about it. They'll forget about it in a couple of days, and you'll be fine."

My stomach sinks. "I don't want to leave them out there for everyone to see. I want them gone!"

He sighs, this time in frustration. "Do you want my professional opinion or what?"

"I want you to solve this problem."

"I'm doing it. If you push against the magazine, it will have the opposite effect." His stern tone is trying to dissuade me.

"I'm not paying you to do a publicist's job. I'm

asking you to fix this thing and make those photos disappear. Money is not a problem," I bark.

The line goes dead. I look at my phone, baffled, and call him again.

"Did you just hang up on me? How dare you!"

The anger simmering in my gut is almost boiling over. Could this morning get any worse?

"Yes, I did, and I'll do it again if you don't stop acting like a fifteen-year-old," he states firmly.

"Are you serious?"

"Absolutely. I'm saving you from a huge mess. You'll thank me when you sober up enough to think clearly. The best way to make those pictures disappear is to not give them a reason to go viral," he says before hanging up again.

This time, I don't call him back. The problem is that he's right, but those photos are a stark reminder that I should feel guilty looking at her like that. It doesn't matter that she is looking at me in the same way. It's just wrong to want her in that way, and I wish I could go back to that moment and do the right thing.

"I'M NOT FUCKING ROXANNE," I TELL RAPHAEL AS SOON as he enters the cigar room at the Hunting Club.

He frowns. "I'm glad to hear that, but I think that's between the two of you."

I know, but I want to be clear with him that I'm not taking my shots with her. I don't want any misunderstanding about it.

"I know, but this magazine insinuates that there's flirting between us, and while Roxanne knows it's bullshit, you don't, and I wanted to clear the air with you."

He grabs the magazine and chuckles. "It looks like you're going to fuck any second."

I groan. "Don't, just don't."

"Listen, I'm not going to give any credit to this kind of magazine. If I have a problem, I'll talk with you. And, by the way, she's an adult; she can do whatever she wants. I can worry about her decisions, be there if she fucks up, but I'll never impose my will on someone else," he points out.

I know. Raphael is one of those men we should clone because he's so supportive of equal rights that he ran for senator to change things from the top.

"But the real question is, why are you stressing about those pictures? You've never cared about something so trivial." He nails me to the chair with a single glance.

I sigh and take a moment to collect my thoughts before answering. There's a lot going on right now, and it's difficult to pinpoint a problem—maybe because they're all equally troubling.

"We're preparing for the acquisition, which is stressful enough. But I asked Oliver to look into the missing money, and he practically freaked out. So now I not only don't have an answer for that missing money, I have a pissed-off head developer making my life a living hell." I look at him and notice the frown deepening on his forehead.

"I know you don't want to hear this, but can you put aside your pride and ask Roxanne for help?"

I look down at my hands in my lap. At this point, the situation is so bad I'm considering it. The only problem is, I don't know how I'd handle her refusal to help me. In her eyes, I'm the bad guy, the monster to fight, and this thought affects me in a way I didn't think was possible.

8

ROXANNE

"**H**e just took you home? You're a liar!" Spike barges into my bedroom without any respect.

I put my head under the pillow and groan. *What time is it?* He rips the pillow from my head and throws something on the bed.

"I hope you have an excellent reason for waking me up, or I'm going to rip your head off," I hiss when I look up at his angry face.

Why is he pissed off? I'm the one who should be in his face about how he woke me up!

He scoffs and picks up the magazine on my bed and slams it down again. That pisses me off even more. Who does he think he is?

"What is it?" I ask because his behavior suggests it's life-or-death.

I pick up the magazine, and I'm suddenly awake. On the front cover of the gossip section, there is a picture of Leonard and me dancing at the party. It wouldn't be a problem if I weren't eye-fucking him. Damn paparazzi.

"So what?" I grumble, throwing the magazine aside.

I turn on the bed, grab my pillow, and go back to sleep. Neither Spike nor Leonard is worth losing sleep over. Not for something as stupid as a magazine that everyone will forget about in a couple of days.

"*So what*? Are you for real? You told me you were going alone to the party. Then you told me he just gave you a ride because your car broke down, and now these pictures come out. Do you think I'm stupid? It's clear as day you two are fucking!" he almost shouts.

I'm done. I'm fed up with this bullshit of a jealous boyfriend.

"Who I fuck is none of your business, but as I told you time and time again, I never did, and I never will!" I spit.

"Yeah, sure," he scoffs. "I don't believe you. Did you see how you're looking at each other?"

"I don't give a shit if you believe me or not. This is none of your business!" I yell, sitting up.

I'm so done with his antics. It's like living with a toddler who throws tantrums for the stupidest reasons.

He's possessive and suffocating, and I'm not even his girlfriend. Not that I would let it go even if I were. I don't tolerate this shit from the person I'm dating.

"You're fucking the enemy, and it's none of my business? He's the kind of person we fight! He's the billionaire who becomes rich fucking over his employees. We don't sleep with those assholes, we fight them. Do you have no moral compass?" he accuses me, disgusted.

"This is rich coming from you. You don't fight those people. *I* do it. You can't keep a job for two days straight. You're not exactly an example of discipline. You screw over those poor owners trying to make ends meet by going to work stoned. You have no right to talk to me like that. Stop acting like a jealous boyfriend." I know I'm being too harsh, and it was a low blow talking about his job, or lack of it, but I'm honestly done with him.

"I'm not acting like a jealous boyfriend," he mumbles, his voice filled with defeat and vulnerability.

All the fight leaves his body, and a wave of guilt crashes over me. I hadn't intended to wound him, but the unspoken tension had to be addressed. Perhaps I could have been gentler.

"You are. Maybe you don't realize it, but you judge all my interactions with men, and I'm not comfortable with it. You are a friend, nothing more," I explain, this time with a firmness that can't be misunderstood.

"Okay. I'll leave you alone," he mutters, scurrying out of my room like a beaten dog.

I sigh and rub a hand over my face. That wasn't how I meant to bring up the topic. As I take a shower, I replay the conversation in my head, thinking of at least ten better ways to handle it.

When I eventually leave my room, I can't find Spike, but I do see Candy sitting at the kitchen table. She lowers her eyes shyly after she meets my gaze. I'm certain she overheard my argument with Spike earlier, and I feel bad for her. Candy has had a crush on Spike since the day I met them four years ago, but he is oblivious to her feelings.

"Do you want to come for a walk?" I ask, hoping to lighten her mood.

She nods and grabs her phone from the countertop.

We walk in silence for a while, letting the chatter of people around us keep us company. I don't know how to start the conversation because the situation we're in is not ideal. She likes Spike, but he's interested in me, and I'm not attracted to him at all. How do you get out of a love triangle that isn't even love?

After a while, she asks, "So, you punched Spike in the guts this morning, huh?"

I wince. "I suppose so. But I really don't know how to handle this situation."

She chuckles. "Better would have been a good start."

I laugh. "That's for sure. You should ask him out."

She stares at me, eyes wide and mouth agape.

"Come on. You're in love with him. What are you waiting for?"

I grab her elbow and drag her away from the trajectory of a skater heading for the skatepark. She is so lost in her thoughts she would walk straight into the ocean and not even notice right now.

"I don't know how. He's so into you he doesn't even know I exist." She giggles.

I shrug. I'm not an expert in relationships, but I'm not shy either.

"Just ask him out. 'Spike, I like you, and I want to go on a date with you,'" I suggest.

It's her turn to laugh. "Yeah, sure. Easy for you to say. You're gorgeous and confident. I'm just...me."

"You're gorgeous, too, and don't even try to deny it."

She shrugs but says nothing.

"I know it seems like a big deal, but what's the worst-case scenario? He says no. So what? At least you tried and you can get over him. Pining over him will get you nowhere—with him or anyone else who is less complicated than him."

She sighs. "You're right, but I suppose it's easier this way. If I don't ask him, I don't have to face rejection."

"What if he says yes? You've wasted a ton of time because of your fear," I counter.

"Do you always have a comeback for everything?" She looks at me, a mischievous smile playing on her lips.

"You know, I've always been a practical person. I don't shrink back from asking questions for fear of what I could find out. I'd rather know and face the consequences. Like when I didn't know where my sister was, and if she was dead or alive. That uncertainty made me the person I am today. It taught me the value of taking risks and facing the unknown."

She says nothing after that. She knows my history with the witness protection program and she gets my point.

"Have you seen these new apartments?" Candy asks when we reach the new building.

It's fancy, with Venice Beach vibes but Beverly Hills amenities. Something I could never afford. I stare at the phone number on the leasing sign. I already committed it to memory, dreaming of having the money to move here, in a space I don't have to share with anyone.

"Do you want to move out?" she asks, following my line of sight.

I turn toward her. "I'm twenty-five, and I live with a bunch of kids who play video games all day. What do you think?"

She chuckles. "Yeah, I get it."

"But I don't have the money. It's just a dream for now." I point out.

She grins "He could solve your problems with that." She nods toward a stand where my face stands out on the cover of the magazine—the same one Spike showed me this morning.

I grimace. "Don't remind me," I plead.

Leonard is so gorgeous in that picture I can't keep my eyes away.

"Do you like him?" Her tone is serious.

I don't know if Candy and I are friends. We talk about everything, and we don't have secrets, but we rarely talk about our feelings. I guess this morning is an exception.

"He's objectively gorgeous and has a sex appeal I can't deny. I mean, it's clear how I look at him in that picture. It's obvious to anyone."

"But?"

We start to walk again, away from that sexy as-sin face that distracts me.

"But as Spike put it, he's the enemy. He stands for everything I hate and I can't get over it. Not even for a gorgeous face like his."

"Why? Because he's rich?" She frowns.

From the moment I met Leonard Walton, I knew there was something about him I couldn't stand. It's difficult to explain why I feel this way about him.

"He's the kind of person who keeps launching new ventures, not out of passion, but because he's insatiable for more wealth. His greed knows no bounds. Not even the lives of his employees are spared," I vent, my words dripping with contempt.

"One of his companies was voted the best place to work last year," she points out something I already knew, but it only fueled my anger when I discovered it.

"By who? Him and his cronies?"

She stifles a laugh. "He comes from a typical family. His parents aren't wealthy. He did it all himself."

"And he forgot where he comes from," I mumble.

"Jesus, sounds like you hate his guts."

I chuckle. "And you seem to like him. Do you want me to put in a good word for you?"

"No! Please. I already have one delusional crush. I don't need a second one. He is sexy, though."

I grin at her. "Yes, he is."

"How it was dancing with him?" she asks dreamily.

I look back on our dance and can't shake the feeling in my gut. I've never felt so good in a man's arms.

"I felt protected. Like I was the sexiest woman on the earth," I reluctantly admit.

"Do you ever wonder what it would be like to be with him? Even though it's just a fantasy, it's fun to imagine." She is serious.

"Probably spoiled in every sense. In and out of bed."

And the feeling of his lips on yours would be something you remember for years, even if you had just a taste. Even if you regret it, you will want more of him, and you will make a fool of yourself to have another bit of him. But I won't tell her that. She's having a fantasy and it's not my intention to spoil it.

Leonard Walton is the perfect devil's package: gorgeous and tempting on the outside, savage villain on the inside. And I'm not going to make that mistake twice.

9

LEONARD

"What the fuck do you want?"

I didn't expect to come across this rude guy who thinks he's entitled to insult me when I mustered the courage to go out tonight and potentially be humiliated. His conceited scowl looks straight out of the worst reality show. If he intended to intimidate me, he's failing miserably.

I take my time to study him. He's half my age, good looking and probably attractive for the girls his age, but I don't even know where to start to approach someone like him. Even picking a fight over his rude behavior is embarrassingly easy. I have a hard time trying to hide a smile.

"Are you dumb? I asked what the fuck do you want," he repeats when I try to peek over his shoulder and spot a bunch of guys playing video games. Am I even in the right place?

"I'm looking for Roxanne," I say, bringing my gaze back to the rude boy.

"Well, she sure as fuck isn't looking for you," he spits.

I tilt my head, contemplating whether I would get into trouble if I physically remove him from the doorway. It probably isn't worth the trouble. How can Roxanne live in a place like this?

"Are you going to call her, or do you want me to shout until one of your neighbors calls the cops?" My mouth kicks up in a smug smile.

The guy snorts. "Like anyone would do that. This isn't your bougie neighborhood. Here, people shout all the time."

"Should we try?"

He crosses his arms over his chest, challenging me.

"Fire! Please help! There's a fire," I shout loud enough for someone to hear me.

His pales. "Shut the fuck up, you idiot!" he whisper-shouts.

"So, are you going to call her?"

"What do you want from her? To end up in another magazine?"

So, this is his problem. He's trying to defend Roxanne from the big bad guy who gets her in trouble. I didn't know she was upset about that. She didn't say anything about it, though she could have reached out through her sister.

"I don't have to explain anything to you, but I'm feeling generous tonight. I don't plan to get her in trouble, no," I reply.

He scoffs again. What's wrong with this guy? "Your name and the word *generous* in the same sentence is not even believable."

Jesus, he's annoying. "Should I start shouting again?" I smirk at him, just to be irritating too.

He doesn't have time to reply because a mop of curly black hair peeks out behind his back. A stunning girl with flawless brown skin and two huge, sweet hazel eyes widen even more when she sees me.

"Are you looking for Roxanne?" she asks and rolls her eyes at the guy's scowl.

"Yes, can you get her for me? I don't want to come in and disrupt your evening." I pull a charming smile to mess with the boy.

She lowers her gaze shyly, and the guy is utterly disgusted by the scene. Good.

"Like we would let you in at almost midnight," he murmurs, and the girl punches him in the ribs before scurrying in.

It takes two long minutes where the blond guards the door like I'm the villain, and finally Roxanne strolls to the door. She has a bewildered look, and I can't blame her. I would be surprised, too, if she showed up at my door at midnight.

"I need to talk to you," I say when she comes out the door, leaving it open for everyone to see.

A couple of kids turn around and do a double-take, noticing me standing here like an idiot. I hadn't thought about not having privacy when I came begging.

"About what?" she barks, now more annoyed than surprised.

I glance at the guy, and his smirk has a "told you so" vibe. I never thought I'd be so bothered by the mere presence of a kid half my age.

"Can we go somewhere more private?" I beg, returning my eyes to hers.

She scoffs. "I'm not inviting you into my bedroom."

"I told him so, but he wouldn't listen," the irritating boy chips in.

"No, you didn't, and this is a private conversation. You can return to your games." I have no qualms about calling out his bullshit.

He grinds his teeth, and his grin sours like I've touched a sore spot. My smirk reappears on my face.

"Sweet Jesus, can you stop this dick-measuring contest?" Roxanne murmurs under her breath. She grabs my hand and guides me far from the front door.

"I'll be right back," she says over her shoulder to the fuming blond.

When we are far from the door, I take charge and guide her to my limo. She stops dead in her tracks when she sees it.

"Can we just talk here?" She is pissed now.

"It's a confidential matter. I don't talk about work in the middle of the street," I point out, and this gets her attention.

"What is this all about?" She crosses her arms over her chest and waits for my answer. She is a stubborn little thing.

I sigh. "I need your help."

There, I said it out loud, and I didn't choke on my words. This is significant progress.

She raises an eyebrow, interested in the turn the conversation took. She enters the limousine without further complaints.

"Only you would come to Venice Beach in a limo." She shakes her head. Her tone is amused, but she tries to hide it.

"Would you rather I came in my helicopter or one of my luxury cars?" I challenge her. I know she despises my money, and I take pleasure in poking her with that.

"You're such a show-off," she mutters.

"Maybe, but here you are."

After our exchange she keeps silent until we enter the downtown area.

"Where are we going?"

"My office."

"Why?"

"Because you have to sign a nondisclosure agreement"

"You have got to be kidding me," she whispers but doesn't add anything else.

I brace myself for a confrontation, but to my surprise, she seems intrigued by what I'm about to ask. Although she tries to appear uninterested, I can sense that she's up for a challenge. I believe my job would be an excellent opportunity to test her abilities.

We park in the garage below the building and ride the private elevator up to the top of the building. I don't miss how she rolls her eyes when I swipe the keycard on the reader and the doors open before us. I have a hard time hiding a smile.

When the elevator opens with a ping, we walk silently to my office. The same keycard opens it. She steps inside and takes in the art on the wall. I let her gawk over the expensive couch and signature desk that cost more than a car. She notices the two-hundred-dollar pen on my desk, next to the monogrammed paper laying on a leather folder. She says nothing but she can't hide the fact that she is impressed.

I don't know if she expected tacky golden furniture or sculptures of myself, but I'm not that kind of billionaire. I pride myself on collecting tasteful objects.

"Have a seat." The words come out of my mouth bossier than I intended. She looks at me with a raised eyebrow that reveals all her contempt for my tone.

I gesture to the chair in front of my desk without apologizing for my behavior and she reluctantly sits down. I'm not the kind of person who tiptoes around her.

"So, why am I here?" She finally gives in to her curiosity.

I reach for a nondisclosure agreement contract in the desk drawer and give it to her along with my expensive pen. She rolls her eyes and doesn't even read the contract before signing it.

As soon as she gives it back to me, I explain. "Someone's stealing from my company."

She stares at me for a long moment before she frowns. "You're going to need to be more specific. I'm not a mind reader here."

I take a deep breath and exhale slowly. "One thousand four hundred seventy-six dollars disappeared from this company without a trace."

She scoffs. "You're wasting my time for that ridiculous amount? You're a billionaire!"

"The keywords here are without a trace," I point out calmly, studying her reaction.

Her frown deepens. "What do you mean? That's not possible."

Now I have her full attention. I know her insatiable brain wants to know more. This is how genius works, and she is undoubtedly a genius. She may have pink hair and a sharp tongue, but you don't get that kind of reputation in this industry by having a pretty face.

"I thought so too, but apparently nobody can track where that money went; we just know that it got out," I say, and I'm surprised when she starts to chuckle.

"Come on! You can't be serious. I'm sure you'll find a solution if you take some time to look into it. Aren't you the genius behind this empire?"

She thinks I didn't look into it. "I've lost sleep over this for the past month. I have exhausted all my resources."

She sobers up pretty quickly. "You mean you personally looked for that money?"

I nod.

"And you came up with nothing in one month? I don't believe it," she scoffs.

"Well, this is why I'm asking for your help. Your sister told me you're a computer whiz, a true genius." My lips curve up in a hopeful smile.

I don't want to give her the satisfaction of telling her I looked her up and spent the last week debating whether I should risk the humiliation of rejection. She is smart enough to understand how desperate I am and how much I need her help.

"What if I say no?" she challenges me.

"I'll strongly ask you to reconsider," I say without hesitation.

I would do anything to discover who stole from me and how they did it. At this point, it's a personal matter, and I won't stop until I have all my answers.

"Start begging because I'm not doing it." She says this like she's already made her decision, and there's nothing I can do to change her mind.

I knew it wouldn't be easy to convince her, but I hoped there would be room for negotiation. Asking me to beg sounds more like a way to humiliate me than playing hard to get.

"I'll give you fifty thousand dollars now and another hundred thousand when you finish the job." I lay out my first proposal.

Her eyes widen when she hears the amount I suggest, but she recovers quickly, hiding behind a smug mask. That smirk is so irritating I almost kick her out of the office. But she knows it's a lot of money; she probably needs it, considering where she lives. All is not lost, and I can feel the hope rising timidly in my chest.

"I don't work for money or I'd be rich by now. Plenty of billionaires have offered me money to do their dirty jobs, and I've never accepted. Why should I help you?"

I tilt my head and look her straight in the eye. "Because I'm not asking you to do something illegal. If this news gets out, this company will crumble like a sand castle, leaving millions of people without the protection of our systems." And my heart will break, but I can't tell her that.

She snorts. "That's hardly a problem. There are plenty of companies that can do your job."

"How much time do they need? And are they equipped to handle massive clients like the government, or the privacy of patients at the biggest hospitals in this country? Because what we do for them is tailored to their needs, it takes months to switch from one system to another made exclusively for them," I point out and see doubt darkening her eyes.

"You can't go down that fast. You'll have time to support the transition."

"Are you sure about that?"

She doesn't answer, and this is enough for me to go a step further. I pick up a second contract and push it across the table at her.

"What's this?" She picks it up and scrolls through the pages.

"If you assist me in uncovering the whereabouts of the funds, I am prepared to provide you with the financial backing and resources necessary to establish your own business. I'll guide you in navigating the legal boundaries of your actions, but how you help others will be entirely up to you. I won't interfere in any of your decisions unless you want my advice."

She gapes at my proposal. For the first time since I've known her, I've surprised her in a positive way. I don't know how to feel about that. Am I so terrifying that people expect the worst from me?

"Why are you doing this?" She frowns.

Does she want me to spell it out? "Isn't it obvious? I'm desperate to save my company, and you're the only person who can help me do it."

She shakes her head. "I mean, why are you doing this?" She waves the contract in her hand. "Why a company? You could have covered me in money."

I inhale deeply. I didn't want to expose myself so much, but this conversation is turning more truthful than I anticipated, and I can't lose her trust now.

"Because I did my homework. Like you said, you could be rich. You have skills that go way beyond common knowledge, but instead of using them for profit, you still live in a shitty apartment with those kids." I can see the shame cross her eyes when I mention it. "If you wanted an easy way out, you could have had it years ago, but you want to help people. I'm offering you the opportunity to do it like never before."

A long silence follows my speech as she studies me. She is interested in my proposal. I know I went in the right direction because I learned a long time ago to read people. The only doubt comes from her hatred toward me. I don't know how deep it is, and I can't foresee if she will throw the opportunity away because she doesn't want anything to do with me. That is a real possibility.

"And you won't have a say in it?" she finally asks.

"No. Not even a share of the company. I'll give you the money, and that's it. No need to give it back," I assure her.

"You're really desperate, aren't you?" She sighs.

There is no need to answer her question; it's more than clear that I wouldn't have asked for her help if I had another way to solve it.

"Fine. Give me that fancy pen." She finally accepts, and I feel a burden lifting from my chest.

"You can take your time reading the contract," I point out.

She arches a brow, pinning me to the chair with her stern gaze. "Are you trying to screw me over?"

"Have you heard a single word of what I've said?"

"So, there's no need to read the contract." She smiles smugly, lowering her gaze over the paper and signing it.

I watch the pen rolling over the paper in a smooth motion, and I wonder how we will manage not to rip each other apart while working together.

10

ROXANNE

"**A**re you sure you don't want me to call movers to help?" I ask for the umpteenth time this morning.

Silver, Raphael, and her bodyguard, Sven, showed up this morning at my door to help me move into my new apartment, the one I dreamed of renting when I walked by it with Candy.

After I cashed Leonard's check, I decided to splurge for a new living situation. I can't imagine working in my bedroom anymore, with a bunch of what Leonard called kids playing video games in another room.

I'm excited about the opportunity to have my own company, and I need to start thinking and living like a grown-up. Moving out of that house was the best decision I have ever made and the first step in that direction.

ERIKA VANZIN

"Why pay for movers if you have two men helping you out?" Raphael's strained voice comes from behind a big box he carries up the stairs.

"Because it seems like you're dying?" It sounds like a question, but it's more of a statement.

They completely underestimated the amount of work they had to do. Next to me, in my new living room—now full of boxes—my sister chuckles while she points Sven in the general direction of my bedroom. He nods and carries the box of who knows what in the other room. He never talks or complains, but I can see he is as tired as Raphael.

"How did you manage to hoard all these things in a single room?" he asks, putting the box on the pile beside me.

"I honestly don't know. I was thinking the same thing when I was putting everything in the boxes," I mumble.

"Well, now you have more room for everything, and you don't have to share that shitty house anymore." My sister scrunches her nose.

She was never a fan of my living arrangement. She thinks the guys are immature kids who want to play all day without taking on any responsibility, and I agree with her.

"You know? I'm happy you agreed to work with Leonard," she adds, glancing in my direction. She knows we don't get along, but she doesn't know why.

I shrug. "He made an offer I couldn't refuse." And it's true. The money alone was a massive reason to accept, but the contract for my company is something I can't let slip away.

"Be patient with him," she murmurs, and her statement gets my full attention.

I turn toward her.

"He's grumpy most of the time, but he's a good man. He is completely losing his shit about that money problem," she continues.

I'm surprised by the worry in her voice. I never understood why she loves him so much, but I suppose she knows him better than me. Raphael's friends are tight-knit, and I'm sure they will protect each other to the end. For this reason, I'm happy for my sister.

"It seemed a bit desperate when he made me the offer." I smile, but she doesn't reciprocate.

Mine dies on my lips.

"He's worried about losing that company. I don't know what he would do." She smiles sadly. "That company is his whole life."

"He has another—what? Fifteen? He won't die of starvation," I point out.

"It's not about money. It never was," Raphael chimes in.

I didn't even realize he came back with another box.

I don't know how to respond. Their picture of

Leonard clashes with my idea of him. I store the information for later; I'm sure I'll need it when things get hard working with him. Because I *know* they will get ugly.

"Can you please not tell him where I live?" I ask. I feel like I need to keep this place my sanctuary, and I don't want to bring my fights with him to my doorstep.

They frown and look at each other curiously, but they don't ask for an explanation, and I'm grateful for that.

"Come on! You can't really be asking us to go through this hell," Raphael complains, even if a smile is tugging at the corner of his mouth.

They offered to help me pick out furniture for my apartment, or at least, Silver volunteered the three of them to do it. Raphael followed her just because he's still head-over-heels for her after four years of marriage.

"How will I sleep without a bed? I need a new one!"

"The sign outside claiming they have the best vintage furniture defies the concept of new," he fires back with a grin.

"You are a smart-ass, aren't you?"

I walk into a section with couches of all shapes and sizes. I run my fingers over the texture because I want to be sure to choose the most luxuriously comfortable one.

"I'm pretty sure it's illegal to insult a senator," Silver points out, chuckling.

I roll my eyes. "Of course, he married the other smart-ass."

This time, even Sven laughs with us. I admit it's fun spending time with them. I could have told them to go home, considering they're tired, but I wanted to be a bit selfish for once and enjoy their company a bit longer.

I plop down on the couch, and my sister sits beside me.

"What do you think? Is it comfortable enough?" I ask her.

"Yes, I like how it hugs you when you lean on the back cushions." She confirms what I already noticed about this sofa.

"You're not really considering buying this thing, right?" Raphael asks me with a disgusted face.

"Why not?" I look at the couch to see if I missed something I should consider before buying it, but I see nothing peculiar about it.

"It's bubble-gum pink," he points out.

"You have stuccos and mosaics in your bathroom. Don't judge me!"

Sven can't help but chuckle, earning him a side-eye from Raphael.

"Fair enough," my sister's husband concedes.

Sven's smile fades a bit when he listens to something

in his earpiece. He moves toward Raphael and whispers something in his ear, too low for us to hear, but I already know what it is, and my sister does too. She stands up at the exact moment Raphael's eyes land on mine with an apologetic look.

Before he even speaks, I already know what he's going to say: Party's over. Everyone needs to go home.

"Word got out that we're here and people are gathering to take pictures. Silver and I should go home before the crowd grows. We don't have full security with us," he explains.

I don't blame him for wanting to avoid the craziness of the crowd. Only in the United States are politicians treated like celebrities, and the frenzies surrounding them are disconcerting, but Raphael can't change reality—not this one, at least.

So, I have to accept not seeing my sister as often as I'd like, but this time I'm grateful to have spent almost all day with her.

"Not a problem. You helped me a lot today. I can take it from here." I smile at him, but I can see the disappointment in my sister's face.

"It's okay, really!" I try to reassure her, but her frown doesn't disappear.

"Are you sure?" she asks sweetly.

"That I want to avoid being judged by your husband

about my taste in interior design? Absolutely positive." I grin and give her the thumbs up.

I manage to get a laugh out of her and Raphael, and when she hugs me, she promises to make up for this interruption. I know she will. She always keeps her promises.

I watch them disappear out the back door, with Sven urging them inside a car already waiting in the parking lot. It hits me just now how alone I am. Tonight, I won't go back to my crowded apartment, and while I'm excited for this new adventure on one hand, this is the first time in twenty-five years I won't have someone to come home to.

I've been adulting for less than five minutes, and I already feel alone. Maybe I'm not fit for this grownup thing.

"May I help you?" The smiling eighteen-year-old salesgirl diverts my attention from the back door. I'm still staring.

"I'd like this couch delivered. Is that possible?" I smile back at her.

She beams. "Of course, we can arrange a delivery. You just need to fill in some paperwork. By the way, I love this couch. I was looking forward to buying it when I get my own space." She winks at me while I follow her to the register counter.

"Sorry to steal your furniture!" I chuckle.

She giggles. "Don't worry. It'll take me awhile to save enough money to leave my parents' house. And with the commission from this sale, I'll be closer to reaching my goal!"

"I'm glad I could help."

It doesn't take long to buy the couch, fill out the papers, and walk out in the Los Angeles sun. *It's time to go home.* My stomach flutters at the idea. A mixture of excitement and anxiety makes my insides quiver. But first, I need some takeout food because I can't cook to save my life. I guess some things are hard to change.

I PROCRASTINATED ALL DAY TO THE POINT THAT I started unpacking my boxes instead of diving into my job, but now I need to face the reason why I can afford this place. I have to try to crack Leonard's system to figure out how they get in to steal that money. I'm reluctant to do this because the moment I'm in, things will start to become real. I'm working for the devil, and I need to face this reality.

I grab my laptop and sit on the only piece of furniture I have in my new home: the mattress lying on the floor, which I brought from the old apartment. I lean my back against the wall and start digging into his systems, starting from the most obvious: the website.

I crack my knuckles, stretch my neck, and take a good sip of my energy drink. I'll need it to stay up all night—or at least for a few hours. I hope I'm done way before the sun comes up.

My hopes of being done by morning die when the sunbeam hits my legs and the birds outside my window are in a cheerful singing contest. I start to lose hope when noon comes and goes. I'm on the verge of tears when the sun goes down again, and there are at least ten empty cans of energy drinks scattered over my bed.

I've always appreciated a good challenge, and I never back down when things get hard, but right now, my eyes are burning from staring for almost twenty-four hours at the computer, and my stomach hurts from way too much caffeine and lack of food.

"I can't believe it," I mutter to myself, standing up and stretching. My back hurts, and I need to take a shower to relieve my aching muscles.

This is the most challenging job I have ever had, and though I expected no less from Leonard Walton, I thought I was better than him at this, and it pisses me off to no end knowing that I'm not even close to winning this battle.

When I walk into the hot spray of the shower, I curse the day I agreed to work for that genius with the devil's personality.

11

LEONARD

"I thought you disappeared with the money," I say as soon as Roxanne enters my office.

It's been fifteen days since she signed the contract, and I hoped she would start to work right away, but she just walked out of this room and went MIA.

I stare longer than I should at her long, tanned legs showing off in those cut-off jean shorts, not to mention the white tank top that does nothing to hide her lace bra. And the sparkly pink sneakers—shoes a twelve-year-old would wear—somehow make her look even cuter. *Since when do I find a woman* cute?

"I had to try to hack your system first," she says, sitting on the chair in front of my desk.

"And did you succeed?" I'm curious.

"No," she grumbles, and I can't hide a grin forming on my face.

"I know, it's perfect!" I beam.

She raises an eyebrow. "You wouldn't be missing that money if it were perfect, right?"

Fair enough. That's why she is here, and while I'm happy someone like her didn't get access from the outside, I know that this complicates everything. At least if she had found a way in, we know there is also a way out. Right now, we're back at square one.

"I need unrestricted access to all your company networks," she finally says.

I study her. Does she really think I'm going to give her free rein to stick her nose in my business?

"For starters, I'm giving you *partial* access to *some* of my networks; then, if you need more, we can discuss it," I counter.

She crosses her arms under her breasts, pushing them up and showing a bit more of the swell, begging for my eyes to stray there. It's a titanic effort not to lower my gaze.

"Do you want me to solve this problem or not? I can't do my job if you treat me like a kid that can't touch your computer. I'm a grown-ass adult, and you're acting like a grumpy old dude who wants to ruin the fun just because you can," she fights back.

I struggle to hide a smile. She is so riled up her cheeks are turning pink and her brows are knitted in a scowl. With that pink hair, she isn't even close to being menacing.

"Are you done?"

She says nothing, but at least she doesn't come back with a remark.

"I can't give you access to everything for privacy reasons. There are some parts of the network where we keep employee-sensitive data; I'm not giving you access to that."

"Fair enough. Everything else?"

"Nope. Not the research and development department and some other areas. I don't trust a hacker with industrial secrets that could destroy my company."

She scoffs, clearly offended by my insinuations. "So you think I'd steal your secrets and sell them to the highest bidder?"

"I'm not risking twenty years of work because of you. Do you want my trust? You have to earn it," I tell her without remorse. "I know who you are, and I know you'll go to prison if you even think to peep a word about what you find in here, but I can't risk my company, not even for Raphael's little sister-in-law."

I stand up and give her a piece of paper with a password and the directories of some of my networks. She is smart enough to figure it out from there.

I walk out of the office without turning around to see her reaction. This is my company; she is a guest. If she needs more, she has to show me why, and she has to be convincing. I still have to figure out which side she's on.

WHEN I RETURN BY NOON WITH A TAKEOUT BAG, I FIND her sprawled on the couch, her shoes on the armrest. I should be pissed because that piece of furniture cost more than the check I gave her, but those legs going on for days and the shape of her ass peeking out from the jean shorts is a vision that makes my dick twitch in my pants. She is sexy as sin, and the image of her naked body sprawled under me on that same couch is so vivid I need to close my eyes to regain my focus.

"If you ruin that couch, you won't have the money to pay for a new one." I startle her when I enter the room and close the door behind me.

She studies me, a bit pissed, then she rolls her eyes and stands up. *She is a brat.*

"Sorry, I didn't know this was a piece of art. I thought it was something people can actually sit on and enjoy." Fake sweetness drips from every word.

How I'd like to tame that little brat. *Give her something to keep her mouth busy. Jesus, where did that come from?* If I don't get a grip, I'll do something stupid.

"Exactly. It's to sit on it, not put your shoes on," I point out, gesturing for her to sit at my desk.

"Yes, *Daddy!*" she teases, and my dick twitches for the second time. She has no idea what that word rolling out of her mouth does to me.

"I brought salad and bread sticks. I didn't know what you like, so I just played it safe." I change the subject before my mind goes places I can't get out of.

"You didn't have to do that. I can survive on energy drinks and caffeine. But thank you." She smiles as she digs into her salad.

I study her for a few long moments. I have no idea how she survives without taking care of herself, like having a decent meal and, based on the dark circles under her eyes, a decent night of sleep. If I imitated her lifestyle, I'd be dead by the end of the week. This is what a fifteen-year age gap does to a person. At twenty-five, I could go for three days straight without sleeping or eating if I was focused on a project I really cared about.

"Did you find anything interesting this morning?" I ask when the silence becomes too long and awkward.

She grabs a notepad and puts it in front of me. "I need access to these directories," she says.

I take a look at the list neatly scribbled on the page. "Pen and paper? You know computers exist, right?" I grin at her.

She raises a challenging eyebrow. "Would you prefer

an email so if you get hacked again, it'll be even easier for them to get around with all the instruction they need?"

Touché. She is probably more paranoid than me, which is a point in her favor. I like how she doesn't leave anything to chance. She's usually on the other side of the fence, and she knows the damage an email like that could do in the wrong hands.

"I'll take a look after lunch and give you what you need."

"Access to everything?" She widens her eyes.

"I said what you need, not what you want."

She rolls her eyes while munching on her salad. She savors it like it's the fanciest plate in the world. I wonder when she last ate a decent meal.

"I understand what you mean when you say the money just disappeared. I couldn't find anything from the inside," she says after a while.

"You didn't believe me?" I playfully challenge her.

"I thought you were just too busy to dig into it. I don't think there's anything you can't find if you set your mind on it."

I'm surprised. "Is that a compliment?" I smile.

"Just a statement. There's no doubt your IQ is way above average," she says so easily I have no doubt she thinks it and I feel somehow empowered by it. I don't know why. I shouldn't care about her opinion.

I sigh. "So, nothing, not even a tiny hint?"

She shrugs. "I only worked for a few hours. I didn't expect to find a solution by the end of the morning."

I rub a hand over my frustrated face. I somehow hoped she *would* find something that fast.

"But there is something peculiar. It's a very specific sum, fifteen different transactions in the span of a year. The numbers are so random that they don't seem random at all."

"What do you mean?" I'm curious about her approach.

"When you look at the entirety of the transactions, there's a pattern, some numbers appearing more than others. I can't help but think they're not purchases—something that was paid for, and the money went out. You usually see round sums or a ninety-nine-cent decimal place—ninety-five sometimes. But who prices something at exactly fourteen dollars and seventy-three cents?" She frowns, like something is bothering her, but she can't grasp it yet.

She is right. I always looked at the numbers but not at the meaning behind them. A sense of excitement flutters in my stomach. I haven't felt this hopeful in a long time.

"So you mean they didn't use it to buy something? It's not like credit card fraud." I try to follow her reasoning.

She shakes her head. "I don't think so. I haven't dug into the credit cards yet, but I feel confident ruling that out."

I nod.

"And then there's the fact that it stopped. There was a regular pattern to how the money was going out, but then it just stopped with a random sum of five dollars and sixty-two cents. Like they had to reach that precise amount. Does the amount mean anything to you—one thousand dollars?" she asks.

She gets it. This is the same direction I was going, like it's not so random after all.

"It's the capital we had in the bank account when we founded the company. We started all of this with one thousand, four hundred seventy-six dollars." I smile, remembering that day.

She thinks about it.

"So, this is personal. It's not just someone stealing from you. This is someone wanting to send you a message," she points out.

I didn't think of it in those terms, but she has a point. The dread sinking in my chest dries my throat and suddenly I'm not hungry anymore.

"Does anyone know about this sum?" She softens her voice, maybe because she senses the sudden change in my mood.

"It's not public knowledge, but people working in

this industry know it. We were quite a legend back in the day because we started literally from scratch and built an empire," I admit.

She chuckles, and her reaction surprises me.

"What?" I ask.

"Nothing, you talk about 'back in the day' like you are an old dude. It's funny." She smiles.

I can't hide a smile tugging at my lips. "Why? Isn't it true?"

"You know you're far from it. Don't fish for compliments. It doesn't suit your devil-billionaire persona."

With that, an honest laugh rips from my chest.

IT'S ALREADY TEN O'CLOCK AT NIGHT, AND WE ARE STILL struggling with the ins and outs of transactions, firewalls, and networks. The feeling of desperation is creeping in. I helped Roxanne search through every directory she could think of, leaving no stone unturned. I granted her access to more information than I am comfortable with, but at this point, I'm not sure anymore what to keep confidential.

"I'm done for today," she mumbles, rubbing her eyes. They are red-rimmed, and she looks tired. I am too.

"We can pick this up tomorrow. Do you want to have dinner? I can order something delivered. It's the least I can do after keeping you hostage all day," I suggest feeling a bit guilty.

I liked picking her brain so much that I didn't want today to end. Finding someone who intellectually challenges me like she does isn't easy. She's more than just brilliant. She's a brainiac in the most unique way. She uses her intelligence to think through the most ordinary things and gives you a new perspective on those problems. She can turn all your certainty upside down with simple reasoning. She's used to thinking outside the box, and I love that in a person.

She seems to consider my offer and then she finally nods.

"If you don't have somewhere else to be, I mean. I didn't even ask," I add, not sure if I'm disrupting her night.

I'm used to not having plans for the night, and sometimes I forget that other people may have other things to do.

"No, it's fine. I usually work during the night." She dismisses my concern, revealing a glimpse into her nocturnal routine.

"Really? How so?" I'm genuinely intrigued, my curiosity piqued by her unconventional work schedule.

She shrugs. "When you always have a bunch of people playing video games in the other room with no regard for others, you get used to working when it's quieter."

She doesn't seem happy about that living arrangement, and I can understand why. The place, from what I saw, was a chaotic den of video games and noise. I can't fathom why she doesn't move out, but it's none of my business, and I don't pry.

I nod and turn to my computer to browse the restaurant website. "If you trust me, I can order from my favorite restaurant. Italian"

She grins. "Go ahead, I'm sure you have good taste."

I shake my head at her, teasing, but a smile rises on my lips.

"So, why Roxanne? Out of all the names you could have chosen when you had to change yours?" I'm curious about it. I always wondered where it came from.

"It's one of my father's favorite songs, one he listened to all the time when I was a kid. So it stuck with me, and when I had to choose, I thought, why not?"

It's a very sentimental choice that makes perfect sense coming from her.

"You know it's about a prostitute, right?"

She rolls her eyes. *Brat.*

"Do you have something against prostitutes? They're just normal people who decide to make money that way. Why demonize them? Because they don't live up to your moral standards? Did you ever think that maybe judging people for having sex is wrong and normalizing it would put an end to all the slut shaming toward women?" She is cute when she is all riled up.

"Jesus, it was just a question. Don't make me out to be a sexist prick because I'm not."

"So, why ask?" she challenges.

"Because most people don't know. It's mortifying when people think it's just from the *Moulin Rouge* soundtrack and don't know the story behind it. How it was banned from BBC, and how it launched the band into stardom," I explain. It's painful, every time, to listen to those things.

"Did you know that the name Roxanne comes from Cyrano's unrequited desire for her? They were in Paris, playing in a club and there was this poster of the play in the hotel." She almost beams, telling me this.

"I heard that too!" I agree.

"Sorry to interrupt." Jack knocks at the open door, startling both of us.

"Come in!" I wave at him toward the chair next to Roxanne.

He gingerly sits and puts a bag over my desk. "They delivered this for you and I told them I would bring it up."

"Thank you. It's our dinner."

He looks at Roxanne with a fatherly gaze.

"You should take him out or tell him to go home. I

find him here day and night, seven days a week. It doesn't matter when my shift is; he's always in this office. Tell him that life is short and it's a waste to spend it in here." He winks at her.

She smiles and looks between us.

"You're wasting your time with her. She works more than me and during the night too." I chuckle.

He shakes his head. "What happened to you young-sters? You should enjoy life, travel, and have a family, not spend your best years in an office."

She sighs. "Capitalism happened. We have to work to pay bills and don't have time to enjoy the small things."

She says it playfully and without any trace of bitter-ness in her voice, but I know this is a cutting remark toward me.

"So, Jack, how is your daughter doing? Is she ready to go to college?" I divert the topic to something safer.

The attempt is successful, and Jack starts to talk about the frenzy, the excitement, and the challenges. Roxanne laughs, asks questions, and seems happy about the situation. She almost looks proud when he tells her all his kids went to college with a full scholarship.

It's such a grounded, common conversation that it feels almost homey to be here, with the two of them, discussing our private life like we are old friends.

When Jack goes back to his job and I start to open

the boxes of food, I find Roxanne looking at me with a smile on her face.

"What?" I ask.

"Nothing."

But it feels like anything but nothing. I feel like I shared a part of my private life with her that I jealously keep to myself, and I haven't even realized it. I don't know if I'm angry or scared about it.

12

ROXANNE

"Are we having this conversation *again*?" I glare at Leonard.

He keeps staring at his computer, frowning because of a problem we incurred this morning. He stubbornly refuses to give me access to the part of his company that concerns his employees, and I'm here, waiting for him to check those files.

"As long as you keep asking me to stick your nose where you shouldn't, yes, we are having this conversation." He never moves his gaze from the monitor.

I study him, his disheveled state. We have been working nonstop on this project since he hired me, and we are running in circles, chasing dead ends. It's frustrating for both of us.

I discovered a side of Leonard that I didn't know

existed. A less perfect version with messy hair from constantly running his hands through it. He doesn't wear a tie because he had almost ripped it off in frustration after hours of coding a patch that didn't yield any promising results. His shirt sleeves are rolled up to his elbows since he needed to keep busy while I searched through yet another directory that turned out to be a dead end. I discovered a Leonard who is more human and less tycoon, someone almost relatable.

"You know that I can do it anyway, but I'm being nice and letting you trust me, right?" I challenge him.

He glances over at me, and his lips slightly curve upward. Another novelty about Leonard: he can smile!

"Of course, I know it. But if you do, you'll be escorted out of this place by the FBI," he threatens me. His tone is playful, but I know he can do it. He has so many connections all it would take is a phone call to lock me up forever.

"Really? You feel so threatened by a girl you'd have to call the big bad guys?" I tease.

"Don't get ahead of yourself. You don't threaten my masculinity by showing off your skills," he counters.

"Strange. I didn't mention your masculinity, but you felt the need to point it out." I grin when he rolls his eyes.

"I pointed it out because you always go there. You never cease to mention that men and women are equal and that all this toxic masculinity is getting inside our heads."

He has a point. I remind him daily of this. "It's true," I scoff.

He finally turns toward me and pins me to the chair with his magnetic stare. *Jesus, those eyes.*

"I know it's true, and I never once led you to believe I think otherwise. I'm well aware of the disparity between men and women, especially how you're treated in tech. I'm doing everything I can to erase this divide and change men's mentality in every one of my companies."

That is also true. To my annoyance, he proved me wrong when I said he keeps perpetrating the same toxic work environment as most of the companies I had to deal with.

A knock on the door puts our conversation on hold.

"Come in," he says, and his secretary—a beautiful woman in her fifties—enters the room.

"Sorry to interrupt; I'm going out for lunch. Should I bring you back something?" she asks, as she does every day.

To my surprise, Leonard shakes his head.

"No, we're going out, thanks." He smiles at her.

"We are?" This is the first time we haven't eaten our meals in front of the computer.

"Don't be so surprised," he scolds.

"Are you serious? This is the first time we're walking out of this office with the sun still in the sky. Are you sure you're not going to burst into flames?"

"Ha. Ha. Ha. Very funny. I need to get out or I'll kill you with my bare hands," he says, standing up and walking around the desk.

When I turn and face the secretary, I almost laugh, noticing her wide eyes and bewildered expression. She is probably not used to this kind of banter with her boss.

When we're in the elevator I can't stop a laugh from bubbling up in my chest. "I think we shocked your secretary," I say.

"Probably. She's not used to this familiarity." He smiles.

"Always playing the boss card with her?" I roll my eyes.

"No, she's just not comfortable mixing her professional and private life, and I respect that," he explains simply and I feel a pang of guilt in my chest.

I assumed *he* was the one keeping his distance.

"So, where are we going?" I ask when I step out of the elevator toward his car. The driver is already waiting for us by the back door. I wonder if he lives in this car. Sometimes he looks like part of the amenities this luxury vehicle offers. He never talks either, like he is not human at all.

"You'll see." A smug smile appears on his face.

I'm guessing today I'll get to eat at a fancy restaurant I couldn't afford unless I go out with my sister and Raphael.

I COULDN'T BE MORE WRONG. WHEN THE CAR DRIVES into a neighborhood that doesn't scream super rich, I start to suspect I'm not getting a fancy experience.

When it stops in front of what looks like a family diner, I'm relieved. I won't be ashamed to wear shorts and sneakers while eating my meal.

"What is this place?" I ask when he helps me out of the car.

"Something I discovered a while ago," he says cryptically.

It's typical Leonard. He never gives you a straight answer, and I've learned not to push him. He likes to be mysterious, but in the end, he'll answer your question.

We enter the place, and I was mistaken. It's not a diner. It's a bakery. My mouth hangs open in front of shelves loaded with at least ten different kinds of bread, pastries, but also sandwiches. A small fridge on the left contains bottles of water and sodas.

"This is a paradise," I say while deeply inhaling the smell of freshly baked bread.

Leonard chuckles. "I know. It smells so good, and it tastes even better."

I turn toward him and encounter a genuine smile on his face. He looks almost younger with that dreamy, nostalgic gaze. I don't know what this place reminds him of, but I am sure it's a good memory.

"Leonard!" A black-haired, olive-skinned woman hollers from behind the counter.

She is in her mid-sixties, maybe older, with a smile that takes over her whole face. She walks around the counter and hugs him. And he hugs her back. Leonard willingly hugs someone. I'm astounded.

"How are you doing?" he asks as she walks back around the counter.

There is no one besides us in this place, and it's a bit surprising, considering how good those things look.

"Good! How are *you* doing?" she asks, but Leonard stays silent for a long moment, studying her.

"How are you *really* doing?" he asks again, and this time, the woman looks almost shy.

"Business is a bit slow lately, but we'll be fine." She smiles as though she's almost convinced of her statement, but it doesn't lessen Leonard's worried look. His eyebrows are still knitted in concern.

"What can I get you?" she asks me, clearly wanting to change the subject.

For a moment, I think he won't drop the subject,

prying information from her, but then he puts a hand on my back and guides me to the counter.

"Their burrata and sun-dried tomato sandwich is the best," he suggests.

"I'll go with his suggestion," I tell the woman.

"Do you want a bit of pesto in it?" she asks.

"Yes, please!" It comes out more needy than I intended.

We wait for our orders in silence, even though I'm dying to know how he discovered this place.

When we finally sit down at the small table near the window, I ask him.

"I was looking with some investors for a place to develop a new business, and we ended up in this neighborhood. We didn't go through with the project, but I love their sandwiches, and I come here quite often," he explains.

His explanation unsettles me. On one side, he looks really concerned for the well-being of the woman behind the counter. On the other, he knows this place because he wanted to tear it down to build another mall and make a profit, becoming even richer at others' expense.

There are two sides of Leonard I can't reconcile in my head. The one I've discovered recently, who's less-than-perfect and worries about other people, and the ruthless mogul who will do anything to satisfy his greed.

Every time I start to reconsider my opinion about

him, something reminds me why I hate him in the first place. I decide not to show my distaste and let the subject drop for the sake of the woman who is looking at us with anticipation from behind the counter.

"This sandwich is amazing," I moan when my taste-buds are hit with the savory pesto and sundried tomatoes, giving the burrata a new layer of flavor.

"Isn't it?" Leonard gives me a smile that almost makes my heart stop.

He rarely smiles, especially not at me, and the sudden brightness in his face is almost enough to make me forget the morning's turmoil, from our heated arguments to the revelation about this place. Almost. Because no matter how attractive he may be, I can't envision a future where my disdain for him goes away.

"If only you'd use the same wise judgment and give me access to all your files," I taunt him.

He stops eating and studies me with an unreadable expression. Sometimes his thoughts are so inaccessible that he drives me crazy trying to figure out his next move. Most of the time, he surprises me with something I would never expect from him, adding to the intrigue of our relationship.

"I'm working with you. I'm the one doing the job based on your directions. You have to trust me."

"I know you *can* do it. But why? It's not a matter of your employees' privacy because I understand that, and I don't ask you to go in there anymore," I point out.

He takes a deep breath like he is undecided whether to tell me what is going on in his mind or not.

"Because I risk ruining our future collaboration," he concedes.

I'm a bit lost. "What? Why?"

"Because there's information in there that concerns my clients. You can't access their personal data; privacy violation is out of the question, but you can access the structure of their security systems, giving you an advantage over your competitors, who would have to ask for a warrant from a judge to have the same information. Giving you access to that means you can be accused of unfair competition and a couple of more serious charges I won't dig into," he explains, and I'm surprised again by his reasoning.

"Why are you so sure we'll have the same clients?"

"Because I personally know a bunch of them, and I'm sure that, at some point, they'll need your help. It's just a matter of time."

I didn't think about the implications for my job when I agreed to work with him. It makes sense. He sells security systems, and I try to breach them. Some clients will overlap for sure.

"Why are you doing it? You could get rid of me and my contract in one go and not break a sweat doing it."

He tilts his head to the side. "You really have a bad opinion of me, don't you?" His tone sounds almost defeated.

I don't know what to say. Yes, I don't expect anything good from him. He built his empire answering to no one, sometimes making questionable decisions regarding his companies. He suffocated every competitor, causing them to collapse and leaving thousands of families without a primary source of income.

It's impossible to erase years of bad behavior with his current actions. How can I trust him? He doesn't trust me in the first place. I suppose the sentiment is mutual. We are going nowhere in the trusting department.

We finish our meal in silence, and before walking out, Leonard approaches the counter again.

"It was amazing," he tells the woman. "Do you also have the other bill?"

I frown, trying to understand what he is up to.

"Thank you. I feel bad every time I ring up this sum for you." She is almost ashamed when she hands him the credit card reader to pay more than two thousand dollars.

Now, I'm definitely curious.

"How many times do I have to tell you that it's not a problem?" he says playfully, clearly having had this conversation a bunch of times.

I keep quiet next to him, not wanting to disturb this moment that feels so intimate.

She tries to reason with him. "I know, but we can find another solution."

"This is the easiest one, and I don't mind paying a bit," he says more firmly.

The woman nods, and we walk out of the place, waving our goodbyes. When we get into the car, I can't contain my curiosity anymore.

"What was that about?" I ask.

He gives me a look like he doesn't want to tell me what just happened, but he has to because I was there and he can't deny it.

"Some families and the homeless around here have a hard time getting by, so they come here, take what they need, and I come by once in a while to pay the bill. This is a family-run business, and they're trying to help the community, but they can't afford to give away things for free," he explains almost reluctantly, and I'm speechless.

Every time I convince myself he is the bad guy, he pulls some major hero card that upends all my beliefs. Like this, providing for poor people and trying to hide it.

Who are you, Leonard Walton?

13

LEONARD

"I swear I want to throw this computer out the window!" Roxanne hisses, standing up and pacing around the room.

She is furious. We have reached another dead end. We're running in circles, and I can understand her frustration. We're both used to getting what we want quickly, and this makes us both restless.

For once, I have no words for her. I'm equally disappointed in our results. And I can't blame it on our lack of commitment because we have been here in my office for many days and nights, trying to find out how they got in.

"How is it even possible? We follow the money, the digital traces they could have left, nothing. How is it possible that we can't come up with anything useful? Who are they? Why are they better than us?" she almost shouts. She is so agitated I don't even know if she's breathing.

Those are all valid questions, and I'm disappointed that I don't have any answers for her. I don't know if she is angrier at not being able to finish this job or because she thinks there is someone better than her out there. I know a thing or two about pride, and she seems to value her skills to the point of honing them to perfection. Apparently, someone is more perfect than her.

It's similar to the feeling I had when I had to ask for her help. What if she proves that she is better than me? It's a low blow to recover from.

"Unfortunately, I don't have an answer for any of that," I reluctantly admit.

She turns around and stares at me. I don't know if she is pissed with my lack of help or just pissed in general. Difficult to say when she is so angry.

"What are we getting wrong?" she asks.

"We are doing nothing wrong. That's the problem. We've tried different approaches to the same problem. We checked, double-checked and we compared notes. If one of us made a mistake, the other should have noticed, but nothing."

She scoffs, disappointed, starting again to pace my office.

"Well, there must be something we're missing, or we would have found a solution by now, don't you think?" Disappointment drips from every single word like acid, corroding her happiness and her ability to think straight.

She's gone down this rabbit hole we are working on, and she can't get out. She won't find anything useful until she can clear her head.

"We have to take a step back and try to see things with a fresh perspective," I suggest.

She scoffs again. "How many times have we already done that?"

"And we'll keep doing it until we find something. Staying on the same path won't help us find anything useful," I insist, and she rolls her eyes.

She won't listen to me. She is so focused on her rage that she can't think of anything else.

I stand up and get her attention. When I walk toward the door, she starts panicking.

"Where are you going? We haven't finished here," she complains, following me to the elevator.

"We're going to a place that can help us focus on work again. I don't know about you, but I'm completely spent, and I'm not able to think about anything at all," I explain.

"And you have a magic place to do that?" There is amusement in her voice.

At least I distracted her from her bad mood.

"Sort of."

When we reach the garage, she is smiling, and when I approach the old Porsche, she has a grin on her face.

"So, you can drive after all," she taunts me.

I open the door for her and walk around the car to get in.

"It's midnight; I can't keep my driver on stand-by all day. He has a family," I explain.

"He does?" She fakes surprise. "I thought he was a robot. Does he smile sometimes?"

I chuckle. I have the same question too, but apparently, he has a wife and kids, and he is pretty damn smiley with them.

We drive in silence in the less chaotic traffic of the night until we reach our destination.

"What is this place?" she asks, peeking up at the anonymous warehouse in the commercial area.

"Jesus, it's a surprise. Can you wait literally one minute until we're inside?" I chuckle as she rolls her eyes.

I grab the keys from my pocket and walk to the side of the building. The door opens with a squeaky noise, and when we step inside it's completely dark. The smell of dust and spray paint is particularly strong, but Roxanne doesn't complain.

I grab her hand and drag her with me until I find the light switch on the wall where I know it is.

"You must come here often if you know where to find the lights," she observes, and I nod.

"The owner is a friend, and he gave me a key to come here after hours," I explain while I guide her to another door.

"Why?" she asks.

I answer, opening the door. "It's a rage room. If people knew I came here to smash things, they'd think I've lost my mind, and my company stocks would drop."

She looks at me with pity in her eyes. "With all the money you got, you're not even free to live. Is it really worth it?"

Her words are a punch to the gut. Not because she said them in an offensive way but because they are true. Sometimes I want to disappear and live a normal life, but even that is impossible because everybody knows my face.

I don't answer, and fortunately, she doesn't push the subject. "We need to put these on before we start smashing things." I hand her coveralls, a helmet, and glasses.

"You willingly put these on over your tailored suit?" She chuckles.

"I know it sounds blasphemous, but yes. I do." I remove my jacket and put it on a chair in the hallway.

She starts to dress in the clothes I got for her and they

are clearly not her size. They are huge on her, and I lower to roll her pant legs just above her ankles.

When I look up at her, I find her wide-eyed. "What?" I frown.

"You just dropped on your knees to help me."

"Yeah, so?" What did I do wrong?

"How do you even know how to do that? Don't you have someone doing that for you every morning?" she asks.

"What? Dressing me? I'm capable of putting on my clothes without assistance," I answer, a bit pissed over this ridiculous idea she has of me. Like I have someone to take care of even the most stupid tasks just because I have money. For Pete's sake, I'm an independent adult.

She grins. "I'm joking, but it's funny to see the outrage on your face."

"Brat," I murmur, standing up, and she sticks out her tongue.

I turn around to hide my smile and start putting on my clothes. When I face her again, she starts to laugh like I've never seen her do before. She is even more beautiful when she laughs, and I almost feel the urge to make her laugh more. The mere idea is terrifying.

We finally face the room full of plates, an old computer, an even older TV, crates of all sizes, and other unidentified objects that have already been violently affected by the baseball bats we hold.

"So, what are we doing? Smashing things?" she asks.

She doesn't seem eager to break what is inside this room. I get it. The first time I came here, I spent the whole time feeling guilty about destroying perfectly intact objects. When you grow up paying attention to care for the things your parents give you, there is something unholy in taking out your rage in this way. But when you go home after doing it, you feel so relieved you can't wait to come back a second time and a third after that.

I approach the old TV and smash the front glass in one go.

"Okay. That's an answer." She chuckles, and I watch her choose what to start with first.

She hesitantly hits the computer.

"Come on. Put some of the anger you had in my office into this crap," I egg her on, and instantly see her mood change.

She grabs her bat with both hands and swings at a pile of plates stacked on a crate. The white porcelain flies all over the wall at the back of the room, breaking into dozens of pieces. A satisfied smile appears on her face.

She focuses her anger on a wooden crate used to carry fruits and vegetables. It takes more swings to smash it, but when she does, she looks at me panting and grinning like crazy.

"Well, I have to admit this is fun," she says.

I nod. "It's somehow therapeutic."

I hit the bat over the TV again, smashing the back part. It's one of those old pieces with a cathode ray tube that they removed for safety reasons. I hit the external shell until it's hanging on one side. My arms burn from the effort, but I'm smiling like I always do in this room.

All the stress, anger, and frustration fly away with every swing I take. It doesn't matter if I'm sweating in my thousand-dollar suit. The energy burning inside me is taking away all the bad thoughts, problems, and worries I carry on my shoulders every day.

I turn toward Roxanne, and I watch her laughing like crazy while she hits the computer again and again. She is beautiful and carefree. I envy her pink hair and printed T-shirt, her idealist heart and her noble purposes. There is something still pure in her, untouched by the ugliness of this industry, something I have learned to admire since I started working with her.

I watch her laugh and witness the switch in her mood. Her smiles fade as if an undesired thought has snuck into her mind. In the beginning, she is startled, almost physically unbalanced by the sudden image appearing in her head. Then the rage takes over, and the anger distorting her beautiful smile is something that tears my chest open. The sorrow, mixed with fury, fear, and something like shame, is branded in my brain. She hits that computer again and again; she doesn't stop when the object is completely destroyed. She doesn't stop when tears stream down her face and hiccups shake her chest.

I didn't mean for her to have such a bad experience. I wanted to help release some stress, but this is deeper and more complex than frustration. I grab her elbow, and she drops the bat. She loses her balance and falls into my arms when I pull her against my chest.

I hold her tight while her tears keep coming, and her arms envelop my waist like I'm her lifeline. She sobs uncontrollably, and I feel responsible for her meltdown. But I don't know how to fix my mistake.

"It's okay," are the only words I can think of, and also the most stupid.

Nothing is okay. She is upset and crying in my arms; nothing is even close to being okay.

"You'll be fine," I whisper, kissing the top of her head.

This, too, is a stupid thing to say. How can I know? I don't even know the reason for this change in her mood.

"Are you going to keep rattling off the worst rom-com clichés you know?" she asks between hiccups.

I stifle a chuckle. "I hope not."

She rests her forehead on my chest and breathes in deeply. It takes her a few minutes to regain composures.

"Sorry about that," she murmurs, drying her tears with the back of her hand.

I want to reach out and clean her streaked face with my thumb, but I refrain from doing such a stupid thing. Too intimate. Too close to care for her.

"Do you want to talk about it?" I offer to listen to her story.

"No, but I think I owe you an explanation," she admits.

"You don't owe me anything," I point out.

I don't want her to feel compelled to confess something so private she looks ashamed about it.

"I *want* to give you an explanation. Even if I don't want to talk about it. If that makes any sense," she clarifies.

"Do you know how I started as a white hat?" she asks as I invite her to sit on one of the crates beside me.

I shake my head, not trusting my mouth to say another stupid thing.

"It was when we entered the witness protection program. I was a kid with a computer and a lot of time to spend in my room. I was terrified to go out in the beginning because I thought someone was coming to kill me, to kill my family," she explains.

I can't even imagine being so scared so young. She was barely a teenager when her sister testified at the trial that completely changed their lives forever.

"I missed my sister. I didn't know if she was dead or alive, but I was scared to search for her because I didn't want to lead someone to her if they tracked me. So I decided I wanted to do something to remove the problem. Remove the person that ruined our life," she confesses.

She gives a quick glance in my direction, probably to gauge my reaction. I hold her gaze for a second before speaking.

"Did you want to kill him?" I ask. There is no judgment in my voice. I'm only curious to know what went through the head of a scared fourteen-year-old.

She shakes her head. "I don't think so. I didn't think that far ahead. I wanted to find information about him and understand if there was something I could do to free my sister and my family."

I believe her. Sometimes you want to know more to put your heart to rest. I guess her parents tried to protect her young mind from all the brutal information about the trial, but doing so fed her fear. She wasn't a toddler unable to understand; she was a teenager with a vivid imagination. And considering the adult she is now, she was a smart one.

"So I tried to hack the FBI." A small smile curves her lips.

I chuckle. "Of course you did."

"I didn't succeed, but from that day on, I dedicated my whole life to this, to find a way to reunite my family. When this nightmare disappeared years ago, I felt empty.

I don't have a purpose in my life anymore and I feel lost. And I feel angry because I should be happy, but I feel just…lost."

I study her face, her big eyes full of shame and somehow regret. I always thought she was a spoiled brat, but the truth is that behind that pink hair and cocky attitude, there is a woman scared about her future and scared of what she became.

"You can do for others what you did for your sister," I suggest.

She frowns. "What do you mean?"

"Use your skills to help people. You have no idea how many injustices there are in this world. Bad things happen to good people, and justice often isn't served. Help those people. Use your skills to find a way to give those victims the life they deserve, a life without fear. Help those people to heal."

"You're suggesting I do something illegal?" She smiles.

"I'm suggesting you find irrefutable proof to put the perpetrators behind bars."

She nods and lowers her gaze to the concrete floor. Her brows are furrowed as if thinking about it. I hope she will consider it.

"Thank you for listening. It's difficult to find someone to tell these things to. Not even my sister or Raphael know," she confesses.

I study her and understand her reluctance to say something like that to the person who involuntarily caused all this.

"I'm glad to help."

But the truth is that I feel powerless in the face of her struggle. I can give her money and a company, but I will never be able to give her what she really needs: the answer to a future she can't see in front of her—the most terrifying thing of all.

14

ROXANNE

When Leonard invited me to spend the day with him and his friends, I didn't imagine waking up at six in the morning for a limo picking me up at seven. But here I am. On the dock, waiting for Raphael's bodyguard to secure the boat before heading out for a sailing trip.

"Is this something you old people do all the time?" I ask, yawning.

Raphael chuckles while Leonard fights a smile pulling at his lips.

"What?" Elijah asks, grinning.

"Waking up before noon on Saturday," I explain.

"Yes, it's something they do a lot," Mia, Elijah's girlfriend and around my age, answers.

"Hey! I'm not that old!" Silver complains.

"Yes, you are," I answer, with Dakota and Mia nodding in approval.

Thank God there are a couple of girls my age, or I would be bored to death listening to these career men talking business all day.

Aaron and Raphael laugh as Leonard scowls.

"What? You didn't think you were young, did you?" I raise my eyebrow, challenging him.

"Jesus. And I invited her," he murmurs under his breath, making everyone laugh.

The truth is, I'm happy to be here. After my meltdown at the rage room, Leonard went easy on me. He reduced our office hours, took me out for lunch more often, and even some dinners. And yesterday, he invited me on a sailing trip he had planned with his friends. It's like somehow I stepped up to be part of his circle—a stark difference from the guys I was hanging out with until a few weeks ago.

"You can go." Raphael's bodyguard gives us the thumbs up.

I grab my bag from the dock and follow the others toward a sailboat. Leonard gets in first, then helps us jump into it until the eight of us are all on board. Raphael, Aaron, and Elijah help with the ropes while Leonard stands behind the boat's wheel.

"Where's the captain?" I ask when I see him tampering with the instruments.

Leonard frowns. "What do you mean?"

"Who's...driving this thing?" I wave toward the massive boat.

"I am." His face contorts with confusion.

"You know how to do this? I thought there was an expert helping us."

He points toward Raphael and the others busy helping him sail this boat. "We do it all the time."

"Of course you do," I murmur as I reach the girls sprawled on the bow.

I sit between them, and I don't miss the curious glance Silver gives me.

"So, I'm happy you two are getting along," she says, nodding toward Leonard.

I glance toward him, and my breath catches in my throat. He is gorgeous in his khaki shorts, polo, sailing shoes, and sunglasses. Even dressed more casually, he has a sophisticated bearing that's difficult not to notice. His tanned skin almost glows in the morning sun.

"Getting along is a strong statement. We tolerate each other," I point out, and they all exchange a look I can't figure out.

"What?" I ask, confused.

"If he asked you to come, he likes you," Dakota explains.

"He's very protective of his free time and picky about the people he surrounds himself with," Mia chips in.

I shrug, attempting to brush off their insinuations. I don my sunglasses and lie down, hoping to bask in the sun's warmth, but their words persist in my thoughts. I never anticipated this invitation to carry such weight, or I would have thought more before accepting.

It takes us half an hour to leave the dock and the harbor. When we finally hoist the sails, a light breeze helps us move smoothly over the flat ocean. It's a perfect day to be out at sea.

"Here we go," Mia giggles and the others follow suit.

I turn my gaze toward where they are all looking and grinning, and my mouth goes dry. All the men have taken off their t-shirts, giving us a view worthy of the best swimsuit ad. How many times do they hit the gym to have those bodies?

"This is not fair. You can drool over your partners, and I should just shut my eyes?" I complain, and they laugh.

"You can always check out Leonard. It's not that bad, is it?" my sister suggests, and my eyes automatically land on him.

He is a piece of art. With his suit on, he is sexy, but without a shirt, he is just perfection made flesh. His biceps slightly bulge, gripping the helm, and his pecs are so defined that I would trace that curve with my fingers for the rest of my life. And those abs? Is it even possible to have an eight-pack?

"No. I cannot." My tongue trips on the words.

"Why not?" Dakota asks. I turn toward her, sheltering my eyes from the sun and studying her curious face.

"What do you mean why not? I work with him. I can't just stare at him like he's a piece of meat." A very, very hot one.

They giggle, and my sister playfully pushes my shoulder. "Come on. You have noticed how sexy he is. Don't play dumb," she challenges me.

I'm not used to talking with my sister about men, especially those I work with for the most part of the day. I can't start to think of Leonard like that, or I won't be able to focus on my job. However, it might be too late. Every single rippling muscle is branded in my brain, living rent-free in each one of my wet dreams.

"Yes, I noticed. I'm not blind. But I can't look at him like that." It comes out like a whine.

The girls laugh at my expenses, and I cover my burning face with my hands. And it's not because of the sun.

"Why not? It's not like you're jumping him. You're...window-shopping," Mia suggests, and we burst out laughing.

"Do you know how hard it will be to work with him after seeing what he hides under those suits?" I point out.

"Well, that's easy. Ditch the suits and bend over his desk!" she giggles.

"Mia!" I scold, but there is no seriousness in my tone.

They all giggle like schoolgirls, and the guys turn toward us with curious looks.

"Don't worry, honey! I was telling them about the first time we used your desk," she hollers toward Elijah, and a flash of lust crosses his eyes. A grin appears on his face.

"What are they talking about?" Leonard asks.

Elijah smirks at him. "Sex. They're talking about how I bent over the desk and fucked the shit out of her," he explains so casually that I'm baffled.

"Elijah!" I scold.

Mia laughs, and I turn toward her. She doesn't look upset about her partner telling others about their private life, and I'm surprised.

"We have sex in front of other people at the sex club. I don't mind if he talks to his friend about it," she explains, and it's like she just slapped me across the face.

Seriously?

"Too much information, Mia. She's not used to our conversations yet." My sister looks at me sympathetically.

I open my mouth a couple of times, trying to think of

something intelligent to say, but my brain has gone blank from the turn this conversation had taken.

"And I thought I was the one living the teenage era because I shared an apartment with a bunch of hormonal guys. You're like puberty on steroids." I'm finally able to elaborate on my thoughts.

"Well, when you start to date men instead of boys, things improve in that department too." Dakota's smug smile is unmistakable. We all get the idea of how Aaron is in the sack.

"Jesus, I need to find a man ASAP, or I can't keep hanging out with you," I murmur, and the silence that follows is almost comic.

The girls are all staring at me like they know something I don't.

"What?"

They are so synchronized, turning toward the boat wheel, that what they are suggesting would almost be comical if it weren't terrifying.

"No, absolutely no," I say resolutely.

"Why are you so stubborn? We see how you look at each other. You're already fucking with your eyes. Bring it on a physical level," Mia pleads like her life depends on my romantic status.

"What movie are you talking about? We're doing nothing with our eyes," I point out.

My sister snorts. "We almost hit the dock when you

took off your dress because Leonard couldn't keep his eyes off you."

"That's absolute bullshit." Is it? I turn toward Leonard and catch him checking me out.

Am I missing something here? We are constantly fighting, always at each other's throats. Yes, I find him hot, but that doesn't mean we have to complicate things. And when Leonard leaves the helm to Raphael and strolls toward us, I can feel all eyes on me.

Did he hear our conversation? It's possible. I mean, the wind can carry voices. But he would have said something, right? His shadow lands over us and I'm sure I'm not breathing at all.

' "We're going to drop anchor in a few so we can eat. Are you okay with that?" he asks no one in particular.

I keep my mouth shut because I don't trust my voice to be firm right now.

"Sure, do you need help?" Silver asks.

He smiles sweetly at her. "No, stay here and enjoy the sun. It's just sandwiches; we can manage."

He turns around and walks away while I'm almost purple from keeping my breath.

"You can breathe now," Mia teases.

"Who? Me? I'm perfectly fine," I lie.

They laugh, calling out my bullshit.

When they call us, we join them and sit around a basket full of sandwiches, fruit, and various sweets some of their chefs prepared. I'm the only one who doesn't have a personal chef on my payroll, and I have to admit it's something I would consider if I were rich. Preparing meals is not my strong suit.

"This is amazing," I moan, biting on a tuna and cucumber sandwich.

"That's my favorite too." Leonard says, almost whispering in my ear.

I'm so close to him I'm practically sitting on his lap. There is not much space for eight people to access the basket, so I can't complain about the situation. It's him or one of the other men, and I don't think their partner would be happy about that.

"Thank you for inviting me. I'm having fun." I haven't had a chance to tell him this yet, but I'm really relaxing and enjoying my time outside.

"I'm glad you came. I would have felt guilty knowing you were bent over the computer working on a Saturday." He winks at me.

I don't know if it's the playful wink or the '*bent over the computer*' thing, but my cheeks burn in response. The sun, it's probably the sun, right? I can't be affected by his flirty ways, or the image branded in my head of me bent over his desk and his erection buried deep inside me. I'm definitely not someone who lives in a delusional fantasy about their billionaire boss.

"So, this isn't for me. It's to quiet your conscience."

My voice comes out remarkably firm, considering the turmoil wreaking havoc in my chest.

The laugh rumbling in his chest does funny things to my lower belly. The sudden need to jump into the water to quench my dirty thoughts is stronger than ever. I can't survive an entire day on this boat with no escape from my needs. It's been a long time since I got laid; I have to do something about the matter.

"Of course it is. I have to keep up the appearance of the selfish billionaire." He winks again, and I'm done.

I can't hold his burning gaze any longer and divert mine in front of me. I meet my sister's smug smile, Mia's grin, and Dakota's wagging eyebrow. I can't believe they are focused exclusively on the two of us. Do they not have a life?

Elijah rescues me from my misery. "I'm jumping in. Anyone else coming?" he asks the group.

There is general enthusiasm for the suggestion, and I'm the first one to jump to my feet. Leonard is the only one sitting relaxed.

"Aren't you coming?" I frown.

He shakes his head. "I'm staying on the boat in case of an emergency. When one of the guys comes back, I'll take a swim too."

"Oh, that makes sense. Thank you," I say, but a pang of disappointment hits my gut. I shouldn't feel let down because he is not coming, but I can't stop the feeling from creeping in.

He holds my gaze for a moment, then gestures towards the side of the boat where everyone is leaping into the water. "Go on, I'll follow later," he says, his voice carrying a hint of reassurance.

I hesitate for a moment longer, then decide not to make a fool of myself by staying on the boat with him. I walk gingerly, trying not to slip, but when I'm almost there, I trip and fall overboard, head-first into the water. Graceful as a seal trying to climb stairs.

When I come up for air, sputtering salty water, I look up to see Leonard's worried face. "Are you okay?" he asks without a hint of amusement in his voice.

I'm still trying to free my face from the mess that is my hair, but I manage to give him a thumbs up. *Great. This is my personal version of 'I carried the watermelon.'*

"Well, that was one way to jump in," my sister laughs, and I give her a side-eye.

We swim for a while, enjoying the cold water and the lulling movement of the small waves. This day couldn't be more perfect.

"What if there are sharks?" Mia suddenly asks. Well, that is an excellent way to ruin the moment, considering we are swimming in a freaking ocean.

"Well, there probably are somewhere," Elijah answers, and we all groan in response.

"Is this your way of reassuring her? Because you're not doing a great job," Raphael points out.

Elijah rolls his eyes but follows Mia to the stern of the boat, where Leonard lowers the boarding ladder.

A few seconds later, a loud splash startles me. I turn around in time to see Leonard emerge from the water, shaking his head and dragging a hand through his hair to shake off the water. I have to check my mouth because I'm sure it's hanging open. Can this man be more gorgeous? The droplets running down his face make him even more sexy. He looks like he came straight out of a perfume ad. One of those fancy brands that uses half-naked models to make women buy cologne in bulk.

"And this is our cue to leave," my sister murmurs.

Jesus, can she be more obvious? She chuckles when I give her the stink-eye.

"I'm cold. Can we go up?" she whines at a clueless Raphael, who eagerly follows her onto the boat.

I turn around in time to see Dakota dragging Aaron toward the boarding ladder. I need to have a few words with those traitors. It's painfully obvious they're trying to set us up.

"If you stare at her like that a bit longer, she may bleed." Leonard's husky voice comes from close behind my back. Too close. When I turn around, he is at arm's length.

He is staring at me like he wants to devour me, and I would totally let him do it. I swim back a bit toward the boat to put some distance between us, but he follows me. His eyes never leave mine, burning with a desire that ignites mine. Suddenly, everything around us disappears —the waves, the cracking sound of the boat, the voices from our friends. When my back hits the side of the boat, I have nowhere to go to escape his magnetic gaze.

And I don't want to. I almost crave his touch when he puts a hand on the boat beside my head and lets the waves push his chest toward mine, close but never touching. He makes no effort to keep some distance, and I'm so gone that I wrap my legs around his waist. His eyes widen in surprise, but a small grin tugs at his lips. *What are you doing? I don't know, and I don't have the will to care.*

His arm wraps around my waist in a firm grip, but he makes no move to drag me to his chest. I wrap my arms around his neck and enjoy the friction of my hardened nipples brushing lightly against his toned pecs. He doesn't get closer, but he doesn't loosen his grip either. We are dancing on a fine line. Neither of us is willing to push the boundaries, to tip the balance on one side or another. Give in to our burning desire and kiss or put some distance and break the spell.

A bigger wave pushes Leonard even closer. His lips are a breath away from mine. He is so close I can see the droplets of water on his long, dark eyelashes. His eyes are hooded with a desire matching mine. The cold water does nothing to dampen the heat rising in my lower belly. I'm surprised the water between us isn't boiling already.

"Are you still alive down there?" Raphael's voice comes like nails on a blackboard.

It takes us a moment to return to reality, but the spell is broken, and Leonard puts some distance between us.

"Jesus Christ, Raphael, can you mind your own business?" my sister intervenes.

"What? Why? They disappeared down there," he complains.

A small smile appears on Leonard's lips, listening to the banter on the boat, but a flash of disappointment also crosses his eyes. Is he annoyed like I am by the interruption? Every sign tells me he is when he reluctantly lets his grip on my waist go and detangles from my legs.

His eyes never leave mine, and a silent question I have no answer for dances in them: what the hell are we doing?

I have no idea.

15

LEONARD

"When you told me we were going for a change of scenario, I thought you meant a café or a restaurant," Roxanne says, peeking out of the window at my mansion.

I help her out of the crappy yellow thing she calls a car and guide her to the front door. She curiously looks around, taking in the raised flowerbed my landscaper insisted on installing and the expensive olive trees. If she thinks I'm the typical spoiled billionaire who throws money into frivolous things, she doesn't let it show.

"Do you want to discuss something confidential and delicate in a crowded café?" I challenge her.

She shakes her head, her eyes still wide with awe, and follows me into the house, her gaze drawn to the corridor adorned with a breathtaking art gallery.

"I guess you're right," she murmurs. "Is that a real Picasso?"

When I turn toward her, I almost laugh at the shocked expression. "If it's not, I definitely overpaid for a copy."

She is cute when she opens her mouth once, twice, but nothing comes out. She takes a deep breath and shakes her head. "How? Aren't you worried it will be ruined or stolen?"

"An auction. And no, that room has controlled humidity, temperature, and light. And there is an alarm system that will notify me if a fly goes inside, let alone a human being," I explain, and she frowns.

"You talk like it's normal for someone to have a gallery in their own house." She shakes her head in disbelief.

We resume our walk toward my office. "To be fair, many people I know have at least one in their main residence."

She scoffs. "Let me guess, some of them have one in their vacation house too?"

"*Houses*, but yes. That's the idea."

"Unbelievable," she murmurs under her breath.

We have just entered my office and turned on the computer on my desk. As she sits on the leather couch, one leg bent under her butt, with an arm sprawled over the back cushion, I can't help but feel a bit strange having her here in my home. She appears so comfortable, as if she lives here. A strange feeling is expanding in my chest—a pleasant one as if I'm getting used to having her around. However, this could become very dangerous territory to navigate.

"So, how are we proceeding?" she asks.

"First of all, I need to eat," I say, going around my desk to reach the door we just came in.

She scrambles to stand up and follow my long strides. "Are you serious? It's ten in the morning."

I turn to look at her without stopping. "Do you need a schedule to eat?"

She frowns. "No, but…"

"I reason better on a full stomach," I explain. The truth is, this problem is obsessing us both and we need a distraction. We are way too deep trying to track down that missing money to be effective in doing it. We need a fresh start.

"So what? Are you calling your personal chef for a snack?" she taunts.

She always does that. Asks me the most absurd thing, like billionaires have the strangest habits in the world. It has become our inside joke.

"It's Saturday. She's with her family."

"You're not keeping her chained to the pantry. Impressive."

"Very funny."

She grins and I can't stop thinking about how much fun she had in the boat. And then my mind strays toward the red bikini she was wearing, and my blood flows under my belt. Damn! I had to take care of my erection like a fifteen-year-old when I got back that day. I can't stop thinking about how perfect that body is and how much I wanted to kiss her when her legs wrapped around my middle in the water. I almost gave in to temptation.

I open the fridge to scan what is inside and to hide the lust I can't contain in her presence. It was the right move to invite her along. We are both obsessed with my problem, and I know she would have stayed inside her bedroom, working her ass off to find a solution. We both needed a break to recharge and sharpen our focus. But since we came back, my energy has been depleted trying not to think about that tiny piece of red fabric that nothing does to cover her curves. Not to mention that I overheard their conversation about her bent over my desk and that was a vivid image I didn't need.

"Steak and salad?" I ask.

"Okay. A full meal. But yes, why not?" She sounds puzzled.

I grab the beef from the fridge and walk to the kitchen counter where she is propped on a stool.

"What's wrong with you and eating at scheduled times?" I'm curious.

She shrugs. "I don't know. I suppose it's something I carry from when I was a kid. Our mom scolded us if we ate outside of meals. We always ate at the same time. I think my parents still do."

"Do you miss them?"

"It's not like they're dead. We talk a lot on the phone, and we see each other a lot. I miss them, but I'm not homesick."

She watches me prepare the meat for the grill. She is fascinated, like I'm some rare experiment, trying to gauge whether it will explode or not.

"What about you? Do you miss your family?" She gives in to her curiosity.

"They'd like to see me more." I chuckle. "But they know that after I founded fifteen companies besides this one, I don't have as much time to get together as often as they want."

She stops with her fingers in mid-air as she was trying to steal some of the seasoning I have in front of me to read the label. The frown that obscures her smile makes me alert.

"What?" There is a hint of concern in my voice.

"Nothing, or maybe everything. You said you have fifteen companies besides this one. There are fifteen transactions," she says, and I can feel my gut twist in a vice of unease, my heart pounding in my chest.

"And the sum of all those transactions is exactly the one we used to start this company, the first one." Her words hit me like a thunderbolt, and I quickly grasp the implications.

She raises an eyebrow. "It can't be a coincidence."

I shake my head, dropping everything I'm doing and wondering if there is a connection. "No, it's not a coincidence. But right now, this is just information that doesn't take us any further."

She stares at me, hope in her eyes. Her brain is running a thousand miles per hour—I can see it from here.

"We focused on this company because we thought they wanted to prove they could beat your cybersecurity system, but maybe it's something more personal. They want to beat *you*," she suggests, and the dread sneaking into my chest is unbearable.

I can't even imagine someone going to that length to hurt me. I've made many enemies along the way, but never someone so resentful as to hack into my systems and hurt me where I'm most vulnerable. My work is my life; if you take that from me, I'm lost.

"It's worth a try." My voice is firmer than I thought.

Roxanne is off the stool before I even finish my sentence. We almost sprint toward my office. When I close the door behind us, she is already picking up her laptop from the backpack she put on the floor near my desk. I drag the chair from the front around my desk next to mine. We both sit behind the monitor of my computer and dig into the network we know like our pockets.

"Do you use your system to protect the other companies?" she asks when I'm already checking the first one.

"Yes, but we didn't receive any notification about that. If someone tries to access one of them, the ticket escalates to me. They page me day or night, no exceptions," I inform her, and a grin appears on her face.

"You are a pain-in-the-ass boss, you know that?"

"I'm proud to be one," I reply with a smug smile.

She shakes her head without any further comment. We work side by side like the trained team we have become since she started to work with me. We dig into every single system for hours until the steaks are forgotten in the kitchen and the sun is deep over the horizon.

"Okay. On one hand, I'm happy we proved your system is solid fifteen different times. On the other, I thought it was a good hunch to follow," she says when the last check confirms what we already know: they didn't hack the other companies.

I stare at the computer. Something is missing, but I can't grasp what.

"I think we should keep going in that direction. I

don't believe in coincidence," I state, and the idea that someone is trying to hurt me is even more disconcerting.

"Me too, but where's the common pattern between the fifteen companies? Besides your system, I mean," she asks.

I ponder it, my mind racing. "I'm not sure," I mumble, my uncertainty palpable.

"Come on. Not even software?" she insists, and it's like being hit by a stone.

"Wait, there is something. The software we use to handle the employee paychecks. Different accounts, obviously, but the company we use is the same." The hope that explodes in my chest shines through my words, a possible solution dawning on me.

"See? Ultimately, you do have to show me your employee files." She chuckles, and I can't stifle a laugh.

"Fair enough."

"Should I hack into their software, or are you?" She grins.

I roll my eyes. "I don't need to hack into anything. I have access to them."

"Party pooper," she singsongs under her breath.

We go straight for the logs, searching for those around the dates we have for the mysterious transactions, and there it is. One of the small sums appears on the screen at the exact date and time it goes out.

"It's strange. This isn't a transaction," Roxanne points out what I already saw.

I log into another company account and we find the second sum. I proceed to check all fifteen companies and we find every single sum missing. My heart hammers in my chest, ready to leap on the keyboard on my desk.

"I only have one doubt: it's not money going out. They aren't transactions. It looks like the bank generates them, or something, through the payroll software. Where is the money?" She is puzzled, and I feel my heart plummet into my stomach.

"It's still there," I say.

"What do you mean?"

"They never stole from me. Not money, at least."

"It's still in there? What exactly are we looking at?" Her voice carries a concern I wasn't expecting from her. These aren't her companies. It's not even her job, but her desire to uncover the truth is enough to make this research personal.

"We still have to check how they got in, but my guess is that they hacked the bank system to access the employee software on our servers and open the door to every single company," I explain with a numbness that overwhelms me. I don't even feel the fear creeping up my spine at this discovery.

She slumps back in her chair. I swear she is a shade paler than she was five minutes ago.

"And from there, they can steal something way more valuable than money: information," she concludes in a murmur.

I stand up and walk to the wet bar in the corner of my office. I grab the whiskey bottle and pour two generous glasses.

"Here, to celebrate." I hand her one of the tumblers.

She frowns but accepts the alcohol. "You want to celebrate them potentially stealing industrial secrets from you?"

I grin and lean back. "We're celebrating that we have found where to start digging. We're far from finished, but at least we have a clear path in front of us," I say, my voice laced with a hint of intrigue.

Roxanne takes a sip, and her face contorts from the taste of the alcohol. The second one goes down smoother. "You're weird, you know that?" she says, her voice a mix of amusement and disbelief.

"Probably, every genius is." I tease.

"And humble too!" she fires back.

We stare at each other for a long moment, and a silent conversation goes between us. Like the one we had in the water: what is happening between us? The comfortable routine-non-routine we have is something I never thought I would experience with a woman. She doesn't mind my dedication to my job because she has the same attachment to hers.

"So, those steaks," she says, standing up and stretching her back. "I hope you have a good bottle of red wine because I don't want to go home until I'm so drunk I forget the shitstorm we are about to raise."

She walks out of the office, and I can't help to stare at her ass. I will have to be very drunk too, if I don't want to do something stupid like, for example, kiss the hell out of her.

16

ROXANNE

"Holy crap," I murmur, trying to open my eyes.

My head is pounding like an entire work crew hammering in my brain. I take a deep breath, trying to calm my nausea without much success. It's been a long time since I had a hangover like this. I remember the fantastic steak Leonard grilled, the bottle of wine, and the second one. I also remember his gin collection and the tasting. We were on the patio, enjoying our night. But I don't remember much after that.

Especially not ending up in this bed.

"Where the hell am I?" I whisper, finally opening my eyes and looking around. This is definitely not my home. This room is as big as half of my new apartment.

I'm not ready to do the walk of shame in front of

Leonard. He's the only one that could have put me in this comfy bed. I look down, and fortunately, I still have my clothes on. I'm glad I didn't try to seduce him. At least, I hope not. Luckily, I don't remember him turning me down. *That* would have been embarrassing.

I sit up and take a moment to give my stomach a bit of a rest. On the nightstand, I notice a glass of water and a couple of aspirins. I smile. He is quite the attentive one. A flutter in my stomach I don't want to acknowledge makes me nervous. *It's the hangover. It's definitely the hangover.*

I stand up and look around for a bathroom. It's easy to spot the door that leads to it, and when I catch my reflection in the mirror, I cringe. My makeup has run, forming dark streaks under my eyes, and my hair is a tangled mess I'll have some difficulty fixing without a shower. But Leonard thought of that too. On the counter sits a comfy robe and fluffy towels.

"It's like being in a spa," I murmur. Must be nice having all this money. I could never afford something this expensive at home. My towels have seen the washer and dryer so many times that they're not even recognizable.

I turn on the hot water and step into the shower, taking my time rinsing away the signs of the night before. I use the shampoo and body wash I find inside, and I'm sure this is a guest bedroom. They are expensive and coconut-scented. A far cry from the manly fragrance Leonard's skin smells like. The fact that I know how he smells should be a concerning enough sign I spend way too much time with him.

The shower is so long and hot I need to dry the mirror with a towel to see my reflection in it. Better. At least now I'm somewhat presentable. Still wearing the clothes from yesterday, but at least I don't look like a runaway.

And now what? Should I try to sneak out of the house and drive home, or should I at least say goodbye? The temptation to disappear to avoid a potentially awkward conversation is strong, but we have to meet anyway tomorrow. It's better if I face the shame now.

After walking in circles for a good ten minutes in this massive mansion, I finally find my way to the kitchen where Leonard sits at the counter sipping coffee and reading his iPad.

I stand in the doorway to admire him, but he doesn't notice me yet. He is gorgeous. With his dark hair and sculpted physique, it's like staring at the perfect human being. It's like one of those Artificial Intelligence pictures where you ask the computer to generate the perfect male specimen. Everything about him fits the quintessential sex appeal attractive to both males and females—from the bulge of his biceps under the polo to the cupid's arc of his lips. The only thing that makes me stay away from him is his personality, but I'm not sure about that anymore.

"There you are. I was starting to think you were dead up there," he says with a smile.

"Nope. I wanted to die, but no such luck." I grimace.

He chuckles. "Why?"

I should just get the awkward conversation over with. It won't get any better if I wait. I study his face. He doesn't seem angry or embarrassed, but he has a poker face to begin with, which could explain his blank look.

"Because I don't remember half of last night and don't know if I made a fool of myself," I confess, and he chuckles.

He puts his iPad on the counter and looks me straight in the eyes with a smug smile on his face. I'm not used to his happy face, and it unsettles me. Where is the stern mogul I hate so much? I almost don't remember him anymore.

"If by making a fool of yourself you mean rambling on about the weirdest facts you know, then yes, you did." He grins.

"That's it? Just rambling?" I want to be sure I didn't act on my attraction to him. No matter how much I convince myself I don't like him, he is someone I would approach at a bar if he were a normal person.

"Just rambling. You know you're interested in the weirdest things, right?"

I pour myself a cup of coffee and sit next to him. "I know. It's my happy place when I'm stressed. I look up random facts online and go down the rabbit hole of how pink flamingos can stand on one leg for hours."

"That was an impressive explanation."

I chuckle. "They're cool."

He stands up and walks around the counter. "Breakfast?"

"Yes, please. I need to put something in my stomach to avoid fainting in your kitchen." I groan.

He studies me for a long moment, and I swear I can read the worry on his face. It's strange coming from him. I expect him to scold me for getting drunk, but the harsh words never come.

"Is it too much to ask you to work today? Try and tackle the problem you discovered last night?" He asks almost hesitantly.

"Do you even have a personal life? It's been a while since we started working together, and I've never seen you doing anything for fun on the weekend besides that boat trip." I have no concern about sticking my nose in his private life, apparently.

He frowns, clearly caught off guard. "I usually catch up with emails, news, and everything else I don't have time to do during the week. It's usually not work-related —not directly, at least."

"Oh, really? I'm a bit surprised. I thought you might

have some other hobbies or interests outside of work. Isn't there anything you enjoy doing in your free time?" I ask, trying to sound genuinely curious.

I'm a workaholic, I can't deny that, but at least I take some days off. Even if only to get a break and recharge to work harder later.

"Keeping up with the latest tech innovation *is* fun!" he complains, his voice laced with a hint of frustration as he deftly turns the sizzling bacon in the pan.

"No, that's research and development. Work," I point out.

He opens his mouth twice, trying to come up with a reply, but then he closes it without a word, maybe realizing I'm right.

"You know what? Today, we don't work. We are tourists." I say resolutely, not accepting a no for an answer.

Of course, he has to fight. He raises an eyebrow and stares at me. "*We* are not. You do whatever you want. I can't force you to work, but I'm going to try to figure out what is going on—not in just one of my companies but all sixteen of them."

"Do you think you'll be able to plug the hole, identify the culprit, and find out what actions were taken during the past year?"

"No, but I can start breaking down the issue," he asserts.

"But won't tomorrow be the same, just another day added to the year when the system was compromised?" I can be more stubborn than him.

He nods. He doesn't look defeated, but I know he is fuming because he hates to admit that I'm right.

"There you go. You have no reason not to take the day off."

"Fine. Can you shut up about it now?" A small smile tugs at his lips. I don't think he's totally against taking a break; he just needs someone to tell him it's not a waste of time.

He strikes me as someone who was scolded as a child for "being lazy" in front of the TV and grew up as an adult who feels guilty for relaxing and taking some time for himself.

I grin as I steal a piece of bacon from the plate where they're resting while he's scrambling eggs and moan. "This is amazing. You're an extraordinary cook, you know that?"

"Of course, I know. I may have a personal chef for practical reasons, but I don't eat shitty meals when she's gone," he points out.

I roll my eyes. "And you're so humble too."

"I never pretended to be humble. It doesn't suit my tycoon image." He grins, and I laugh.

"No, ABSOLUTELY NOT. YOU MADE ME DRESS LIKE AN idiot, I won't ride in that piece of crap too," he complains when I open the door to my car and get ready to drive him around the city.

"You're far from looking like an idiot, trust me." If I'm being honest, he is hot as hell. With those cargo pants, polo, sneakers, and baseball cap, he looks like an athlete on vacation. Even the backpack suits the image of a carefree tourist.

He raises an eyebrow and mumbles something I can't discern while I jump into my car. I wait for him to get in too, and smile when he finally decides to humor me.

He puts on his seatbelt while I admire his figure. He is so big that his knees almost touch the dashboard. Our elbows brush together for a moment, and I tingle from the contact all the way down to my core. *It's the hangover*, I need to remind myself.

I drive out of his property and down the canyon road leading to Beverly Hills, rolling my eyes when he grabs the handle over his head like his life depends on it. I'm not that bad of a driver—most of the time.

"You can relax, you know," I say after the umpteenth grunt he lets out.

"You just hit the third curb since leaving my house. How can I relax?" he complains.

"Jesus, you're so dramatic sometimes. This is Los Angeles. We all know that curbs are always in the way.

How often do you see someone hitting one parking on these narrow hilly roads?" I glance at him and see disbelief plastered all over his face.

"Never! It's literally never happened to me, and I've never witnessed anyone else doing it."

"Because you have a driver, and you don't pay attention."

"Why are you parking here?" he asks, puzzled.

"Because we're doing the Walk of Fame." I smile smugly at him.

He stares at me like I've grown another head. "You're serious. So we're hitting all the tourist traps?"

"Yep." I open the door to step out of the car, and I hear him mumble under his breath. It sounded a lot like "unbelievable."

It turns out that after a few minutes of embarrassment and looking like a fish out of water, he actually enjoys his tour. Especially when he compares his hands and feet with the imprints in front of the theatre. He grins smugly when he realizes his hands are bigger than most of the handsome actors' there. Everything is a competition for him, and he hates to lose.

"Why are you going in there?" he asks, looking suspiciously at the souvenir shop.

"Are you always like this? Asking why for everything?"

"Yes, if someone drags me around the city, making me do stupid things."

"You're acting like a toddler."

"I am not."

I look at him, raising my eyebrow. "You just proved my point."

He scowls, and I chuckle.

"Try these." I hand him a pair of pink flamingo-shaped sunglasses.

He opens his mouth to say something, but I quickly cut him off, my eyes twinkling with mischief.

"If you ask why again, I will stab you with this Hollywood sign." I point at an ugly piece of metal that doesn't even resemble the original.

He sighs but humors me and puts on the sunglasses. The pink flamingos perched on his nose make him look utterly ridiculous, and I can't help but find it endearing. He is cute, and I feel my cheeks heat up. *Since when do I consider a man cute?*

"Happy now?" he asks, diverting my thoughts from a very dangerous path.

"No, we need proof of this moment." I grab his hand and drag him toward the photo booth.

"You gotta be kidding me," he mutters when he understands my intentions.

"Come on, have some fun!" I chirp, knowing it will

annoy him even more, and I get, in fact, a side-eye from Leonard in response.

I open the curtain, then realize that pushing his boundaries might backfire. There is no way we can both fit side by side on this tiny bench. Leonard seems not to notice or care. He drags me inside, sits down, and then makes me sit on his lap. I'm petrified.

"Come on, put on those pineapple sunglasses so we can get over this craziness," he grumbles.

The deep voice resonating against my back makes me realize how close we are, his strong arms wrapped around my waist, heat emanating from his perfect body. *Jesus, is it hot in here, or is it just me?*

"At least smile so it looks you're enjoying it." I turn my head to him. That was the wrong move. He's so close, our lips are mere inches apart.

I can't see his eyes, but a muscle twitch of his jaw and his grip on my waist tightening gives him away. He realizes how close we are, how intimate this situation is.

I'm barely aware of the camera taking pictures because when his hand reaches out to move a loose strand from my face, his fingers brush my skin, leaving a sizzling hot tingling that shoots sparks down to my core. My eyes stray down to his lips, and the temptation to kiss that luscious mouth is almost unbearable. Just one small taste.

His fingers linger on my skin, tracing my jaw and

cupping my neck. His thumb lightly outlines my pulse, stopping to enjoy the quickening of my heartbeat.

He licks his lips, and I feel mine burning with the desire to taste them. So close. We are so close I only need to bend a bit to give in to my craving for him. I squirm on his lap, squeezing my legs shut in the hope of relieving myself from the aching need to ride him in this booth.

"Are you done in there?" A girl's voice startles us.

It's like a slap in the face, and from the tightness of Leonard's jaw, I know the feeling is mutual. I was going to kiss him. If I had a few more seconds, I would have done it. I stand up, open the curtain and notice an annoyed teenager ready to go in with someone I assume is her boyfriend. He smirks when he sees Leonard coming out of the booth behind me.

I grab the strip of pictures without even looking at them, put them in my back pocket, and walk out without saying a word. I don't want to address what just happened in there and from the way Leonard follows me out of the shop, I'm guessing he doesn't either.

"TAKE CARE OF THOSE CHEEKS; PUT ON SOME AFTER-SUN cream, or your skin will peel off," Leonard says to me when I park in front of his house.

"Sure."

The silence that follows is awkward. We spent our day strolling around the Santa Monica Pier and Venice beach. We had lunch at a café, talking about everything and nothing but never addressing that moment in the photo booth. It's like we silently agreed that it never happened. But now, in front of his house, everything is coming back.

Leonard should leave my car, and I should go home, but neither of us is making a move to end this day.

"If this were a date, I'd ask you to come in, but *this is not a date*, so I'll just say goodbye here and see you tomorrow," he says, looking me in the eyes.

I don't know why he needs to point it out. Does he really assume I'm delusional enough to think otherwise? Still, I feel a pang of disappointment making its way into my chest.

Going in right now is the worst idea ever because the tension that was rising in that photo booth never got released. If I go in now, we'll make the worst mistake we can possibly make. Leaving is the wise choice, but my body hasn't gotten the memo.

"Yeah, sure." I shrug, putting on my best poker face. "Wait!" I stop him from getting out of the car.

I grab the strip of pictures in my back pocket, rip it in half, and give half to him. He says nothing, but he stares at the pictures for a long moment. I watch his jaw twitch, his knuckles turning white around the door handle, and then he gets out without another glance at me.

I look at the pictures in my hand for the first time and my heart hammers in my chest. We're just inches apart, my hand on his chest, his on my neck. Seconds away from the most sizzling kiss in history. And we look like long-time lovers.

This is not good. This is not good at all.

17

LEONARD

I stare at the two small square pictures in my hand. We look like we are going to fuck each other's brains out. *What was I thinking when I dragged her onto my lap?* The truth is, I didn't think at all. My body took charge and I gave in to my desire to have her close. Since the boat trip and after carrying her to bed the other night, my body has been craving her skin against mine. And this is a very bad urge to deal with.

I stare at Roxanne, biting her lower lip slightly, my mouth just a bit open, and the desire to kiss her returns, crashing like a wave against all my resolve to stay away from her. Every single reason I told myself about why it is the worst idea ever to give in to my desires has lost its significance. For every bad reason, I can find a good one to strike it down.

Yesterday, for the first time since college, I spent a day enjoying life without thinking once about work. It was refreshing. And she was responsible for that miracle.

For some unknown reason, two workaholics together are very good at enjoying their free time. Who knew I needed someone with my same toxic approach to work to find a way to turn off my brain?

"Why are you smiling like that?" Roxanne's amused voice startles me. I hadn't even noticed her coming into my office.

"I'm not smiling." I totally am, and didn't even realize it.

"Keep telling yourself that, but I saw it. You can't fool me anymore with your mogul charade." She plops into the chair in front of my desk and crosses those long legs, showing off her sparkly pink shoes.

When I finally move my eyes from her inviting legs to her face, I notice her reddened cheeks.

"Did you put on after-sun cream like I asked?" I'm surprised by the concern in my voice. I feel a strange grip in my gut. Since when did I start caring about her? I know I've rescued her a couple of times since meeting again, dancing with her after the creep molested her, or giving her a ride when her car broke down. But I chalked those up to something I did to protect Raphael's little sister-in-law. This time hits differently. I care about her on a level that has nothing to do with my friend.

The brat rolls her eyes. "Yes, Daddy."

My cock twitches in my pants. *Why should I stay away from her again?* Difficult to remember the reason right now.

"Don't say that again," I growl.

A smug smile appears on her face. "Why? Does it turn you on?"

"You don't want to find out," I tease.

"Maybe I do," she challenges, and I need to change the topic of this conversation before I bend her over the desk and fuck that attitude out of her.

The stare contest lasts for a long moment, but she's the first to look away. I smile. I decide to drop it and steer the conversation toward a safer topic: work.

"I think we should ask Oliver to work with us on what we discovered about the money," I suggest, and her smile immediately drops.

"Why should we do that?" She frowns.

"What do you mean why? He built this company with me. He knows the ins and outs of every single file in our systems," I answer even though it's pretty clear the reasons behind my decision.

She abruptly gets up and begins pacing my office, disrupting my train of thought. Her resistance to the idea puzzles me. Why is she so opposed to this suggestion? Three minds working on this problem could yield better results than two exhausted ones. A fresh perspective might be just what we need.

"We don't know if it was an inside job, and you want to spread the word? I don't feel comfortable with this turn of events," she says bluntly.

Is she serious? She thinks someone inside my own company could do something like this, and the mere thought of it is offensive.

"Don't even think something so twisted," I warn in a stern tone.

She turns around, crossing her arms under her boobs, making them stick out even more. *Damn! I need to focus on this discussion, not how good her tits look!*

"Why not? Are you so sure of their loyalty that you trust them blindly?" She raises an eyebrow like this would be the most stupid thing in the world.

I feel the anger boiling in my gut and make a huge effort to keep it down, avoiding making a scene. I assume she's used to untrustworthy people, considering she's a hacker. But even she should have some people she can rely on, or she will become paranoid.

"Yes, especially the ones who started this company with me. We have more than twenty years behind us trying to grow this—" I gesture around with my hands. "No one wants to throw it away," I point out with a finality that leaves no room for argument.

She stares at me for a long moment, studying my

face. I don't back down from her evaluation, and I feel almost reinvigorated by how she challenges me. It's the first time I've been around a woman who isn't trying to appease me just because of what I represent.

"Fine, but I'll hold you personally responsible for any fuck-up related to this decision," she concedes, sitting again in the chair in front of my desk.

I can't hide a smile. "It won't be necessary, but you have my word," I assure her.

She nods, and her mood seems to lighten again, though I know she disagrees with my decision.

"So, what's next?"

"I'm calling Oliver, and we'll figure out together how to dig deeper into what we found out."

HALF AN HOUR LATER, WHEN OLIVER WALKS INTO MY office, one glance at Roxanne changes his mood completely. Tensions rise as he mutters under his breath, "You have got to be kidding me."

Roxanne raises an annoyed eyebrow at me, and I look at her, trying to convey all my prayers not to make this moment worse with her sharp tongue. Luckily, she gets the hint and humors me.

"Hi, Oliver. We need to talk to you about what we discovered about this missing money." I smile at him, trying to be as accommodating as possible. It's always a gamble these days with him. One day, he's nice and kind; the other, he is grumpy and shouting at everyone. I honestly find it impossible to gauge what his mood will be, but today I have a good clue from his pissed face. I prepare for all hell to break loose.

"You are obsessed with this freaking money. You're a billionaire; get over yourself and start to think about the people who work for you! You're wasting time and resources for nothing," he growls.

Roxanne scoffs, and I stare at him in disbelief. "We found out they're not stealing money but information, and you think it's nothing?" I raise my voice.

He shrugs. "Do you have proof? Maybe it's just a mistake by the bank. You just said they're not stealing money; maybe it's just that: nothing. You're so wrapped up in *her* that you can't see beyond your nose!" he spits.

"Excuse me?" Roxanne's outraged tone forces him to turn toward her.

He sneers at her—an actual creepy sneer that I've never seen before on his face. "You play the big bad hacker but you're just a kid who knows nothing. You came here, stuck your nose in our systems, and God knows what you're doing with that information. You bat those pretty eyelashes, wriggle your young ass in front of him, and get him to do whatever you want. You're good at it, I'll give you that."

"This's enough!" I shout, getting his full attention.

He looks at me with sad eyes. "You've become so greedy that you don't even care about this company anymore. You want to get bigger and bigger, losing focus on what our initial goal was."

"That's not true, and you know it. Don't play this card with me because it won't work. I know exactly what I'm doing, and I haven't forgotten where we came from and where we're going. If you can't see that, it's not my fault. It's yours," I fire back and he looks like I slapped him in the face.

I feel bad for him, but I'm tired of sugarcoating everything because he snaps at the least inconvenience. He turns around and walks out of the room without another word, and I clench my fists, glaring at the door closing behind him.

Roxanne studies me with worried eyes. Neither of us breaks the silence for a long moment.

She speaks first with a stern expression. "I would say 'I told you so,' but I think his behavior speaks for itself."

I don't say a word because I'm so dumbfounded by Oliver's outburst that I can barely think. I'm missing something, and I can't put my finger on it. It seems like I'm doing that a lot lately and this realization is concerning enough.

"Are you convinced there's something off about this situation? Oliver included?"

Her implication snaps me out of my dizziness. "Don't even think about it. He's my most trusted partner, the co-founder of this company, and I don't want you spreading completely baseless rumors," I bark out with more bitterness than I intended. I don't want to be rude to her, but the turmoil rumbling in my chest makes it challenging to be levelheaded.

"Are you serious? He just freaked out because we're digging our noses into the problem, and you don't find it even slightly suspicious?" She presses the subject.

Anger and discomfort mix in my gut, making me boil. "No! I've known him forever. He's under a lot of pressure because of a big step we're taking with the company, and he just doesn't have time for this."

She scoffs. "Your relationship with the people around you blinds you. You haven't even considered it's one of them fucking you over, have you?"

It's my turn to be offended. If there's anything I'm proud of, it's the fact that I can read people better than anyone else. I surrounded myself with the smartest and most loyal people I had ever met, and I would bet my life on their integrity. Especially Oliver, who is the most idealistic of the bunch. He would never stoop so low as to damage his own company for some petty reason I can't even imagine.

"How many companies did you build from scratch? How many people do you work with? How many people can you count on? You know nothing about this kind of relationship because you've never experienced anything like this. You can't understand what loyalty or integrity mean because your job is full of distrust, trying to hack other people's systems. Trying to fuck other people's lives," I spit, and immediately regret my choice of words.

Her face hardens as she stands up and grabs her things.

"If there's anything I've learned in my life, it's that the people you love the most will make decisions that most fuck up your life, and you can't do anything about it. They'll do it *because* they have the most personal motivation. Until you understand that, I can't help you," she says with a coldness in her tone that chills my spine.

I don't stop her as she turns around and walks out the door with a calm I should have.

I stare at the point where she left for a long time, mulling over what she said. It can't be true. She had a rough life growing up, but that doesn't mean ordinary people react like she does. She didn't have a normal childhood, and what she experienced scarred her deep down to her bones. She'll always be distrustful of everyone.

How the hell did this go so wrong so fast?

I grab my phone and call the only person I can talk to.

"Can you come to my office, please?"

After he agrees, I put my phone on the desk and stare at the door, leaning against the chair.

When Benjamin comes in, his face instantly becomes serious. His frown deepens the lines on his forehead. "What happened?" he asks, worry dripping from his words.

I take a deep breath and tell him everything. I need to get this off of my chest, it's crushing me. He studies me with a concerned gaze and doesn't breathe or move, as if either could worsen the situation. After I finish, he stares at me for a long moment, aggravating my already bad mood.

"It's worse than I thought," he murmurs as though to himself.

"That's not exactly reassuring," I point out.

He shakes his head and takes a deep breath, raising his gaze to the ceiling before lowering it back to my face. "He's going to lose his mind between the acquisition and the divorce."

"Divorce? What divorce?" I feel my stomach squeeze in a tight grip.

He stares at me, surprised. His frown deepens even more, fraying my already tense nerves.

"You don't know? His wife asked for a divorce a year ago. I thought he told you about that."

My heart drops. How did I miss something so crucial

in the life of one of my oldest friends? The fact that he didn't come to me for support like we always do for each other is concerning.

"He didn't say a word," I whisper, and Benjamin's gaze softens.

"I'm sure it's because he doesn't want to add more stress to your life right now. He knows how much you're caught up with everything going on here." He tries to explain away something that is way simpler: Oliver didn't want to tell me. For whatever reason, he's lost faith that I could understand what he was going through. Maybe because I never had a wife or a relationship, but it doesn't matter. He decided to keep me out of this part of his life. And it hurts.

"One year. He decided to keep it from me for one year, and I didn't notice anything unusual. I mean, he was difficult to deal with, but I never stopped to under-stand why. What kind of a friend does that make me?" The words are like fire in my throat. How could I have missed something so massive?

Benjamin doesn't add anything. It's difficult even for him to find an explanation that doesn't sound like an excuse. I'm a shitty friend, and I have to deal with it.

18

ROXANNE

I sit in my car for a long time, simmering with anger and disappointment. How could Leonard not say a thing when his dear friend started to rant against me? His bewildered expression can't compensate for his lack of words. I don't understand; he's one of the most intelligent people I know, yet he's easily influenced by his feelings for his friend. It doesn't make sense. Nobody achieves so much without a ruthless mindset. No matter what, you have to sacrifice your personal life to reach that kind of success. Leonard has indeed shown me he cares about things other than his job, but blindly trusting a person who is clearly hostile towards both of us is a rookie mistake he shouldn't be making.

There's more to this story, and I can't shake the feeling that I've been blindsided by the same man who shared so many secrets with me. Professional secrets, not personal ones, but this doesn't change the reality that he trusted me with those. I take a deep breath, not sure if I'm angrier about what happened in his office or because I felt excluded from his world as soon as Oliver entered the room. Before Oliver showed up, we were a team, but afterward, I felt like an annoying spectator of their long-lasting friendship. I felt personally betrayed, and that thought scares me the most.

I start the car and drive into traffic without any specific destination in mind. After the turmoil of the past hour, I need a distraction to calm my anger and clear my thoughts. I take random turns, changing the scenery, which helps to ease my anger. As I begin to calm down, I start recognizing some of the buildings around me. The bakery where Leonard took me to eat is just a few yards away.

I park close to the entrance and walk down the sidewalk to reach the place. Compared to the luxury I've experienced recently, it's a poor neighborhood, but it's not as run-down as one would expect. It's certainly not fancy but everything is well-kept, clean, and the overall vibe is that people enjoy living here.

I reach out to grab the door handle but hesitate, feeling like I'm somehow spying on Leonard's personal life coming here alone. It's a strange feeling, but I dismiss it along with my lingering anger. The baked

goods are amazing here, so why shouldn't I enjoy them?
I shake my head, smiling at my silly thoughts, and walk
in. It's still quite early, and the place is not busy, just like
the other time we came here for lunch. The doorbell
rings, and the two people behind the counter look up
with a smile. I recognize them from the previous time I
was here.

"Welcome! We'll be with you shortly," the woman
says cheerfully.

I nod and smile at her while peering from behind the
customer she serves to decide what to eat. My mouth
waters at the display case in front of me full of savory
and sweet pastries to choose from. I can't decide what to
try first—because there will absolutely be more than one
pastry on my plate today.

"What can I get you?" the woman asks me with a
genuine smile.

"Difficult question. I want some of everything," I
giggle, and she chuckles.

"Do you trust me?" Her tone is almost conspiratorial.

I nod, intrigued. I take a moment to study the dark
circles and fine lines around her eyes. She is not old, but
she's definitely tired.

"Do you have any allergies?" She tilts her head.

"Fortunately, not," I shake my head.

"I'll make something up for you." She winks at me
and fills a plate with way too many things to count. She

doesn't hesitate as she chooses sweet and savory delicacies for me.

"Jesus, I don't know if I can handle all this," I chuckle when she hands me the plate filled with everything I could possibly want.

"You can. Trust me. And if you don't, we can give you a box to take it with you." She chuckles.

"Okay," I finally agree.

"You're Leonard's friend, right?" she asks before I have the chance to turn around and sit at one of the small tables.

I'm surprised she remembers me. It's been a while since I was here, and it was the only time. Leonard must be very close to them if she pays so much attention to the people around him.

"Yes. Do you mind if I ask you how you met him?" I give in to my curiosity. I know I shouldn't pry, but, to be fair, she started this conversation.

She smiles fondly like it's a memory she is glad to relive, like the expression you see on a sister or even a mother.

"He came here because he wanted to buy our shop. But we said no and offered instead for him to try our pastries. He's been coming here regularly since then."

"Really? He was trying to talk you down in price, wasn't he?" I prod, though I'm not proud of it. But this is my only chance to understand him a bit more without asking him or Raphael. He's so closed off that I'm sure he wouldn't tell me something like this, even if I insisted.

The woman laughs and shakes her head. "No! On the contrary. He was very generous." She must notice my confused face because she continues with the explanation. "He offered way more than what this place is worth, but we explained we were just too attached to it. We wouldn't sell it for any price, even if we were drowning in debt. It's a matter of feelings, not money."

"And he gave up just like that?" I can hear the incredulity in my voice.

She chuckles. "You don't know him very well if you think he just gives up. He paid off our debt, became a regular customer, and always pays for the homeless peoples' meals."

"It sounds like his stubbornness hit you full force," I say.

She barks out a laugh. "You got that right."

"Tell me about it," I murmur, but she hears it and winks at me.

I grab the plate from the counter and sit at one of the small tables next to the window. I dig into the salmon and mushroom pastry and moan.

"This is amazing," I tell the woman.

"I told you to trust me." She smiles.

I watch as she serves the next customer, and I can't stop thinking about what she just shared with me. If you had told me this about Leonard a few months ago, I would have been sure it was pure bullshit. Now, I think it's the most Leonard-like behavior I've ever heard.

After working with him, I believe he did something like that for this family. He hides behind the heartless mogul facade, but he cares about people. He's willing to sacrifice his business and personal assets for strangers—because I doubt he used the company's money to pay off their debts. He takes care of the meals of an entire community, for Pete's sake.

So, what happened with Oliver? I feel guilty for having doubted his judgment. Maybe the guy is just an asshole and has nothing to do with the shit that is going on with the company. Maybe he is just stressed, and I'm judging him for the wrong reasons.

Leonard knows him best, and I should at least listen to his explanation. I stand up, ask for a to-go box, and head back to where I can find some answers.

WHEN I WALK INTO THE OFFICE, LEONARD LOOKS UP IN surprise and I feel a pang of guilt hit my chest. He should know I wouldn't leave him alone to solve this mess. He should trust me. But maybe I haven't given him many chances to. Have I?

I show him the box in my hand. "A peace offering." I try to break the awkward silence between us.

He smiles and asks me to sit across from him at his desk. I open the box in front of us, and we start to dig into the fantastic meal.

"Tell me about Oliver," I say, and his eyebrows shoot up in surprise.

He takes a deep breath and leans back in his chair.

"We met at college. We became friends over a project we did together. He was with me through all the ups and downs, and he kept being my friend even when I dropped out of college."

"Was that when you started this company?" I'm curious.

He shakes his head. "That came a few months later. We had an idea but not a solid project at the time, let alone a business plan. He was the one who pushed me to do something with my life when I thought I was making a massive mistake."

I nod. I've second-guessed my career so many times I know the feeling. The only difference is that I didn't have a dear friend to lean on. I had nobody growing up because I couldn't tell my parents I was doing something illegal—and they were the only ones I could trust at the time.

"Was it your idea or his for this company?"

"Both. We knew we wanted to make the world a

safer place, so we brainstormed ideas. With our expertise in technology and software, this was the natural path we chose."

"Was he always this… challenging?"

He gives me a tender smile—something I've never seen him do. He shakes his head, and his gaze becomes distant, like he's remembering something that happened when they were young.

"You're being generous with him. But no. He wasn't like this. Yes, he is a bit…how can I say, unique. He was peculiar in every way but never so angry. Quite the opposite, he was a chill guy," he explains, his gaze back on me.

"So, what happened to him? Because the man I met is someone with huge anger issues." I want to know the extent of his problems and if they will put us in a difficult spot.

He lets out a long sigh. "He had a particularly rough year, both personal and work-related challenges that made him bitter. And I wasn't there for him."

His confession comes in a whisper, and I wonder if he feels somehow responsible for what happened to him. The way he looks down at his hands instead of meeting my gaze is enough to tell me that his friend's outburst shook him pretty deeply. This is not the fearless Leonard that I know, and it's pretty obvious he is out of his depth in this situation.

I reach over the desk, grab his hand, and let him know I'm here for him if he needs me. I may not be the best person to advise him about this, but I'm good at listening.

His surprised gaze lands on mine, and we stare at each other for a long moment like the world around us doesn't exist. My stomach clenches in a pleasant grip, and my heart stutters in my chest, trying to keep a stable rhythm and miserably failing. He is always attractive, but the vulnerability in his eyes at this moment makes me want to go around this desk and kiss all the sadness from him. The mere thought is terrifying.

"I'm sorry for how he treated you. I shouldn't have let it happen. In my defense, it was so out of character for him I was completely stunned into silence," he admits.

I nod, understanding, especially after his confession.

"I felt like I was suddenly put aside. Like I didn't exist anymore, and…it hurt," I say candidly.

He frowns, and his face darkens. The grip on my fingers intensifies, and I realize we are still holding hands. I feel like if I let go, this connection between us will disappear, and I'm not ready for the emptiness that will follow.

"We are a team. I know we started on the wrong foot, but I want you to be certain that no matter what, we are a team," he states with so much intensity that a pleasant shiver runs down my spine.

"Starting on the wrong foot is a bit of an understatement," I chuckle. I need this tension between us to dissipate because it is becoming suffocating, and I don't trust myself when the need to kiss him is so strong I can hardly find a reason why this is entirely wrong.

He laughs, letting go of my hand and breaking the spell holding us captive. "I was trying to be nice."

"It doesn't suit the mogul persona." I wink at him, and his eyes darken with lust.

His gaze is so intense that I have to look down at our meal spread over the desk. I'm sure he can see my cheeks burning with what I hope he interprets as embarrassment, but it's just pure sexual longing.

It will be a long, tortuous road to the end of this collaboration, and I don't know if I can resist the impulse to give in to my desire.

19

LEONARD

Roxanne and I are in my office, seated on my couch, tracking down every bit of code to understand what they installed into the software we use. After a couple of weeks, we are practically sure that they used the payroll software to breach our systems and gain access to my other companies. Now, we just have to figure out how they did it and what information they are stealing.

Roxanne bends over her computer to grab a piece of sushi and pops it into her mouth, bringing her focus back to her monitor. She is wearing a pair of shorts and a loose tank top; her glittery pink pair of Converse are tossed on the carpet, and her feet are tucked underneath her on the couch. I get a peek of her lacey black bra from the wide sleeve hole and my dick, which has been at half-mast since she walked into this office this morning, is hurting.

I make a massive effort to bring my gaze back to my computer and focus on my task instead of her long, smooth, tanned legs. I've dreamed way too many times of those limbs wrapped around my waist while I fuck her against the wall.

A knock on the door distracts me from my inappropriate thoughts. I look up and see Jack's smiling face.

"Mr. Leonard. Still working?" he asks and I motion for him to come inside and sit in the armchair in front of the low coffee table.

He sits down, bending his knees with some difficulty, and I make a mental note to ask him about his health. When we are alone, we can talk freely without him feeling embarrassed about sharing his personal life with a stranger.

"Should I drive the Miss home? You keep her here so late, working on that infernal machine." He waves at the computers. It's always funny how he scolds me. He acts more like a father than my night security guy. But it's somehow comforting, his concern about my life. I'm used to having people bowing down before me, agreeing to everything I say. It's refreshing when someone calls me on my bullshit.

"I am feeding her...if that helps my cause." I chuckle, and Roxanne does too.

"I promise he is treating me well," she interjects.

Jack doesn't seem convinced and studies her intently, his dark eyes like laser beams taking in her every expression as he scrutinizes her for long moment.

"But you're still here this late," he points out.

"I'm used to working this late. Even if I'm not doing it for him," she says, and the frown on Jack's face deepens.

He turns his scowling gaze on me, and I suddenly feel like a kid being scolded. Very few people can make me shrink in my chair like this.

"When I suggested you find a woman, I meant someone who drags you out of the office, not someone who keeps you in it," he points out, and I bark out a laugh.

I think Roxanne wants to point out that she is not my woman, but when she opens her mouth, she closes it without a word. She is intimidated by Jack. This is the first time I've seen her show respect for someone. It's amusing.

I don't correct him either, and I don't know why. Maybe because, during this time, I've come to know Roxanne enough not to consider her a kid anymore. She's smart, challenges me, and is sexy as hell. Everything I want in a woman.

"How is your family?" I ask, changing the subject.

Jack has been with me long enough to know not to

press a subject if I don't respond. But the question is so close to his heart that he completely forgets what we were discussing.

"I completely forgot to tell you. My youngest was awarded a last-minute scholarship. She is going to college for free like my other kiddos. She is thrilled about it, and I am too. Now she can focus on studying and not worrying about paying off her debts," he says proudly and I'm happy for him.

Out of the corner of my eye, I notice Roxanne studying me with a curious look.

"I'm happy for her. She's a good kid; I'm sure she'll take advantage of the scholarship and make you proud. Has she already decided what to study?" I'm genuinely pleased for them. They are a great family, and they deserve a chance to do great things.

"She wants to become a lawyer." He beams, and I can see his eyes watering. He's a good father.

"I'm sure she'll be a great one."

"Considering how much she argues her case to avoid being grounded, she's had a lot of practice," he chuckles, and we laugh with him.

"Well, I'd better be going. You don't pay me to stay here and chat." He stands up slowly. I'm a bit worried about his health, considering how slowly he moves.

"Good night, Jack."

"Good night, Mr. Leonard. Goodnight, Miss."

"Goodnight," Roxanne replies.

He walks out the door, closing it behind himself. Roxanne turns toward me with a smile.

"What?"

"There isn't a 'last-minute scholarship', is there?" she asks.

A small smile crosses my face as I shake my head. I should have known she'd be smart enough to see through this.

"You paid for her scholarship." She says out loud what she clearly already figured out.

"It's difficult to get a scholarship, especially to Ivy League colleges, so I just made it happen," I confess.

She shakes her head and looks at me like I'm some sort of hero. And I don't deserve it. I did nothing special.

"Why don't you tell everyone what you do? Why hide it?"

I shrug. "Jack wouldn't have accepted the money."

She shakes her head. "Not just this, everything you do. The debt you paid for the bakery, the homeless meals. Nobody knows about it."

"So what? It's nothing special. I have loads of money; it's the bare minimum I can do to give back."

"Because people think you are a heartless asshole, but you're not," she says softly, and my heart clenches in my chest. She makes me feel seen and vulnerable, and it's scary as hell.

"I don't give a crap about what people think, and you're the one that says I'm an asshole." I raise an eyebrow in challenge.

She scoffs. "Yes, because you made me feel like an idiot."

"When? I came to you begging for your help!"

The outraged look on her face tells me that's the wrong thing to say. She is almost scary. Almost.

"At my sister's wedding. I kissed you, and you rejected me. It was humiliating!" she burst out.

Oh, *that*. "You were a kid! What should I have done? Let you go even further?"

She rolls her eyes. "I was twenty-one, far from being a kid, and you had a hard-on in your pants. I could feel it!"

Yes, I clearly remember how I was feeling that day. I completely lost my mind as soon as I saw her in that dress that left her back naked. I would have licked every single inch of that glorious skin.

"Because you were sexy as hell, and you talked to me about all your projects. I get hard when you talk nerdy to me," I confess.

Her expression is priceless. She's so surprised her mouth is hanging open. I could almost laugh if I didn't realize what I just admitted out loud to her.

"Really?"

It's useless to backtrack now. "Really. I'm a sucker

for smart women. And that dress was killer."

She smirks. "It was fabulous, wasn't it?"

I would have ripped it off with my teeth, but I can't say that to her. I've already babbled enough for tonight. I just nod.

"Then why did you reject me? I'm right, you're an asshole!" she remarks.

"You were young, and you are Raphael's sister-in-law," I explain, almost exasperated.

"So what? I was more than legal, consenting, and Raphael has no right to say anything about how I live my life!" she fights back.

She's right. Everything about what she just laid out is the truth, and I can't find a single reason to counter her reasoning. Damn, I *was* the asshole.

"Fuck it," I whisper right before grabbing a fistful of hair at the base of her neck and crashing my lips on hers. The couch creaks under my sudden move.

I catch her by surprise. She goes still in my arms for a long moment, almost making me wonder if she's changed her mind since that day. Fuck, what if she doesn't want it anymore? But then her hands shoot behind my neck, and she presses her body against mine.

A small whimper leaves her lips and when she parts them to take a breath, I take the chance to deepen the kiss. It's like a fire ignites in my veins. She is so perfectly soft between my arms that I can't resist running my hand down her spine as she climbs on my lap.

She straddles me, and I growl in response. I'm not usually one to give in to primitive instincts, but she draws the caveman out of me and I want to brand her as mine. She is so sexy, and sweet, and clever. I can't resist.

I drag my hand lower down her back to reach the soft curves of her ass. I squeeze and press her against my erection. She moans.

I end the kiss to look her in the eyes. Lust and desire are swimming in that bright gaze, signaling that she is into me—even if the eager kiss didn't give her away—a lot. I'm surprised about how much I like this realization.

She lowers herself against my chest and drags her lips against the skin of my neck. She slowly moves from the collar of my shirt to my ear and slightly bites my lobe. I let out a slow breath and tighten my grip on her hair as her breath catches in her throat.

"Was it so bad kissing me?" she whispers softly, tickling my skin with her breath.

I almost scoff. "This wasn't something we could do at the wedding reception. Not if we didn't want to be shot by Raphael's bodyguards." I let out a low chuckle.

"There were plenty of rooms to hide in," she points out, but I can't answer because her mouth is peppering my neck with soft, languid kisses. Her tongue darts out from time to time and tastes me. I shoot back my head and enjoy every single second of this moment.

She is so perfect. I have no idea how I found the strength to push her away all those years ago. Because right now, I want to sink deep into her and make her mine.

I crush my lips on her again, lashing my tongue against her in a battle neither of us wants to lose. She challenges me in more ways than I expected, and I'm here for this. I love the way she matches the fierce woman she is in everyday life.

She moves her hands on my loosened tie, unfastens it, and snaps open the shirt button.

"I can't," I murmur against her lips.

She stops abruptly and detaches from my chest just enough to look at me with a frown. "What?" She is as puzzled as I am.

What did I think would happen after I kissed her like this? That we would stop and go back to work? I didn't take a moment to think; that's the problem. I just gave in to my desire and fucked up big time.

"I can't have sex with you," I blurt out.

"Why?" She is baffled.

Good question. I can't find a good enough reason, just excuses that don't add up. She is way younger than me, Silver's little sister. I know there is a good reason somewhere I should give her, but my brain is frozen between lust and the urge to stop this.

She takes my silence as an answer. She stands up, grabbing her things. "Unbelievable," she scoffs.

"Roxanne," I try to stop her, but she slaps my hand.

"I don't know what is wrong with you, but I won't stay and be rejected again." She storms out of my office barefoot.

I stand up and watch her disappear around the corner, but I don't follow her. I know I just fucked up, and this time, there is not enough groveling I can do to make it better.

20

ROXANNE

"He is an asshole," I mutter under my breath as I walk toward the elevators. I push the button to get out of here as soon as possible, and I remember I still have to put on my shoes. I stare at the pink sneakers, and a pang of shame hits my chest.

Anyone seeing me would assume I just had sex with him, and that he kicked me out before I could even dress properly. Why else would I be doing this walk of shame? The man always gets away with it, never the woman.

The ding of the elevator and the doors sliding open should remind me that it is time to walk away and face the reality that he is not into me. But the truth is that there is a chance that he wants me. The erection that I felt in his pants tonight is the same that he had years ago.

Nothing changed in that department. And I want answers. I won't accept this second rejection like the stupid girl I was the first time.

Instead of stepping forward and going home to nurse my bruised ego, I spin and charge down the hall I just came from. I push the door open and find Leonard standing behind his desk. His hands are pressed against the dark wood, and his head is slumped between his shoulders. He seems defeated. He raises a surprised gaze as soon as I step inside.

"Why? I want a reasonable explanation for why you pushed me away again," I say more firmly than I expected, considering the turmoil agitating my chest.

He shakes his head and looks down.

"If it's because you're not attracted to me, fine, but tell me. If it's because of my age, fine, but I remind you I'm a consenting adult. And if it's about Raphael, he's not my father. He has no say in my personal life," I press, stepping forward until I reach his desk.

He shakes his head again and looks up at me with tormented eyes. I didn't expect such vulnerability from him. He's always so put together that now I'm doubting whether I did the right thing coming here.

"I don't know," he admits.

Well, I didn't expect that. His face is honest. There is no way he is lying his way out of this conversation. And I'm confused.

"How is that possible?" I ask, genuinely curious.

He plops into his chair and crosses his hands on his lap. A small smile appears on his face. Is he embarrassed by this conversation? This is a first.

"Every single motivation to stay away from you just crumbled tonight," he explains. "You're right. There is no reason for me not to consider you a woman I'm attracted to."

"So you are attracted to me?" I double-check. You never know. I walk around the desk and stand in front of him.

He chuckles briefly. "Wasn't it obvious?" He beckons towards his pants.

"Well, yes, but then you pushed me away, so..." I let him draw his own conclusions.

He lets out a sigh and rubs a hand over his face. He seems almost defeated. "I don't know why. Maybe because I've never had sex in my office, and I don't want to treat you like a cheap fuck. You're not."

He is so serious he's almost cute. *Jesus, I have to stop thinking this man is cute.* He is Leonard, for Pete's sake. He is hot, exudes power, is cold as ice, is an asshole...he is most definitely not cute.

I walk closer to him, my chest barely containing my racing heart. This is it. This is my chance.

"I never thought you considered me a cheap fuck. We were both into it. It happened here, so what? It's a place like any another." I grab his tie and pull it off his neck. "On the contrary, I think it's flattering that someone like you can't resist fucking me in his office," I purr in his ear as I grab his wrists and wrap the tie around them.

"Someone like me?" He smirks, but his breathing is more erratic than before.

"Yes, powerful, sexy, gorgeous." I smile, standing up and bringing his tied wrists over his head. I walk around his chair and secure the other end of the tie to the back of it. I hear him suck in a breath.

I grin. I love this game.

"What are you doing?" he growls when I walk in front of him.

I curve my lips in a mischievous smile. "I'm making sure you won't push me away and run this time."

He lets out a deep chuckle. "Believe me, I don't want to go anywhere."

"Good, because I have plans for you tonight," I purr while I slowly unbutton his shirt without ever moving my eyes from his.

"Fuck," he whispers. His gaze drips lust.

I part his legs and go down on my knees. His hard cock is straining against the fabric of his pants. A big, mouthwatering cock. I slowly unbutton his shirt until I can open it, push the fabric aside, and admire his chiseled body. How is it possible to have such perfection in one single person?

His lustful gaze never leaves my face, taking in every inch of me and biting his lower lip when I move forward and kiss each one of his abs. I go down to the edge of his pants and then lick my way up the delicious cleft between his perfectly defined muscles.

A smattering of dark hair covers his lower belly, disappearing under his pants and showing the way for my lips, where they will indulge in trying to drive him crazy. I don't think it will be difficult for me to achieve that task. His lustful eyes and erratic breath suggest that he is reaching his limit.

His abs twitch under my touch, his skin ripples, and when I grab his belt and unbuckle it, his arms strain to free himself.

"You're going to kill me," he murmurs breathlessly.

I grin. "Not my intention," I say, winking at him.

He lets out a low growl and raises his hips, pushing his erection toward my face.

"You're such an impatient man. Always get what you want, don't you?" I purr, dragging my nails over the strained fabric covering his cock.

"You have no idea." His voice comes out so deep a shudder runs down my spine.

He is not the only one wanting to speed things up. I'm so soaked that my panties feel cold against my skin. *Damn, I'll come as soon as I let his cock sink into me.*

I unbutton his pants and grab the hem. He raises his

hips to help me drag them down to his ankles, along with his boxer briefs. His erection springs free in front of my face. Hot, hard, and...massive. I don't know if I can fit all of this glorious cock in my mouth.

I look up at him, and the smirk plastering his face tells me he is pleased by my reaction—pompous asshole.

"Do you think you can handle it?" he asks smugly.

I scoff. "You always underestimate me."

I lick my way up from the base to the tip and kiss the salty pearl leaking from it. My tongue sweeps a couple of times around the hot cock head, eliciting a hiss from his lips.

"Fuck!" he growls when I sink his erection deep inside my mouth.

I take a deep breath, keeping my gag reflex at bay, then sink it even deeper into my throat and suck. I watch his eyes roll back in pleasure.

"Holy shit!" he whispers, lowering his wide eyes to mine.

Pride expands in my chest when I see his surprised and lost face. I bob my head, reaching out my hand to fondle his shaved sack. I keep it going for a few moments until his hips push up, trying to fuck my mouth. I let his cock out with a loud pop of my lips.

"Oh, no, sweetheart, you are not going to come like this. I want to ride you first," I tease, standing up.

He lets out a frustrated huff. "Where did you learn to talk like that?" He grins.

I shrug. "I told you I'm not a kid anymore."

"I can see that. And when I'm free from this chair, I will fuck that brat attitude right out of you," he promises.

"I'm counting on it." I wink at him before grabbing the hem of my tank top and slipping it over my head.

He sucks in a breath, and his eyes widen when I reach back to unhook my bra. I make a show, letting it fall at his feet, and I savor the powerful feeling of seeing him entirely at my mercy.

When I turn around and hook my fingers under the hem of my shorts, I can hear his heavy breath and feel his heated eyes on me. I'm slowly killing him. He is so caught up in this moment. I'm sure he would gladly free his hands to grab me and fuck me like no other has ever done. He's usually in charge, I'm sure about that, but I like that he lets me play with him.

I decide to take him out of his misery and slip my panties off with the shorts, bending down and giving him the full view of my bare ass. I hear him struggle to free his hands, but when I turn around, they're still in place. Only his chest is having a hard time inhaling enough oxygen, and his eyes are roaming every inch of my naked body.

I smile. "Condom?"

I hope he has one. I'm on the pill, but I'm not used to

going without one, even if I'm pretty sure I can't trust him. It's not like he's a guy I picked up at a bar. Still, this is the first time and I feel more comfortable this way.

"My desk, bottom drawer," he answers quickly.

I raise an eyebrow. "Very suspicious for someone who never fucks in his office."

I'm teasing him. I'm glad he's not one of those men who keeps a condom in his wallet. I don't even know if he has a wallet. Usually, unbelievably rich people don't own one, just a small patch of leather that contains all their credit cards.

He chuckles. "I'm a thoughtful man. I also have one box at home and one in the car I use for daily travel. I'm not a teenager who goes around with a condom in my wallet. I don't even have one!"

I knew it! Rich people, no wallet. I bend down to pick up the golden foil from his desk and I notice that there are no missing pieces from the box. He's telling the truth when he says he doesn't fuck in his office.

He growls. "Bend down like that again, and I swear I'll break this chair to put my hands on that glorious ass."

I sway my hips to tease him a bit more; he lets out another deep growl from his chest. He is a sight I'll never tire of seeing. His muscles are tense, giving him a perfectly sculpted body. His pecs are so well defined I could fit them in my palm. The desire to nip them is overwhelming, and I just give in to it, lowering myself, licking and biting my way to his nipples. I suck one between my lips, and he stops breathing, arching his back and offering me his body. I love to have him under my spell. It's empowering and exhilarating.

I stand up and rip the packet with my teeth, my gaze never leaving his lustful eyes. I smile while I bend down, slowly lick his shaft, and then roll down the condom over his hot manhood. I straddle him and tease his erection with slow, calculated movements.

I rub my clit over his cock and moan when a bolt of pleasure runs along my spine. If I keep going like this, I will come before even fucking him.

"Let me suck your tits, please," Leonard rasps, reminding me he is still restrained to the chair. His tone is pleading, his eyes full of an urgency that is difficult to ignore.

"Only because you asked me nicely," I purr in his ear and then suck at his neck.

He pushes his hips against my core, and another moan of pleasure escapes my lips when my clit rubs harder against his shaft.

I arch my back and give him access to my breast. He strains his neck and grabs a nipple with his teeth. He squeezes a little, not too hard to hurt, but enough to sting a bit, giving me a shock deep down in my core. Then he licks it, and I almost come. I look down at him. A smirk crosses his face. He may be restrained, but he knows how to use every other part of his body to give me pleasure. I like that about him, so confident he can make a woman come only with his mouth on her breast.

I respond, pressing my core against his erection, and he moans, sucking at my nipple. It's a war between us for who will come first. There will be no losers, no matter the outcome.

I raise myself, standing a bit, and, with my hand, guide his cock toward my entrance. I slip down so slowly that it's almost a punishment for both of us. He fits me so nicely his shaft reaches places no other man ever got the pleasure to explore. *Damn, it's nice to have a man this packed.*

He lets out a low breath and closes his eyes, pushing his hips upward, trying to fit every inch of his length inside me. And I take it.

"Fuck me, please." His moan is almost strained, his desire clear in his eyes, and I do just that. I roll my hips and fuck him deep and slow, enjoying every inch of his manhood. He thrusts his hips, matching my movement, and I don't even realize I'm now riding him like my life depends on it.

I chase the orgasm I've craved since I started working with him. I give in to my fantasy and ride the man who's made me come time and time again alone in my room. I ride him hard and fast, and with a low, guttural growl, he comes so hard he rips his hands free.

He grabs my hips and squeezes them, almost bruising me, and guides me to the point of no return, where the pleasure explodes in my lower belly and wave after wave of mesmerizing orgasm shakes me to the point I slump spent on his chest. The pleasure is so intense I can feel it deep in my core, in my chest. My breasts are so sensitive it almost hurts.

We are both silent and panting for a long moment, wrapped in a cocoon of rugged breaths and shivers that ripple across our skin.

"Damn, that was my favorite tie." He chuckles as one hand caresses my back and the other puts the shredded piece of fabric on the desk.

I look at him and smile. "I'll buy you another one."

He shakes his head. "You can rip every tie in my closet if you put on a show like tonight. I've never come so hard in my life." He raises an eyebrow.

There is a hint of vulnerability in the smug smile that curls his lips. Something I'm not used to in him, and an unexpected feeling grips my heart and squeezes lightly. I can't tell if it's a pleasant or a scary one.

Doubt creeps into my chest. "Does that mean there will be another round?" Hope drips from my words, and I curse myself for sounding so needy. I don't want to look like a weak girl who needs reassurance, not in front of a man like him, confident and unapologetic.

He frowns. "Of course, there will be. Do you think I

just fucked up all my resolution to stay away from you for a one-night stand?" His tone is almost offended. The look on his face tells me that he took for granted that this would be clear from the beginning, but he already rejected me once, and I don't take it for granted. It's not like we've had time to talk and plan this thing out.

Also, I don't know where to go with this new development in our relationship—it's too soon to process what just happened—but I'm certain his words lifted a weight from my chest.

"I promise I won't shred the contents of your closet." I wink.

He puts his arms around me and drags me to his chest. His heart is still beating fast, and the comfort of this embrace makes mine leap in my chest. I spent so much time hating him that my heart and brain have difficulty processing what happened tonight. But one thing I'm sure of, this contact between us, skin-to-skin, feels damn right.

21

LEONARD

S he is perfect.

I run my gaze over the curves of Roxanne's naked body sprawled on my bed. The depth of the small of her back and the mouth-watering round shape of her butt. Even those pink tips on her blond strands grew on me.

She breathes softly, and I can't resist the urge to lower myself and nip at that perfect ass. Her skin pebbles under my touch, and I continue my assault of kissing and nibbling her soft back.

Her breath catches, and I know she is awake. I straddle her, nestle my hard erection over her ass, and lower myself on her back, nipping at her shoulder, licking my way up her neck, sucking the spot behind her ear I know drives her crazy. In the two weeks since that first time in my office, I've had the chance to discover every inch of her body, and I can't get enough of her. She's like my favorite food—I want to eat her all the time.

I smile when a moan escapes her lips.

"You're gonna make me come if you keep teasing me like this," she murmurs in a sleepy voice.

She hasn't opened her eyes, but a smile lights her face. She's beautiful when she's awake, but she's stunning when she's sleeping. Her skin is soft, her features are relaxed. It's like she steps into another world, one where she's happy and carefree.

"That's the plan," I whisper in her ear, slipping my hand between us and brushing my fingers between her legs.

She is already wet for me. "Good girl," I growl, propping myself on an elbow just enough to reach my nightstand and grab a condom. One of the few I have left. I need to remember to buy a new box, and I smile, thinking how fast we went through this one, and the one I keep in my car...and the one in my office. The number surprises me. Even at fifteen, I wasn't caught up in this much lust and thinking about fucking every waking moment of my day, and sometimes even when I'm sleeping. She pulls the animalistic instinct out of me. I'm insatiable when it comes to her, her body, her mind, her soul.

I rip the golden foil with my teeth, slide the rubber

on my cock and make space with my knees between her legs. She shakes her butt a little, teasing me and raising it from the mattress in time for me to slip my hand under her belly and reach her already swollen clit. She lets out a long, soft groan when I circle it, and she pushes her ass against my hips, slipping the tip of my cock into her soft and hot entrance. She is so wet it's no effort to make my way inside her, and it's like paradise.

It's my turn to groan. I sink ball deep into her with just one slow thrust. I enjoy her tight, hot pussy clenching around my shaft. I take it slow, savoring the feeling that will never cease to amaze me. How can we be made for each other in such a perfect way? It seems like our bodies were made to enhance each other's pleasure. I've had my fair share of other women, but I've never reached such a deep physical connection with anyone else before. It's like my body became aware of a new level of pleasure, and it keeps craving more and more.

"Leonard, please, fuck me," she whimpers, shaking her ass and trying to make me move.

I chuckle. "As you wish."

I pull almost all the way out and then thrust into her hard and fast—the way I've learned she likes it. She's not the type who craves sweet lovemaking. She fucks the same way she lives: wild and carefree, taking all of it and giving back more. She is a generous lover, and I'm sure not complaining about that.

I fuck her like our life depends on it and rub her clit with the same determined intensity. I want her to orgasm over my cock, and squeeze it in a tight grip. She comes hard, letting out a moan deep from within her chest, clenching her pussy around my dick, triggering my own orgasm.

I breathe hard as I roll to her side. She finally opens her eyes, and I smile at her content face.

"I should have put in the contract that you have to wake me up like this every morning," she sighs.

I laugh. "We can make up a new one if you want. I will gladly sign it."

"Every morning from here to eternity? I could get used to that," she says, and immediately, her eyes widen, probably realizing what this suggestion entails.

I think about it, and the most surprising part is that I'm not scared or annoyed by the thought of a long-term relationship with her. Why should I chase away something that makes me feel so good? I don't know if she's serious or still in the afterglow of her orgasm, but I decide not to ask more. I give her time to think about it.

"I'll make sure you won't get bored over time," I answer, kissing her lips.

She lets out a long breath, probably realizing I'm not upset about her statement. We've never talked about what this new development means for our relationship, but it's clear that it's not just professional anymore. And it's not a casual sexual relationship, either. I wouldn't have let her stay the night. Jesus, I wouldn't have let her come to my house if she was just a random hookup.

"Are you sure *you* won't get bored?" she asks.

I love that she doesn't beat around the bush. If she has doubts, she voices them. Sometimes, even when she shouldn't.

"If you're asking me if this thing between us has an expiration date, I'm not that kind of guy," I explain in a firm voice. "If I just wanted a one-night stand, I would have said so *before* we fucked."

She seems to think about it. "So you want to explore this thing between us?" she asks softly. She seems almost relieved that I said it first. And I'm sort of relieved too. When I said it, I realized how true it was.

I touch her cheek and caress her lower lip with my thumb. She leans into the touch, savoring the moment. "You're Silver's sister. I'm not messing around with you. You're not just a random hookup. And not because Raphael would have my ass handed to me, but because you're family, and I don't mess with family."

She chuckles, teasing me. "That sounds a bit incestuous."

I roll my eyes. "Not *that* kind of family."

She kisses me lightly. "I'm messing with you," she whispers over my lips.

"I know, and you will be punished for it, but now you are going to shower while I prepare breakfast," I say, raising my eyebrows when I hear her stomach growling.

She lets out a sigh but doesn't protest. I watch her rolling out of the bed and swaying her hips toward the bathroom. It's really hard to convince myself I need to go downstairs to put together some food instead of following her to the shower and fucking her against the wall.

I'm gathering ingredients from the fridge when the doorbell startles me. It's ten on a Sunday morning; I'm not expecting anyone at this hour.

I drop the food on the counter and walk to the front door and open it, only then realizing I'm wearing just my boxer briefs. Damn. I'm so caught up in Roxanne, I can barely function. Dressing was not on my to-do list today.

Anyway, I don't have time to think about it because I'm too stunned to see my friends' eyes widen at my bare chest.

"What are you doing here?" My voice is hoarse, and it's clear I've just rolled out of bed. But that's not even the problem. Silver, Raphael, Aaron, Dakota, Mia, Elijah, Sienna, and Harrison are all dressed like they're ready for the beach. Am I missing something?

"I don't know. You invited us on a boat trip a month

ago, and when you didn't show up this morning, we came here. We were worried. You never forget an appointment," Raphael explains with a frown.

"Shit," I murmur. "I completely forgot about it!"

They seem even more perplexed now. But I need to think of a convincing excuse because I can't let them know that Roxanne is showering upstairs right now. I feel anxious and guilty at the same time. I didn't think about how to tell her brother-in-law and sister when I first kissed her. I should have thought of that *before* diving deep into her.

"Can we reschedule? My boat isn't ready to take it out," I half lie. I can call someone to fix everything we need in an hour, but I wouldn't have a chance to hide Roxanne. Another pang of guilt crosses my chest at the idea. I don't want her to be my little secret, but I need time before hard-launching my relationship with her.

"Are you okay? You seem...strange." Silver voices what everyone is thinking right now.

Strange doesn't even come close to what I feel right now. I've spent two weeks so buried in Roxanne's perfect body that I completely forgot reality. I completely screwed up the chance to do the right thing and talk to Roxanne about how to handle this news with our friends.

I don't have time to answer because Roxanne's voice from behind me startles us all. "Who is it?" she asks, putting her hand on my bare back and peeking out from my side.

"Shit," she murmurs when she sees them.

A series of reactions cross my friends' faces when they realize we aren't working, considering my extremely naked body, Roxanne wrapped in one of my white shirts, and her hair still wet from the shower. Silver and Raphael are in utter disbelief—eyes wide and mouths hanging open. Dakota, Mia, and Sienna have a mischievous smile that goes from ear to ear; they seem to silently congratulate Roxanne, who is blushing, hiding a smile. Aaron, Harrison, and Elijah are looking at me with a smug smirk on their faces.

The silence stretches for a long moment before Raphael breaks it. "I need a drink for this," he murmurs, pushing me aside and entering my house.

I guess we're discussing this development now. I sigh and let everyone else in. Harrison hits my chest with a playful jab, passing in front of me. The others try to cover their laughter. I roll my eyes and close the door behind me.

"So, are you ready to explain?" I raise an eyebrow at Roxanne with a smile on my face.

She giggles. "Not even a little bit."

"Me neither." I laugh as we run upstairs to put on some clothes.

It will be an interesting weekend.

I hope I survive it.

22

ROXANNE

I finish getting dressed in yesterday's clothes, since I don't have anything else here at Leonard's house, and start drying my hair. It's taking way too long to complete this simple task, which normally takes no more than ten minutes. But I'm dreading having to go downstairs and explain to my sister what's happening in my life.

I saw the shock on her face when I showed up at the door, and even though she insists that Leonard is a good guy, doubt creeps into my chest. What if she's disappointed? I shouldn't be concerned about her opinion. At the end of the day, this is my life, and I should do what feels right for me. Still, I know it will hurt a little if she doesn't approve of our relationship.

"Are you ready?"

I turn around to find Leonard leaning against the door, dressed casually in sweatpants and a t-shirt. He looks surprisingly put together, and I can't understand how he can be so calm knowing there are people downstairs waiting for a complicated conversation.

"Not at all, but we have to face them at some point." I'm not just referring to my outfit; I honestly don't feel emotionally ready.

He smiles, pushes off from the doorframe, and wraps me in his arms, kissing the crown of my head. A warm sensation spreads in my chest, and I realize I really appreciate this sweet side of him. I feel protected, and even my strong, independent self isn't going to make a fuss about it.

"We're not doing anything wrong. Like you said, we're adults, and we're making our own decisions." His words resonate in his chest, and I squeeze him tightly.

"I know, but did you see my sister's face?" I lock my gaze with his.

He chuckles. "Did you see Raphael's?"

A smile curves my lips, and I take a deep breath. Raphael seems on the verge of a breakdown. I've never seen him so flustered. He's a politician; he knows how to hide his feelings. Not this time.

"Let's go, or they'll barge into this room," I say,

breaking away from his embrace and grabbing his hand, pulling him downstairs.

As we enter the living room, conversations come to an abrupt halt, and everyone's gaze shifts toward us. I focus on the two people who matter most: my sister and her husband. Silver seems to have recovered from the shock, with a small smile on her face. Raphael, however, looks as if he's just swallowed a frog.

"Can we just get over with this conversation so we can enjoy the rest of the day?" Leonard sighs as he sits in the armchair in front of the others and pulls me onto his lap.

I can't help but let out a small squeal, which brings grins from Harrison and Aaron. They are clearly pleased at this turn of events.

"What's there to say? You fucked her behind our back, and you got caught." Raphael raises an eyebrow and takes a sip from his glass, which I assume contains liquor.

"I didn't do it behind your back, and I definitely didn't get caught. You barged into my house uninvited," Leonard retorts, clearly irritated by his friend's comment.

Meanwhile, Silver elbows her husband, and he responds with a grunt.

"You didn't tell us!" Raphael grumbles, and everyone suppresses a laugh.

I'm about to explain that this is none of his business, but Leonard cuts in with a scoff.

"Of course, we didn't tell you. It's a pretty new development, and we're trying to navigate it. You shouldn't be upset; you need to respect our timing. This is our personal life, and we deserve respect."

"This is a very mature argument," Dakota says, smiling at Raphael and raising an eyebrow in a clear message that he shouldn't be so childish.

I hold back a laugh, biting my lips.

"Being forty years old has its perks," Leonard winks at her.

We're all making fun of Raphael. No one in this room actually has a problem with our relationship; they're simply surprised that this situation came out of the blue. I believe that Raphael isn't angry with us, either; he's just reacting to the unexpectedness of the situation. He's used to having everything under control, and the fact that we managed to catch him off guard is unsettling for him.

I breathe a sigh of relief. For a moment, I thought I was going to have to fight with my sister.

"Yeah, yeah. But a heads-up before catching my sister-in-law wearing only your shirt as you standing there in boxers would have been nice," he mumbles, and we all laugh.

"That was quite shocking," Sienna admits. "I thought you two hated each other."

I grin at her, not quite sure how to answer that. Yes, last time we talked Leonard and I weren't exactly on good terms, but we weren't openly fighting either.

"Angry sex is the best," Mia chips in.

"Amen!" I agree.

"Please, stop talking about sex. I still have to digest this information. I don't need a detailed visual of those two together," Raphael grimaces.

We chuckle, and he shakes his head, rolling his eyes. He's not angry over our relationship, just horrified because he caught me half-dressed. That's just Raphael's protective side showing up.

"Can we talk about the real elephant in the room?" Dakota asks, her eyes widening.

We all turn to look at her, puzzled. She gestures toward where Leonard and I are seated. "He's wearing sweatpants and a T-shirt. Doesn't that bother you?"

We all burst out laughing, Leonard included. I don't think they've ever seen him dressed less than perfect.

"Blame her," he says, gesturing toward me. "She forced me to buy comfortable clothes, and wouldn't stop pestering me."

Dakota smirks, and Aaron shakes his head. "You were the last man standing—the only one who still refused to bend or change his habits for a woman." He lets out a low chuckle.

I glance at Leonard, wondering if he'll be irritated by Aaron's comment, but to my surprise, he's smiling. This is a refreshing change, and I'm glad I could bring it into his life. He's usually so grumpy and serious; this feels like a significant accomplishment.

"Okay, does nobody want to acknowledge what the real problem is here?" Harrison asks, looking incredulous as we all turn to face him.

"What are you talking about?" Sienna replies, rolling her eyes, likely used to his dramatic antics.

"The fact that at her sister's wedding, she was clearly fawning over *me,* and how she got over her crush so quickly," he jokes.

We all let out a collective groan of amusement. Typical Harrison.

"Quickly? It's been four years!" Silver chimes in.

"I don't want to crush your dreams, but as soon as I saw Leonard at the wedding, I completely forgot you were there," I add, only half-joking.

Everyone bursts into laughter, and Harrison clutches his chest, his mouth wide open in mock disbelief.

"You are so, so cruel," he replies, feigning hurt in his voice.

I turn to Leonard and am surprised to see admiration in his eyes as he looks at me. A blush creeps up my cheeks, making me feel warm. Is it just me, or does he gaze at me as if there are deeper feelings hidden beneath that perfect exterior?

I'm so focused on him that I barely notice everyone standing up around us.

"Silver, you have to teach me how to make that amazing cocktail you prepared last time," Dakota chirps.

My sister smiles. "The secret is spanking the mint." She winks at her.

"What?" Aaron asks, half intrigued and half worried.

"Do I even want to know?" Raphael adds.

I laugh, and Sienna looks intrigued too.

"Yes! Instead of simply breaking the mint's leaves, you have to clap them between your hands to make the flavor pop. Spank the mint!" she explains, clapping her hands.

"Just when I thought I'd heard everything, you manage to surprise me," Leonard mumbles, shaking his head as he helps me stand up to follow the others into the kitchen.

As soon as I pass my sister, she reaches out her hand to stop me. Now that the others are out of earshot, I know she has something to ask. Her silence earlier had been too suspicious.

She smiles at me. "Leonard?"

"It wasn't planned," I reply, nervously shifting my feet.

"I don't think these kinds of things can be planned."
She raises an eyebrow.

"Yeah, I suppose you're right."

"Does he make you happy?" she asks, probing when
I remain silent.

"Yes," I respond so quickly that the realization
catches me off guard. It's true. We had been so caught up
in the intensity of our physical relationship that I never
took the time to consider my feelings for him. And I'd
been angry with him for so long I overlooked the possibility of feeling something else. Am I happy? Yes. Does
this happiness outweigh the resentment I held for him?
The answer is yes again.

"Are you upset because I didn't tell you?" I finally
express what has been bothering me.

She frowns. "Why should I be? As Leonard said,
when you're ready to share, I'm here to listen. We should
apologize for 'outing' your relationship before you were
ready."

"It's not your fault either. But I'm glad you're not
angry with me about…him."

"He's a good guy. If he treats you the way you
deserve and makes you happy, who am I to tell you not
to date him?"

A genuine smile spreads across my face. I didn't
realize how much I valued my sister's opinion until I

thought I had disappointed her. It's surprising, considering we grew up apart.

"Let's go spank the mint before someone does something they might regret." I grin at her.

She lets out a soft chuckle but doesn't protest when I lead her toward the others, bringing our conversation to a close and lifting a weight from my chest.

23

LEONARD

Trish, sitting next to Benjamin across the desk, looks at me. Their deep frowns reveal their concerns about what Roxanne and I discovered.

"So, this is why you're delaying the acquisition," Benjamin correctly assumes.

I nod in response. "I need to learn more about the situation. We still don't know what information is being stolen or how they are handling it."

"This explains the rumors circulating about this operation. We kept everything confidential under a non-disclosure agreement, and yet someone still found out."

I considered that and reached the same conclusion: there's no way someone would risk being sued for breach of contract, especially when this acquisition benefits both parties.

"What do you want to do about it?" Benjamin asks.

I take a deep breath. "Roxanne and I are working to find out who did this, and then we will decide how to proceed with what we discover."

He nods. "The FBI will probably be involved."

The weight in my chest doubles. That seems like the best course of action. Someone is stealing confidential industry secrets; otherwise, they wouldn't have breached the system. This means there will be an investigation and legal actions—something I don't want to deal with, but it seems inevitable at this point.

"I can't think of a scenario where we can avoid this," I confirm.

"What a mess," Trish murmurs, shaking her head.

"Tell me about it," I reply, rubbing a hand over my face.

"Why don't you ask Oliver for help with this? He knows the company better than anyone else," she suggests.

I glance at Benjamin and notice an expression on his face that I can't quite place. Is it anger? Worry? I'm not sure.

I turn back to Trish. "He's not in the right state of mind to help with this. He's made it clear that he doesn't want to get involved and thinks I should just leave the problem alone since they're not stealing money," I explain, simplifying a situation that's much more complex.

She scoffs in disbelief. "What the heck? If this isn't more important than money, then what is? Is he all right? I understand he has personal reasons to be upset, but that doesn't mean he can just turn his back on the company," she states matter-of-factly.

I know she has a point. The sensible thing would be to put him on paid leave until he sorts out his issues, but I don't want him to feel excluded from the company he founded. Any other person in my position would have fired him on the spot, but I can't bring myself to do that, even if it goes against the company's best interests.

"Can you trust this Roxanne?" Benjamin asks.

They are unaware of my personal involvement with her, and I'm unsure if I should tell them. Ultimately, my lack of judgment could jeopardize this company. Right now, I trust her completely, but I understand their doubts, especially if they find out I have crossed that line and my feelings are involved.

I decide to remain neutral. "I have no doubts about her."

"Are you thinking with your brain or your little brother down there?" Trish asks, a smug smile on her face.

I raise an eyebrow, silently questioning her. I never

told her about my attraction to Roxanne. We don't share everything about our personal life.

"Come on, everyone in this office knows there's something going on between you two. They're even placing bets on when you'll go public with your relation-ship," she chuckles.

Well, I didn't anticipate that. I thought we were main-taining a professional facade around here.

I turn toward Benjamin, and this time, *he* is silently asking a question. I let out a sigh.

"My personal involvement has nothing to do with my trust in Roxanne. I hired her because she's an excellent hacker and one of the few people in this world capable of tracking down who is behind this." The confidence in my voice is unmistakable.

"Good, I trust your judgment," he replies firmly, not leaving any trace of doubt about his opinion on the matter.

I breathe a sigh of relief. I don't want to jeopardize my relationship with him because of my personal life. I glance over at Trish and find her smiling.

"I just wanted confirmation about it. I would never question your decisions. I know the integrity you bring to everything you do, so I have no doubt that you're not messing around this time, either. To be honest, I'm relieved you found someone. I was growing increasingly concerned about your lack of a personal life. It's not healthy to live and breathe work."

"Is there anyone who isn't concerned about my personal life—or lack of it?" I ask in disbelief. I never imagined my relationship status would matter to anyone, but it turns out it's a big deal for them.

"Leonard, you're a good guy," she says, fixing me with a steady gaze. "But you have zero self-control when it comes to this job. We're all worried you'll work yourself into an early grave before you even hit forty-five."

I scoff, a half-smile tugging at my lips as I shake my head in disbelief. "Are you already planning my funeral?"

She smiles back, softly but firmly. "We care about you, Leonard. We're just worried."

For a second, I'm at a loss. No words seem big enough to hold the gratitude I feel. All I can do is smile back, letting the warmth of her concern sink in.

I MEET RAPHAEL AT THE HUNTING CLUB. WE ARE sipping whiskey in one of the private rooms where members can converse without being overheard. It feels strange to see him again, especially after he showed up at my door a couple of weeks ago and found out about

Roxanne and me. Honestly, he took the news better than I expected, and I'm grateful for that.

"Do you still have contact with the FBI?" I ask him right off the bat. I'm not in the mood for lengthy discussions.

He frowns and studies me for a moment. I begin to worry that I made a mistake coming to him for this, but finally, he responds, "Yes, I still have my contacts. Is something wrong?" His tone is concerned.

I shake my head. "Yes and no. You remember the issue I'm dealing with regarding Roxanne, right? We've discovered that someone is not stealing money but pieces of information." I get straight to the point.

"Shit," he murmurs, baffled.

"Yeah, we still need to determine exactly what happened and who was involved. Once we have that information, we have to take legal action. There's a chance this situation is so big the FBI could get involved. You know we work with government agencies too, so I can't just pretend nothing happened."

He nods gravely. "I know it's the right thing to do, but I'm worried about Roxanne. I don't want the FBI interfering in her life. How did it all escalate?"

This is the same concern I have. She has done things in the past that were borderline legal, as well as some that were outright illegal. I don't want to put her in a difficult position.

"I haven't told her yet; I wanted to discuss it with you first. That's why I came to you. I want to keep things quiet and controlled for her sake. I wouldn't want the wrong person asking the wrong questions and drawing attention to her instead of the actual problem. That's a risk I don't want to take," I admit.

A small smile appears on his face. "You're in love with her, aren't you?"

I shrug. I've asked myself the same question a million times. As much as we're keeping things casual, I feel like I'm fully invested in her. I hope we're on the same page about that. Maybe this is a conversation we need to have sooner rather than later.

"I don't know if I'm in love, but I care about her, and I don't want to hurt her in any way."

He nods, and his expression turns serious again. "I'll start asking the people I trust to help us, but you need to find that evidence quickly. It better be rock-solid because once they start digging, they won't stop," he warns.

I nod, feeling a weight settle heavily on my chest. This is it. This is the moment when my entire life—everything I've worked for—could crumble into a million pieces, and I'm not sure I can handle that.

24

ROXANNE

"Wow. Did you even sleep last night?" Leonard asks, standing up from behind his desk. He walks over, taking the cups of coffee from my hands and setting them down, his gaze narrowing as he studies me.

I must look terrible, because his usual professional boundaries in the office seem to vanish when he reaches out, pulling me into a quick hug. It's uncharacteristic, and it surprises me enough to make me pause mid-yawn.

"Not exactly," I admit, yawning again.

He places his hands on my shoulders, holding me at arm's length with a mock stern expression that almost makes me feel like a kid caught sneaking out. "When we ended the call at midnight, you promised you were going to bed," he says, a touch of exasperation in his voice.

A guilty pang tugs at my chest. "I know, but...while I was getting ready, I had this idea pop into my head. A solution. You know I couldn't just let it go."

His skeptical eyebrow lifts. "And did you figure it out?"

"Of course I did!" I say, a bit indignant. By now, he should know that when I'm onto something, I don't stop until I see it through.

His expression shifts, and something unreadable crosses his face. He leans back against the desk, gripping its edge hard enough that his knuckles turn white. It's clear there's something he wants to say, but he hesitates as if he's not sure how I'll take it.

"Just spit it out," I urge, sinking into the armchair in front of him. Whatever it is, I'm not sure I'm ready to handle it in this sleep-deprived state—but I brace myself anyway.

"I spoke with Raphael yesterday. I didn't mention it on the phone because it's a delicate matter, and I wanted to discuss it in person. With what we're about to uncover, the FBI will probably be involved." He stares at me, trying to gauge my reaction.

The truth is that I had already considered this possibility, and I'll deal with it if it arises. I don't want to think about going to prison before knowing if they have their eyes on me.

I nod. "Thank you for telling me. I had already

figured that out, and I've decided to go along with it anyway. But why did you consult Raphael? There are plenty of official channels to use." I'm genuinely curious.

He studies me for a long moment. "I don't want strangers sticking their noses in your life. I thought Raphael might have someone trustworthy to work with. I need help trying to protect you while I'm doing the right thing."

His admission fills me with a rush of feelings, and my chest expands. Is this happiness? It feels so over-whelming that I want to smile and giggle like a little girl.

"Thank you. I really appreciate it," I say, my voice trembling slightly, overwhelmed by what I'm feeling inside.

I've never been one for sappy love stories—the kind where people say love changes everything and melts even the coldest hearts. I'd always dismissed it as overly sentimental fluff, words that held no weight for me. But right now, the way he's looking at me, with a quiet inten-sity that says he'd do anything to make sure I'm okay—it hits differently. There's something so genuine, so steady in his concern, that it sneaks past my usual defenses.

For the first time, I feel something shift, like warmth spreading in a corner of my chest I'd forgotten was even there. Maybe I've always believed that to be strong, I had to keep a cool distance and armor myself against the messiness of emotions. But this level of care, this kind of steady, wordless understanding—it does something to me, something I can't deny. It moves my so-called cold heart in a way I didn't see coming, like a quiet promise that maybe I don't have to be so guarded all the time.

Maybe love isn't about grand gestures or perfect moments. Perhaps it's the simple acts of kindness, the way someone's care makes you feel like you are in the safest place in the world. And even though I don't believe in love stories, this...whatever this is feels a little like one.

He clears his voice before speaking again, breaking the heavy silence between us. "So, you said you have a solution."

I shake my head, trying to clear my thoughts before speaking, but with the lack of sleep and the turmoil in my chest, I find it difficult to focus on what I actually came here for this morning.

"It's a long shot, but we should try," I say, opening my laptop and putting it on his desk. Leonard turns around and focuses his gaze on my computer. Now that he is not staring at me, I can almost concentrate. Almost. "We can't trace where the code they put in comes from, but I wrote a script that triggers that code, and it gives us a chance to trace it to the source if the person who put in the code in the first place reacts to it."

Leonard frowns but nods. "So, we don't know if this

person will do something about it or not," he murmurs, thinking hard about it.

"No, but they will know we found it. We bait them, and we wait for their reaction," I explain.

Leonard sighs and shrugs. "It's better than staying here and running in circles without finding anything useful. Let's try it."

I smile and feel the excitement surge in my chest. We finally have some hope to grab onto. And then we go our separate ways, and I don't know if I'm ready to do that.

25

LEONARD

Waiting.

Hours have passed since Roxanne fixed the code, first in my office and now in my living room, as we watch the screen with anticipation, hoping for some kind of result. Anything at this point.

"I really thought this would be it," she sighs, her voice full of exhaustion.

Her eyes are rimmed red from lack of sleep. I tried to convince her to take a nap, promising to call the second something happened, but she is so stubborn that, in the end, I gave up.

"Don't lose hope yet," I say, more to reassure myself than her. "They've only just realized we're onto them.

They're probably scrambling now, trying to figure out their next move. After a year of staying invisible, they're suddenly exposed. They will slip up—but they need time to figure out what happened and what to do about it."

But even as I say it, doubt crawls up inside me. We're finally so close, yet the silence is far too long, making my confidence falter with each passing minute. I can't shake the growing fear that maybe we've missed something, that after all this effort, we're still no closer to catching them.

"I don't know. What if I messed up and it's not working?" Her voice falters, tinged with a doubt I've never heard from her before.

A pang of helplessness hits me. I've always been confident in what I do, always knowing exactly how to fix things, but now I'm at a loss. I don't know where to start to help her, and I can't shake the memory of my last partner, reminding me of what happens when I fail to pay attention. I'm not about to make that mistake again.

I reach out, gently grabbing her chin until she looks away from the screen and into my eyes. "Listen to me," I say in a firm voice. "You are one of the best in the world at this. I've never once doubted that you'd make it work."

I pour every emotion into those words—every ounce of confidence I can muster—determined to crush the uncertainty in her eyes. Her gaze softens, the doubt slowly giving way to something less daunting, and I hold on, hoping she will feel better.

I lower my lips to hers, kissing her softly, letting everything I feel pour into this simple gesture. The kiss isn't rushed or intense, but instead, full of meaning—an unspoken promise that everything will be fine. She responds gently, her fingertips grazing my cheek as if she's feeling the same—as if she understands without a single word.

When we break apart, she nestles against my chest on the couch, her warmth seeping into me as she lets out a sigh. She reaches out, her hand resting lightly over my heart, where it's hammering beneath her touch. I pull her closer, wrapping my arm around her, and she lays her head on my shoulder.

For a few moments, we sit in comfortable silence, her breathing slow and even, her hand rising and falling with each movement of my chest. The quiet is only inter-rupted by the faint sounds coming from outside, but here, in this cocoon, it's as if the world has shrunk to just the two of us.

Her breathing becomes softer, slower, and I realize she's drifting off to sleep. I look down and see her lashes resting softly on her cheeks, her face relaxed, a gentle peace settling over her features. She's finally let go, finally given in to the exhaustion that's been weighing on her. I smile, a warmth spreading through me, relieved that she's allowing herself this moment of rest. She's been so relentless, always pushing herself, always on high alert, never sparing a thought for her own limits.

I adjust her slightly so she's more comfortable, and she unconsciously shifts, nuzzling closer to me. Her wild, free blonde and pink strands spill over my shirt, contrasting beautifully against the dark fabric. The way her hair fans out reminds me of her spirit—untamed, young, and full of life. I trail my fingers lightly through a few of those strands, marveling at how something so simple could make me feel so grounded.

As I sit here with her sleeping against me, it hits me just how lucky I am. Finding someone who shares the same drive, values, and unrelenting will to see things through. It feels like a rare gift, a blessing I never expected. We came to this moment from entirely different paths, worlds apart in some ways, yet here we are, closer than I've ever been with anyone.

I study her face, memorizing every detail in the gentle glow of the lamplight. Her eyes are closed, her lips slightly parted, and a hint of a smile still lingers from moments before. Her expression has a vulnerability, a softness I don't often get to see. She's always so fierce, so determined. But now, asleep and at peace, she looks more like the person she rarely lets the world see.

I let my head lean back against the couch, savoring

the stillness, and allow myself just to be. For the first time in what feels like forever, I don't need to keep up my guard; I don't need to worry about the next challenge or the next step. In this moment, there's no agenda, no need to prove anything. Just her, asleep in my arms, and the quiet, steady rhythm of her breathing against me.

As the minutes slip by, I wonder how we got here. How two people who seemed so different could end up so similar, with lives that feel entwined, like two pieces of the same puzzle. I've never known this kind of connection before, this effortless closeness. It's not just an attraction; it's something deeper that goes beyond words. She knows my flaws, my sharp edges, the parts of me I'm still trying to soften. And yet, she's here, without hesitation, allowing herself to be this close.

The thought stirs something profound within me. It's a kind of contentment I'm not used to, a warmth I don't want to let go of. This understanding we've built feels like a foundation I didn't know I was missing. And as I watch her, feeling her small, steady breaths against me, I realize I don't want this to end.

My gaze drifts to how her hand rests lightly against my chest, right over my heart, as if she knows where she belongs even in her sleep. I cover her hand with mine just to feel that connection, and a small smile tugs at my lips. There's a calm that comes with her presence, an anchor that grounds me, a reminder that even in this unpredictable world, there's something solid, something real, between us.

Time seems to stretch, each second holding a weight I can't describe. I feel the comfort of her warmth, the soothing effect of her breathing, and for once, I allow myself to imagine a future—one where moments like this aren't sparse and occasional. One where I don't have to let go.

In the gentle silence, my thoughts settle, and I feel a peace I've rarely known. I don't want to disturb her. I don't want to risk breaking this fragile moment. So I sit there, holding her close, and let myself feel it all. The gratitude, the awe, the spark of hope that maybe this connection isn't something I'll have to say goodbye to.

The night continues humming around us, but in this little bubble, there's nothing but us, locked in this quiet intimacy. As her head rests against my shoulder and her hair brushes against my cheek, I know that whatever comes next, this moment will be one I'll never forget.

A SOFT, INSISTENT BEEPING PULLS ME FROM THE LIGHT, restless sleep I hadn't even realized I'd fallen into. Roxanne stirs against my chest, a warm, steady presence, and it takes me a few moments to understand what woke me. My mind is foggy, but then I remember—the computer, the code we set to track our intruder. My heartbeat picks up as reality sharpens my mind.

"What is it?" I ask, my voice thick with sleep, hoping this isn't just another false alarm.

She shifts beside me, rubbing her eyes, her body warm against mine. "What time is it?"

I glance at my watch. "Four in the morning."

She groans, sitting up a little straighter and brushing her hair from her face. But then her gaze lands on the screen, and all the sleep leaves her eyes in an instant. Her whole body goes rigid. "It's the code," she whispers, her voice tight with excitement and disbelief. "They took the bait."

A rush of adrenaline surges through me, making me forget my exhaustion. For the first time in days, something real and solid is within reach. After months of chasing shadows, we might finally have a lead. But even as the excitement builds, an undesired sense of unease twists in my gut, a feeling I can't quite ignore.

Roxanne's expression shifts from excitement to confusion, her brows knitting as she studies the screen. I can see her eyes darken as she processes what she's seeing, her whole face tightening in a way that sets off all my alarms. Slowly, she puts a hand over her mouth, her fingers trembling.

"What is it?" I ask, feeling a strange knot of dread beginning to twist in my chest.

Her eyes are locked on the screen, her voice barely a whisper. "I know this IP address."

I frown, the meaning sinking in slowly. "You... know it?"

She nods, her voice wavering. "It's my old address—the apartment I used to live in."

I stare at her, trying to make sense of what she's saying. "Your old place?" The words feel heavy in my mouth. "You never mentioned moving."

She lets out a small breath, and her gaze is a bit ashamed. "I didn't tell you," she admits, her voice soft. "In the beginning, I didn't want anyone to know, especially you, because you were bossy and terribly annoying. Then it just...never came up."

The confession lands like a stone on my chest, her honesty mixed with regret. I can't help but feel a faint sting at the realization that she'd kept something so significant from me. But there's no time to deal with my hurt feelings—this revelation has more critical implications. Why would her old address be tied to the intrusion?

"We need to go there," she says, her voice steadying, her resolve sharpening her gaze. "Whoever is behind this might have left something, or they could still be using it somehow."

I pause, trying to think through the possibilities. "Your old roommate..." I hesitate, searching for the right question. "Could they have done something like this?"

She shakes her head firmly. "No. They don't have the skills. And they don't know anything about this." She glances at me, her expression resolute. "This kind of coding, this level of access...it's way beyond them. Every place I go is like a fortress network. I can't risk letting the information about what I do slip out, so I lock every access from the outside."

The weight of her words settles over us, pressing down like concrete pouring. Whoever is responsible for this wasn't just a random intruder. This was someone who knew Roxanne well enough to follow her steps and keep tabs but with enough technical skill to stay hidden until now.

A shiver runs down my spine as I absorb the implications. Someone isn't just watching Roxanne—they're trying to frame her. Using her old IP address to mask their moves, they've set her up to look like the source of the breach. It's the perfect chance to serve her to the FBI on a silver platter. If they get a hold of this, they'll have a reason to bring her in. Her skills, her background—it could all be twisted into a motive if someone wanted to paint her as the mastermind.

"We're dealing with someone who knows exactly

how to make it look like you're the one pulling the strings," I say, the gravity of the situation hitting hard.

Her jaw tightens, and I can see the fear beneath her steady gaze, just barely concealed. "If they have that kind of access, they could be tracking more than we even realize." She looks down at the computer screen, the IP address still blinking at us, taunting us with its accusation. "The FBI has been waiting for a lead on me for years," she murmurs. "If they find this address in any of the logs…"

She doesn't finish the thought, but I don't need her to. The fallout would be catastrophic. All they'd need is a single connection—a single weak link—and the entire investigation would fall on her. All the careful work she's put into tracking these people down, the months of long nights and grueling hours—everything could be used against her instantly.

I can't let that happen.

"We need to see that place," I say firmly. "There might be something there—some clue they left behind. Or, at the very least, we might get ahead of whoever's setting you up."

Her gaze snaps to mine, and she nods, bringing the resolution back into her eyes. "I set up that network in a way nobody would breach it, like I usually do. They must have had an excuse to go into the apartment and use some computer in there."

In the silence that follows, I feel the weight of what we're about to do, the unknown dangers of facing off with a faceless enemy who's always one step ahead. But as we move together toward the door, something tells me that tonight might be our only chance to set things right. And I know that whatever we find could change every-thing—especially for Roxanne.

26

ROXANNE

I drive toward my old apartment with a growing sense of dread. The early morning light is a contrast against the gray streets. Leonard sits in the passenger seat beside me, watching me worriedly as if he can sense the turmoil raging inside me. I barely notice his concerned glances. My mind is fixed on the IP address we discovered and the reality that someone's trying to frame me.

When we pull up outside, the place looks as worn as I remember, but I haven't been here in months. I left without much of a goodbye, just an excuse about work that Spike didn't believe. I'd always meant to explain things properly, but somehow, I never did. Now, as I step out of the car, I'm not sure what kind of welcome we'll get.

We reach the door, and I raise my hand to ring the bell, but it swings open before I can touch it. Spike's standing there, his eyes red-rimmed and watery, and a scowl already pulling at his lips.

"Well, well," he mutters, leaning against the door-frame wearing a smirk mixed with hurt and annoyance. "If it isn't Roxanne, the great Houdini. Decided to reappear out of thin air, huh?"

"Spike, I'm here because something important came up, not to bring up old arguments," I say, trying to keep my voice steady. I've never liked how confrontations with him go, but there's no getting around it now.

"Right," he scoffs. "And you decided to come at six in the morning with *him*?" He nods toward Leonard, giving him a hard look.

Leonard steps forward, hand outstretched in his usual businesslike manner, but Spike just stares at it with raised eyebrows. I feel an uncomfortable sense of guilt. This was my home for years, and Spike was my friend and my roommate. But I hadn't been honest with him, and now I'm here with Leonard, looking for a back door to a breach in my system I didn't even know existed.

"Spike, I'm not here to fight with you. We need to check something inside. It's related to work, but it's... well, it's personal too," I explain, hoping he'll understand. "Please. This is serious."

He looks between us, still suspicious, but something

softens in his gaze. Maybe the part of him that still had a crush on me hasn't quite disappeared. I feel bad manipulating his feelings for me, but right now, I'd do anything to make this problem go away.

"Fine," he mutters, stepping back to let us in. "But I don't know what you're hoping to find here. The place hasn't exactly been quiet since you left."

I walk through the doorway and into the familiar chaos of a party that died down a few hours ago. A few people are scattered across the living room—some slumped on the couch, others sprawled on the floor. The remains of last night's party are everywhere: empty beer cans, pizza boxes, and, of course, someone still playing on the PlayStation, the screen is flashing with a racing game. I shake my head. Some things never change.

Spike gives me a pointed look. "Good luck finding anything here. The internet went out about a month ago. Had to get some guy to fix it. He was here for ages, messing with all sorts of cables and God knows what."

"A month ago?" My voice is sharper than I intended, and Spike raises an eyebrow.

"Yeah. Why?"

I exchange a look with Leonard, my mind whirring. "After we discovered that the breach started from the third-party software. It can't be a coincidence that it pinged my old IP address. Whoever this technician was must have set it up then. It's easy to mess with the internet and pretend it doesn't work properly."

"Did they call you, or did you call the internet provider?" Leonard asks Spike.

They lock in a staring contest for long moment, but it's Spike that gives up first. I fight the urge to roll my eyes at their childish behavior.

"That's the weird part. He showed up at the door saying they were doing some kind of work in the neighborhood and he needed to check our connection. We didn't even have time to call them," he says, frowning.

Leonard gives me a meaningful look. "Because he couldn't answer the internet provider company's call, so he intercepted them before they could do anything."

Spike's eyes narrow as he processes this. "He was very convincing, and we had no doubt he was someone legit. So, you think this guy used my apartment to hack...what, your company?"

He looks at Leonard in disbelief, and Leonard shifts uncomfortably. I know there's no good blood between them, but the accusatory tone in my ex-roommate's voice is obviously grating on his nerves more than it should. It's not just my freedom at stake right now—his company's credibility is on the line too.

"Not exactly," I say, jumping over a couple of passed-out partygoers as I make my way to the router. "It's more like they used my network as a cover. But they didn't know I have a secret back door to every network I put up. It lets me trace any traffic back to its original source. A bit of a simplification, but more or less, that's how it works."

Spike scratches his head, still looking bewildered. "Okay...so, you're saying you can find out who's really behind this?"

Leonard is unusually quiet. I want to reach out and hold his hand, but I know that while it would be acceptable in the privacy of his home, it's a different matter in public. He has to maintain his business mogul facade, and sometimes I feel sorry for him. The situation doesn't look good for my freedom, but I can't forget that this is his life, and he is watching it crumble before his eyes.

"That's the idea." I pull out my laptop and connect it to the router. The network boots up slowly, like it's too tired of the PlayStation, too, and I begin running a trace through my backdoor software. I can feel Leonard's gaze on me, waiting, but I focus on the screen.

After what seems like an eternity, I pinpoint the ping's origin. My heart sinks as I recognize the source. I don't know whether to laugh or scream.

"It's from your company." The words come out strained, full of confusion and frustration that almost spills out of me in waves. It doesn't make sense. Why would someone from within Leonard's own company be going to such lengths to frame me?

Leonard leans over, staring at the screen, his expression a mix of shock and anger. "This can't be right. I would know if there was someone inside working against us."

"Unless it's someone very high up or very well hidden," I mutter, my mind racing through the possibilities. The company's secure, but I know better than anyone that no system is unbreakable.

Spike crosses his arms, watching us both with a smug expression. "So, let me get this straight. Some big-shot tech company is hacking through my crappy Wi-Fi?"

"Not hacking, exactly. More like using it as a disguise," I say, rubbing my temples. "They're trying to make it look like I'm the one behind this breach. And if the FBI finds out…"

Spike's face darkens as he realizes the gravity of what I'm saying. "So, what now?"

I look at Leonard, who's still staring at the screen in disbelief. "Now," I say, steeling myself, "we figure out who's behind this inside your company. Because if they've gone to these lengths, they're not just trying to sabotage us—they're trying to destroy me."

And that thought is scary enough to consider leaving the country.

27

LEONARD

My fingers hesitate over the keyboard as I type in the final IP address from our employee logs. I didn't think I'd ever have to check this one. My stomach clenches when the line lights up, confirming the match with the pings that have been triggering the recent breaches.

I lean back in my chair, feeling like the ground beneath me has disappeared. The name staring back at me doesn't feel real. Oliver. My best friend. My partner since day one. He's the one stealing from us. From me. It's a betrayal so deep that, for a moment, I can't breathe.

"Leonard…" Roxanne's voice cuts into the silence. It's soft and cautious, like she's as shocked as I am, but she doesn't want to rub it in. Her eyes stay glued to the screen, processing the same information I am. She looks at me, incredulous, as if trying to figure out what to say, but the sympathy behind her eyes only makes this ache deeper, rawer. I want to push her sympathy away. I don't need it, I don't want it. The only thing I need is answers.

"What the hell is he thinking?" The words come out raspy and pained. "Oliver's been with me since the beginning. We built this together. And now he—" My voice chokes in my throat. I can't finish the sentence. I don't want to because it feels too real.

Roxanne lets out a breath, her fingers brushing her lips as if she's not sure what to say. "Leonard, I... I'm sorry. I know how close you two are."

I nod, barely hearing her. Memories of late nights working in our first office, taking calls, drinking coffee, strategizing, and trusting him with everything flash through my mind like a cruel movie. Oliver had been distant lately, tense since the divorce, irritable, and snapping at everyone. But I never thought—I never imagined he would do something so hideous.

"He was the one who wanted more security," I say, bitterness coating every word. "He was the one pushing for tighter systems, more firewalls. And now he's using those exact protocols against us."

"Maybe that's why he wanted them in place," Roxanne murmurs, her voice dark with understanding. "So he could know exactly how to get around them."

I grimace, gripping the edge of the desk until my

knuckles go white. The humiliation of missing the signs, of trusting him completely, burns in my chest. "Oliver's been a jerk for months, and I just assumed it was stress. But he's been planning this the whole time, hasn't he? And I didn't see it. I trusted him. One year. The first transaction is one year old." I don't even dare to look her in the eyes. How was I so blind?

Roxanne's hand hovers near my shoulder, and for a second, I feel like she might reach out to comfort me. But she doesn't. "Leonard, you trusted him because you believed in him. That's not your fault."

"*Believed*," I repeat the word. It tastes bitter on my tongue. A laugh escapes before I can stop it. "He was my friend, Roxanne. We built this from nothing. You don't doubt that kind of loyalty."

She nods slowly, looking away. There's something in her expression like she is measuring her words to not make my situation worse. But I saw it in her eyes, and it hurt more than her speaking. "I get it. But as much as you want to confront him now, we must consider the bigger picture."

The reality of that stings. Confronting Oliver now would feel good. It would release the fury boiling inside of me. But she's right—the stakes are too high for impulsive moves. For this company, for her. I can't risk Oliver turning against us and going to the FBI now.

"I know." I try to sound more controlled than I feel.

"But right now, it'll feel like I'm letting him get away with it."

"We need to gather proof, Leonard," Roxanne says firmly. "If we go to the FBI now without solid evidence, they could investigate everyone in the company, including us. And with what's already hanging over me…" She trails off, but I hear the tension in her voice.

Of course. This isn't just about the company's integrity—Roxanne's life is tied up in this too. Her whole career, but most importantly, her freedom. The FBI could decide to do two things with her: put her in prison or not press charges and force her to work for them. I don't know which is worse. I shake my head, trying to dissipate the fog of anger. I don't want to make this worse for her. But the need to do something claws at my chest to get free.

I know Roxanne can see my struggle, and there's a flash of something like frustration in her eyes. She is quick to hide it. "Look, I understand how much this betrayal hurts you. But we can't rush this. If Oliver is covering his tracks, we need everything on record, or we could end up with nothing."

My jaw tightens, and I nod, understanding even if I hate it. "You're right. Doesn't make it any easier, though."

"No, it doesn't," she agrees, crossing her arms and glancing at the floor. "But we can't let him see that we're onto him. Not yet. We have to keep gathering data, tracking his every move until we can go to the authorities with solid evidence."

The thought of pretending, of working beside him as if I don't know the truth, makes me sick. I don't know how long I can keep up the charade. But she's right. If we blow our cover too soon, we'll be back at square one, and he'll have a chance to bury whatever he's hiding.

Roxanne takes a deep breath, clearly thinking through every implication. "If it helps, I'll be with you every step of the way. We're in this together."

I nod, grateful even as I try to mask the pain and frustration in my chest. "Thanks."

But she doesn't stop there. Her brow furrows, and there's a spark of urgency in her eyes. "We should take the time we need for this. I know you need time to process the entire situation but remember, my life is on the line too. Every day we wait without a plan is a day I could be implicated."

"I know," I say it as steadily as I can manage. "I'm not letting anything happen to you, Roxanne. But I need to clear my mind before doing something stupid. My feelings are all over the place, and I don't trust my reasoning right now."

She studies me, her eyes filled with that same frustration from before. After a long pause, she finally lets out a sigh. "You're right. I just…I needed to hear that you're considering my situation too."

The room is silent, filled with tension. Slowly, she gives a nod as if assessing our options and agreeing with me. I can tell it's hard for her—she's as restless as I am. We don't have time to waste, but at the same time, we can't rush our steps. It's a frustrating situation, to say the least.

"We'll do it your way, Leonard," she says quietly. "Just promise me, when the time comes, we won't hold back. We'll make sure Oliver gets exactly what he deserves."

I nod, tightening my jaw, while the determination solidifies in my gut. "He'll answer for this. I promise."

But when I say it out loud, the ache in my chest sharpens. This isn't just about justice. This is personal. The betrayal has shattered something deep, something I'll never fully get back together. And I'm not sure what's worse—the fact that Oliver did this or that I didn't see it coming.

28

ROXANNE

Leonard's home office is dimly lit, filled with the faint scent of cedar and leather and the quiet hum of electronics buzzing. I'm curled up over his laptop, scrolling through screens of data, each line of code and bank statement leaving me more baffled than the last. I can feel Leonard pacing behind me with heavy steps that no doubt mirror the weight in his chest. He is like a raging storm.

He's not saying much. Since we discovered what Oliver did, he's become more distant and a far cry from the confident, decisive man I've known. It's not like him to be this quiet. Normally, he would be making plans, delegating, and taking charge. But now he just watches silently as I sift through the wreckage his friend left behind. This is why we are working from home. I'm not confident he would handle Oliver well if they met in the office.

I type a few commands, pulling up some logs from the server. Each new line of information adds a weight to my chest. I know this is tearing him up inside, but he won't let me in. He's bottling everything, locking it all away behind that blank face. I wonder how much more he can take before he breaks.

"Leonard," I say, glancing up at him, hoping to coax even a hint of the old him back. "We're going to figure this out. It's just going to take time."

He doesn't respond immediately. His jaw tightens, and he crosses his arms, looking out the window with a distant stare. "Time," he says finally with a low rumble. "I don't know if we have time."

I want to reach out, to reassure him, but there's something in his expression that tells me to keep my distance. This betrayal has wounded him in a way I can't fix. All I can do is keep going, keep piecing the puzzle together. Help him find the truth and hope for the best.

I return to the screen; my fingers move quickly across the keyboard. Pulling up another log, I see more encrypted files buried deep in the server—Oliver's files. I recognize the encryption, something only Oliver would use, hidden so well it's almost as if he dared anyone to find it. My stomach churns as I enter the decryption keys

Leonard found earlier. I have a feeling I'm not going to like what I will discover.

"What's that?" Leonard asks, moving closer, his voice raspy.

"It looks like he's been hiding entire batches of sensitive data," I say, keeping my voice calm. "Data we didn't even know was at risk. Stock market reports, upcoming mergers… It's not just sensitive information. It's crucial for the future of each one of your companies."

I glance back at Leonard, gauging his reaction. He nods slowly, his lips pressed into a thin line, but there's a darkness in his eyes I haven't seen before. "Inside information," he murmurs. "It's worse than I thought."

I click through more files, and the picture becomes increasingly clear and devastating. There's a pattern to the data he's been pulling, all focused on upcoming mergers and financial moves, the kind of information that could make someone millions if used the right way, like in the stock market, for example. Oliver knew exactly what he was doing. And then I see it, a record of offshore transactions, small at first, then escalating in size, all tied to accounts in the Cayman Islands.

My heart sinks. "Leonard, these funds… They're all heading to an offshore account."

He moves closer, leaning in to see the screen. His face pales. "What are you saying? He's stashing money overseas?"

I nod, swallowing hard. "This isn't just a breach. This is inside trading, Leonard. And the amounts are enormous. We're talking about an entire fortune. Millions, if not billions." I click through the records, my fingers moving faster as more files open up. Each one confirms the same thing—Oliver's been using the company's secrets to trade on insider knowledge, and he's accumulated a fortune for himself.

Leonard lets out a long breath, his hands clenching into fists at his sides. "The entire time I thought he was struggling after the divorce. Instead, he was..."

He doesn't finish the sentence, but he doesn't have to. I can see the hurt in his eyes, the betrayal that runs deeper than any business deal gone wrong. This isn't just about money for Leonard. It's about trust and loyalty— things he values more than anything else. And now, everything is shattering before his eyes.

"And there's more." I take a shaky breath, scrolling through the latest transactions. I hate to be the one to give him this information. "He's been selling this information. It's not just for him." The words come out heavy with implications. My stomach churns, I hate to kick him when he's down, to be the one that dismantles, piece by piece, years of friendship and trust.

He freezes, his gaze darkening as the words sink in. "He's been selling our secrets?" His voice is so deep and raspy I barely recognize it.

I nod, nauseated that I have to confirm it. "The records show he's been in contact with multiple parties. It looks like he's shopping your proprietary information around to anyone who can pay. Competitors, brokers... you name it." How could someone betray everything they worked for? Did Oliver ever care for this company, for what they built? It's his company too, for Pete's sake!

Leonard's face goes pale, and for a moment, I worry he might be sick. He sits down heavily in the chair beside me, his head in his hands, and I can feel the weight of his pain filling the room.

"I trusted him with everything," he whispers, more to himself than to me. "He was my friend. One of my *best* friends. We built this company together. How could he do this?"

I don't have an answer. My mind and heart can't comprehend it. Betrayal is the worst thing you can do to a person. I don't know what to say. I can feel his pain, raw and exposed, and it aches to see him like this. Leonard has always been the strongest person I know, unbreakable and confident. But right now, he looks shattered, like the pieces of him are barely holding together.

I reach out, my hand hovering over his shoulder, and for a second, I hesitate. But then I press it down gently, offering what little comfort I can. "Leonard... This isn't your fault. You couldn't have known."

He lets out a bitter laugh, lifting his head to look at

me. His eyes are red-rimmed, a mix of anger and devastation. "I should have seen it. I ignored the signs. I knew he was acting strange, but I kept giving him the benefit of the doubt. And now—" He stops, taking a shaky breath. "Now everything we've worked for could be destroyed."

"No," I say firmly, meeting his gaze. "We're not going to let that happen. We're going to stop him. We're going to make sure he answers for this."

He stares at me, the pain in his eyes softening just a little. "How, Roxanne? We have no proof of his intentions, just traces of transactions and encrypted files. If we go to the authorities now, they could tear the company apart while they investigate."

I pause, biting my lip. He's right. This is delicate. We're standing on a razor's edge, and one wrong move could ruin everything. "We need to keep gathering evidence," I say finally. "We can't make a move until we have everything in place. If we're careful, we can track every transaction, every piece of data he's sold. Once we have that, we can take it to the authorities without risking the company."

He nods slowly, his expression hardening as he regains some of his composure. "You're right. We have to be patient. As much as I want to confront him now…" He clenches his fists, the anger in his eyes sparking again. "He's not getting away with this."

The resolve in his voice makes me feel a spark of hope. Leonard may be down, but he's not defeated. He's a fighter, and I know he won't let Oliver's betrayal break him so badly as to admit defeat. Still, I can't shake the worry rising in my chest. My life is on the line here too, and every day we wait feels like a risk.

"Leonard," I say quietly, looking him in the eyes. "I'm with you in this. But promise me you will consider *my* position here. If we fuck up, I am implicated. The FBI doesn't care about feelings—they'll throw anyone under the bus to get a conviction."

He nods, understanding. "I know. I won't let that happen to you. As cold as my heart has gotten in the last few days, it's not *that* cold. Somehow, you manage to sneak in there and make sure it's warm, no matter what."

I couldn't believe it was possible, but the tender side of Leonard suits him almost as much as the mogul side. His words give me a momentary relief. We have to be methodical and patient. But as I look at Leonard, seeing the strain on his face, the tension in his shoulders, I can't help but feel a surge of determination. I'm not going to let Oliver ruin his life, not after everything we shared. This became personal the moment I confessed my feelings for him. It's time to admit to myself that this thing between us is not just temporary.

I stand, forcing myself to keep my voice steady. "I'm

making some sandwiches, and then we'll tackle every single file on that server."

A spark of something fierce lights up in his eyes, and he gives me a nod, a hint of the old Leonard returning. "Thank you. For everything."

I nod back, feeling a sense of purpose settle over me. I don't know how long it will take, or what else we'll uncover, but one thing is clear: we're in this together, and we won't stop until justice is served.

29

LEONARD

Raphael's house looms large as we drive toward the fountain in front of it. I can feel the tension radiating from Roxanne beside me, her fingers tapping a quick rhythm on her thigh. She's been quiet since we left, but I can sense her mind working a mile a minute, turning over every detail we've uncovered about Oliver's betrayal.

"Ready?" I ask, even though I'm not sure I am. Roxanne just nods, her face set with determination, a quiet fierceness that's been both my strength and my torment these past few days.

Raphael opens the door himself, letting us in with a grim nod. The smell of fresh coffee fills the air, mingling with the sharp scent of flowers coming from his garden. He gives me a worried look. His eyes study me in that protective way he has before his gaze shifts to Roxanne. "You two look like you could use a drink," he says, only half-joking.

"Not yet," I reply. "We need to keep our heads clear for this."

Raphael leads us through the house to a cozy room. In it, a man in his forties, wearing a suit that somehow manages to look both professional and worn-in, is seated on a cream couch. He stands as we enter, offering his hand with a polite smile.

"Leonard, Roxanne, this is Agent Harris," Raphael says. "He's here to help us...theoretically."

"Pleasure to meet you both," Agent Harris says, his voice smooth and professional, though there's a spark of humor in his eyes that tells me he's used to working around the system when necessary.

I take his hand, nodding. "Thanks for meeting with us. We... Well, we're in deeper than I ever expected."

He gestures for us to sit. "From what I understand, it's complicated. Raphael gave me a brief overview, but I'd like to hear it from you. And please, keep in mind that anything we discuss today is purely hypothetical."

Roxanne and I exchange a glance. I know he's saying this because we need to trust him with the information that potentially incriminates us both, but it's a massive leap of faith to even have this encounter. I take a steadying breath before diving into the details. I recount everything we've uncovered about Oliver—his transactions, the encrypted files, the offshore accounts. My voice doesn't shake, but it feels strained, tight with the hurt and anger that keep fighting their way to the surface. This is my friend, my partner. I had trusted him with everything.

Agent Harris listens carefully, nodding from time to time. When I finish, he leans back, considering. "Hypothetically speaking," he says slowly, "you're looking at serious charges here. Inside trading, corporate espionage, not to mention potential sales of classified information. But without concrete evidence, it's all circumstantial."

I tense, feeling the frustration building. "That's why we're here. We need to know what kind of evidence would hold up in court. And…how to get it without tipping him off."

He smiles a bit at that, a glint of respect in his eyes. "Smart approach. If you move too soon, he could cover his tracks, and you'd be left with nothing. What you need, again, theoretically, is a confession."

Roxanne shifts beside me, crossing her arms. "How are we supposed to get him to confess? Oliver's not stupid. He'll be careful about what he says to anyone involved with the company."

Agent Harris nods. "Which is why it's best if the confession isn't coerced. But if there's a way to get him to speak about his actions, perhaps by feigning ignorance or using a third party, he wouldn't suspect…that might work."

"So, we set up a meeting?" I ask, though the thought of confronting Oliver face-to-face after everything I've discovered feels like taking a bullet. The man was practically my brother. Now I don't know what he is.

"Hypothetically, yes," Harris replies. "A meeting where he feels comfortable enough to let something slip, obviously recorded. However, you need to be aware of the legalities here. In most states, if only one person consents to the recording, it's admissible. But since you're potentially involving the FBI, it's better to keep everything above board."

I let out a breath, rubbing my temple. "So, what are you saying?"

He raises a brow. "Theoretically, if an FBI agent were aware of this operation, the recording could be made legally admissible in court. Conveniently, you have one here right now."

A bit of the tension loosens as I meet his gaze, the corner of his mouth quirking in a small smile. For the first time, I feel a feeble spark of hope. This is a plan that could actually work.

"I'll need to be there to oversee the process," Harris continues, "and to ensure everything is done by the book. But if you play your cards right, you could have a solid case. That said, it might take time to get Oliver comfortable enough to speak freely."

"Time," Roxanne says, her voice dripping frustration. "We don't have a lot of it. My life is basically in a choke hold until we clear this up, and every day we wait, I'm another step closer to being implicated."

Agent Harris nods, looking at her with sympathy. "Understood. But rushing into this could jeopardize everything, especially your own position. Right now, Oliver is a clear primary suspect. If we can bring him in with solid evidence and link him to others who bought the information, you'll have a better chance of keeping your name out of it."

I can see the weight of his words settling on her. She's restless, and I don't blame her. This entire situation is pulling us both apart, each in our own way.

Raphael speaks up then, his tone serious. "If we're going to do this, we have to do it right. Leonard, you know what's at stake—not just for you, but for Roxanne, for the company. If there's even a shadow of a doubt about the legality of our actions, it could ruin everything."

I nod, feeling the full burden of responsibility pressing on my shoulders. I know Raphael's right. We have to be careful and strategic. But it doesn't make the anger burning in my chest any easier to deal with.

Agent Harris continues, "Now, there are some

specifics you'll need to prepare for. Does Oliver have any reason to suspect you've discovered his actions?"

I glance at Roxanne, and she steps in, her voice steady. "No. He knows that we're digging into the problem, but as far as we can tell, he thinks everything is well hidden. Leonard and I have been working privately, so there's no reason for him to suspect anything yet. He still thinks he's framing me."

Agent Harris nods approvingly. "Good. Keep it that way. The fewer people who know, the better. What we need is to catch him off guard and get him talking, naturally. Even a hint of pressure might tip him off."

I clench my fists, forcing myself to stay calm. The betrayal still stings, twisting like a knife in my gut. Oliver, the man I'd trusted with everything, was willing to risk it all—for money, for power. I feel Roxanne's gaze on me, a mix of concern and understanding in her eyes, and it helps to steady me.

Harris continues, "When it comes to the recording, there are a few technical details to consider. We'll need a clear connection, ideally with minimal interference, to make sure every word is captured cleanly."

Roxanne steps in again. "I can set up a discreet audio system. I have experience with wireless surveillance tech, so I can ensure we're getting a high-quality recording."

Harris raises his brows, impressed. "You know what

you are doing. Good to have someone with technical expertise on the team."

Roxanne just nods, but I can see a spark of pride in her eyes, and it brings a flicker of a smile to my face. Even in the midst of all this, her strength and determination shine through.

"So, once we have a recording," I say, bringing the conversation back on track. "What then?"

Harris leans forward, his expression serious. "If Oliver implicates himself clearly enough, we move to secure him and gather the rest of the evidence from his devices. That's when we'll bring in the bigger fish—the buyers of the information, the people who enabled his actions. The more connections we can trace, the better your position will be."

Roxanne's face tightens, but she nods. I know she's frustrated by the wait, but I can see that she understands the necessity of it. "We already have more than a few names from the files we discovered. I think he's making sure nobody speaks about it, using proof of their involvement as leverage."

Harris nods, a small smile appearing on his face, like this news is particularly interesting for him. "Good, knowing who we're targeting will make our job easier."

"Leonard," she says, turning to me, her voice soft but resolute. "We'll get through this. You built this company, you can save it."

Her words ground me, and I feel a rush of gratitude mixing with the bitterness. The betrayal of a friend cuts deep, but I have people who believe in me and are willing to stand by my side.

Agent Harris stands, a look of determination on his face. "We'll need to coordinate this carefully. I'll make the arrangements to oversee the recording, and we'll set the meeting as soon as possible."

I rise, feeling the weight of the situation settling on my shoulders. There's a long road ahead, but for the first time, I feel like we have a plan and a way forward.

As we leave Raphael's house, I look at Roxanne, the confidence in her gaze giving me hope and strength. No matter what lies ahead, I know I won't be facing it alone. And as painful as Oliver's betrayal is, it's nothing compared to the loyalty and support of those who've stood by my side in this situation. Maybe something good will come from all this chaos in the shape of a blond, stubborn woman.

30

ROXANNE

After we leave Raphael's place, the tension between Leonard and me is so thick and tangible I could reach out and touch it. The silence on the car ride back is heavy and filled with everything unsaid between us. I can feel his presence beside me, a steady warmth that I find strangely comforting, even as the heaviness of what we've just discussed weighs on both of us.

By the time we get to my place, it's late. Leonard parks in front of my building, his hands gripping the wheel with a bit too much force, staring forward as if the house itself might have the answers to all our problems. I reach over, putting my hand gently on his arm. "You don't have to stay," I say softly, though part of me hopes he will.

He looks at me; his face is closed off, but his gaze is intense, searching mine. "I don't know if I could leave right now, even if I wanted to," he replies, his voice coming out in a low rumble. There's a vulnerability there, a crack in his armor that reaches something deep inside me.

"Come in," I say, hearing the hint of longing in my own voice. I slip out of the car and head up to my door, hearing his footsteps close behind me.

Inside, the house is dark, the only light streaming in from outside. It's quiet, as if the apartment itself is giving us a rest from what we've been dealing with. I turn on a lamp, and the soft glow spills across the room, making it feel almost cozy and safe. Leonard stands in the doorway, his eyes sweeping over the room as if he's committing every detail to memory. I regret not telling him sooner about moving here. Now I realize my mistake. I should have trusted him with this information.

He looks exhausted, but more than that, there's something else—a deep devastation that's like a raw wound. His shoulders sag, his usually confident posture crumbling under the weight of betrayal. I feel a wave of sadness for him, for everything he's going through, for how much he's been forced to carry on his shoulders. I step closer, letting my hand rest on his chest.

"Leonard…" I don't know what to say. Finding the

right words to offer comfort feels impossible when there's no easy solution, no quick fix.

He turns to me, and his eyes catch mine. For a moment, it's as if the walls he keeps so carefully constructed around himself just crumble. He's not the mogul, the CEO, the one who built an empire. He's just Leonard, someone hurt and betrayed, someone who's trying to stay strong even when the world seems determined to pull him down.

"Roxanne..." he murmurs, his voice barely a whisper, as if speaking my name is an effort he can barely pull off. There's a pause, a beat where everything stills, and then he reaches for me, his hand cupping my cheek with an unexpected gentleness, his thumb brushing against my skin, tracing a line that sends a shiver through me.

I close my eyes, leaning into his touch and savoring the warmth that radiates from him. When I open them again, he looks at me with an intensity that leaves me breathless. It feels as though the distance between us is nothing, as though the weight of everything we're dealing with falls away, leaving only this fragile, electric connection.

I tilt my head up, closing the remaining space between us, my lips finding his in a tentative, lingering kiss. He hesitates for a moment, his hand still cradling my face as if he's afraid to let himself feel anything. But then he deepens the kiss, his fingers tangling in my hair, his other hand finding its way to my waist, pulling me closer.

It's like everything we've been holding back, all the tension, all the unspoken words, comes pouring out in that kiss. My hands find their way to his shoulders, clutching the fabric of his shirt as if it were the only thing keeping me grounded. I can feel his heartbeat beneath my fingertips, strong and steady, and it's that rhythm that I cling to as his lips move against mine, slow and searching like he's savoring every second.

He breaks away just long enough to rest his forehead against mine, his breathing heavy, his voice barely a murmur. "I don't know what I'd do without you."

His confession is raw and exposes all his vulnerability. We've had sex many times before tonight, but this feels different and special. Like something shifted between us, something deeper and more grounding than the intimacy between our bodies. This time, our hearts entwine, bridging the space between our souls.

"I don't know what I'd do without you either," I whisper back.

"Are you sure?" he asks, as though he's uncertain that something like this could happen, like he expects some sort of betrayal from me too. My heart breaks for him. He is so wounded by all that's happening he has to ask the question out loud to ensure he trusts the right person.

I nod, unable to form the words. I'm more sure of this—of him—than I've been about anything in a long time.

He lifts me effortlessly, carrying me toward the couch, lowering me onto it with a tenderness that almost undoes me. He hovers above me for a moment, his gaze tracing every inch of my face like he's trying to commit it to memory. I reach up, my fingers skimming along his jaw, feeling the roughness of his stubble beneath my touch.

He leans down, pressing his lips to mine once more, his kiss deepening, his hands exploring the curve of my waist, the arch of my back. His touch is both gentle and possessive, a reminder that, in this moment, we're both exactly where we want to be.

I unbutton his shirt slowly, savoring his gaze that skims every inch of my body. I run my fingers across his chest, resting my palm on his hammering heart. The same heart that broke into a thousand pieces but still hammers for me, for us, in this bubble we are living in right now. He deserves this moment. We deserve to be happy, even if for a few hours. Tomorrow, the problem will chase us with a vengeance, but for now, we are here, safe and happy, sharing this intimacy.

Leonard grabs the hem of my shirt and pulls it over

my head. He then takes my shorts and slips them down my legs, leaving them on the floor. He bends over me and kisses his way down from my jaw to the swell of my chest, slowly, oh so slowly, savoring my skin, every breath that catches in my throat, every goosebump that arises under his touch.

He takes his time, allowing us all the time we need to be happy. There is no rush, no consuming lust, but a strong, steady beat that accompanies our hearts.

I can feel the weight of him above me, the warmth of his skin against mine, and everything else—the betrayal, the tension, the fear of what comes next—fades away. There's only this, only us, tangled together, finding peace in each other in a way that feels both inevitable and absolutely right.

His hand slides beneath my panties, his fingers tracing a path along my opening, leaving a trail of fire in their wake. I arch into him, my own hands exploring the expanse of his back, the strength in his shoulders. There's a desperation in our movements, a need to hold onto something real, something solid, amidst the chaos.

When he slips his hard erection deep into my core and we move together, there's a sense of release, of letting go of everything that's been building between us. His touch is like a balm, soothing the raw fear and grounding me in a way that nothing else has. I can feel his heartbeat, strong and steady, a rhythm that matches my own.

I wrap my legs around his and move to meet his thrust, knowing that here, with him, is the only place I want to be. And when the climax hits me with wave after wave of immense pleasure, I wrap my arms around his neck and pull him into my chest. His arms wrap around my waist in response.

"Don't let me go," I breathe in his ear. And I don't mean just now. I don't want to slip between his fingers when this storm ceases and the sun shines again.

"Never, I will never let you go," he says, staring straight into my soul, and I know he means it.

We lie tangled together on the couch, breathing slowly, our hearts returning to a normal pace. His arm is wrapped around me, holding me close, and I rest my head against his chest, listening to the steady thrum of his heartbeat. There's a quiet peace in the room, a sense of calm that feels almost fragile, like it might shatter at any moment. But for now, it's enough.

He brushes a strand of hair away from my face, his fingers lingering against my skin. "Thank you," he murmurs, his voice soft but filled with a depth of emotion that surprises me.

I lift my head to look at him, studying the lines of his face, the vulnerability that lingers in his eyes. "For what?"

"For being here," he says simply, his hand tightening around mine. "For not walking away."

I smile, feeling a warmth bloom in my chest. "I couldn't even if I tried," I reply, my voice barely a whisper. And it's true. No matter how complicated things get, no matter how tangled our lives become, I know I'm here for the long haul.

31

LEONARD

In the anonymous, plain hotel room, I adjust my headphones, fighting back the urge to smash my fist into the table. Oliver's voice drifts through the earpiece, calm and almost cheerful, as if he's discussing the weather. He's way too relaxed for someone committing a federal crime. How many times has he done this? How long has he been passing information behind my back, taking everything we built together and selling it to whoever would pay his price?

Beside me, Roxanne is facing the monitors, her expression intense and focused. Her fingers tap lightly on the table, betraying a tension as she listens. She glances my way from time to time. Her eyes scan my face as if she's checking to make sure I'm holding up. I can feel her worry, her silent encouragement, but it only makes the anger in me burn hotter because I'm here, powerless, while my world crumbles.

On the other side, Raphael sits with a deep scowl, his arms crossed over his chest and his eyes locked on the screen. Harris, the FBI agent, monitors the recording. His face is unreadable but professional as he takes notes. This is routine for him, just another case, just another criminal to put behind bars. But for me, this isn't just about justice or even business—this is a betrayal on the deepest level.

The audio comes through clearly, and we hear Oliver's voice again. He's talking to another man, our so-called "first buyer," who decided his freedom is more valuable than more money. They've set this up to look like a typical transaction, the man who bought the information in the first place pretending to act as the intermediary for a new client who's supposedly interested in our data. The first buyer has immunity now, thanks to a deal with the FBI, so all we need is for Oliver to give them the stolen data and a real exchange of money through his computer. Once it's done, they'll seize his device, securing every damn piece of evidence.

I grind my teeth as Oliver's friendly tone comes through the headphones. It's the same voice he used every day in the office, the same voice he used to assure me that we were in this together. And now he's selling all our secrets—my secrets, of the companies *I* built from scratch without him—like it's nothing. My fingers curl into fists, and my pulse roars in my ears. If I go in there right now, it will take everything Harris and Raphael have to keep me from tearing him apart.

Harris glances at me, his brow furrowing slightly. "Leonard, you're doing fine. I know it must be difficult for you but we need this to be clean. You can't mess this up with some rash decision."

"Trust me," I mutter, "I'm trying very hard not to kill him."

On the screen, Oliver's face comes into view as he sets up his laptop. They're preparing for the transaction. Harris gives me a nod, indicating that they're doing exactly as planned. Roxanne's hand rests on my arm, a silent reminder that she's here with me, that she understands. It's the smallest gesture, but it grounds me and keeps me from doing something reckless.

I lean forward, my eyes fixed on the monitor, watching as Oliver's expression darkens. His eyes narrow with concentration as he initiates the transfer. I can see the familiar interface on his laptop, the same one we designed together in the early days, back when we were nothing more than two friends with a shared vision and enough stubbornness to keep going when no one else believed in us.

And now he's using that same interface to betray me.

It feels surreal as we watch the transaction going

smoothly. Oliver types a few keys. He's almost smirking as the guy initiates the money transfer—a lot of money. The buyer plays his part like his life depends on it— which is actually true, considering the situation. He acts excited, going so far as to flatter Oliver's skill. Oliver, a man I don't recognize anymore, takes pleasure in the praise, his ego clearly soaring more than ever.

"There we go," Oliver says smoothly, and a notif- ication pops up on the screen, confirming the transfer.

"Payment's cleared," the buyer says. "It's a pleasure doing business with you."

Oliver nods, a smug smile creeping onto his face. "If you need more, don't hesitate to contact me," he replies. I boil at the comment, but he has no idea he's just condemned himself.

Harris moves quickly, signaling to the FBI agents waiting outside the door. "Now," he murmurs into the radio connected to his men's earpieces. His voice exudes command.

In seconds, the agents work in a smooth, practiced motion that will put an end to this torture. I hear the muffled sounds of a door opening and the gasps of surprise through the earpiece. Oliver's indignant voice cuts through the audio, his protests filling the room as the FBI storms in, handcuffs him, seizes his laptop, and reads him his rights. I should feel relief, or at least some sense of closure, but there's nothing. Just an empty pain where there should be...something to fill the void. Disappointment grows in my chest, leaving a bitter taste in my mouth.

Harris switches off the audio, turning to me with a curt nod. "It's done. We have everything we need."

I stare at the empty computer screen, my mind racing to find something to say. I should be grateful—we've caught him and gathered the evidence we need to protect the company. But all I can feel is emptiness, like someone reached into my chest and ripped my heart out, leaving a hole in its place. He was supposed to be my friend, my partner, the man I trusted more than anyone else.

The room is silent for a moment, and the tension blinds me like a heavy fog. I feel like I'm gasping alone, trying to figure out what to do next. Roxanne turns to me, her hand reaching out to touch my arm again. "Leonard, you did the right thing."

I want to believe her, but it doesn't make it any easier. "Did I?" I ask, my voice sounding empty even to my own ears. "Because it sure doesn't feel like it."

Raphael speaks up, his tone gentler than I'd expect. "You didn't have a choice. He dug his own grave."

"Yeah, well, it doesn't make me feel better, especially because I don't understand why he did it. He had every-thing; he had my undying friendship. He could have asked and I would have given him anything he wanted, but still he decided to stab me in the back," I say bitterly. My mind is a storm of anger and sadness, a painful swirl of emotions that I can barely hold inside. I can feel the pressure building, the urge to lash out, to find some release.

Harris gives me a sympathetic look. "Leonard, I know this is hard, but sometimes people do things because they are just bad people. You could have given him the moon, and it wouldn't be enough. But I can assure you, he won't get away with it."

I nod numbly, but the words offer little comfort. How did we even get here? How did the man I thought I knew like a brother, like myself, become someone capable of this level of betrayal? Because he wasn't like this in the past. When we started out, he had such good intentions. I *know* him—or at least that's what I thought. Was it all a lie? I glance at Roxanne, seeing the worry in her eyes, and it cuts me even deeper. She's caught up in this mess too, all because of Oliver's greed and my blind trust.

She must see the storm brewing in me because she steps closer, never dropping my gaze. "We're going to get through this. You're not alone. I will be with you every step of the way."

Her words placate some of my anger, taking away some of the tension that grips my gut. I nod, trying to take in her calm words.

I take a deep breath, turn away from the monitors,

and force myself to regain some composure. "I just need a minute," I whisper in a broken voice.

Roxanne nods, watching me with an understanding that somehow steadies me. I head toward the window, looking out, trying to find some escape from what I've just witnessed. Everything just turned upside down.

Behind me, I hear Raphael and Harris talking, discussing the next steps and the logistics of the investigation. But it all feels distant, like background noise that I can barely hear.

It's only when Roxanne comes up beside me that I finally feel a spark of something. She stands beside me in silence, her presence calming the turmoil brewing inside me. She doesn't say anything, doesn't push me to talk or pretend I'm okay. She just lets me be, giving me the space I need, and somehow, that's enough.

After a while, I turn to her, the weight of guilt crushing my chest. "I should have seen this coming," I admit, the words taste bitter in my mouth. "I should have known."

She shakes her head, her gaze never leaving mine. "Leonard, no one could have predicted this. You had a reasonable explanation for his odd behavior. You trusted him because he was your friend. That doesn't make you weak—it makes you human."

I want to believe her, but the guilt crushes me. It constantly reminds me how badly I've fucked up judging the man I once considered a brother. "Maybe. But it still doesn't change what happened."

"No," she agrees softly, "it doesn't. And it doesn't make it easier for you. Give yourself time to grieve this situation and the friendship that you lost. You are a person with a big heart, and it will take time to heal it." She puts a hand over my chest, where my heart is beating erratically.

We stand there in silence, and for the first time, I allow myself to acknowledge the hurt, the betrayal, the defeat I can't avoid. Roxanne's words resonate in my mind, calming the spiraling thoughts. I need time to heal, and this time, the strength is coming from her.

When we finally leave the hotel, Harris assures me that the evidence we've gathered will be more than enough to bring Oliver down. But even as we step out into the cool night air, the sense of closure feels out of reach. I'm not done; it's not a closed chapter for me, but I know where to start when it comes to healing my wounds.

Roxanne stands by my side; her hand slips into mine, and her fingers are warm and reassuring against my skin. It doesn't make the pain go away, but somehow, with her here, I feel a little bit stronger facing whatever comes next.

And for now, that will have to be enough.

32

ROXANNE

I stare out the window with my fingers wrapped around the mug of tea in my hands, comforted by its warmth. Silver's house feels like a safe haven, almost another world, far away from the chaos unleashed by Leonard and me. After Oliver's arrest, the news spread like wildfire on a windy day, and even this cozy living room, with its colorful sofas and bookshelves, can't dissolve the fear taking root in me.

Silver sits on the couch in front of me, watching me with that worried look only an older sister can give you —it's strange how this situation has brought us closer than anything else we've tried in the last few years. She's already sensed the fear I can't hide, but she waits, giving me time to gather my thoughts and explain my urge to come here.

I take a deep breath and break the silence. "It's…it's just that with the FBI involved now, I keep thinking about my past. I wonder how much they already know, or worse, what they're capable of finding if they really dig," I confess in a shaky tone.

Silver tilts her head, her gaze softening as she thinks about my words. "You weren't doing anything criminal. You were exposing corruption and hacking for good. It's not like you were profiting or hurting people. You're a white hat, that should count for something."

She's trying to be supportive, make me focus on the positive, but still, the feeling of dread is nagging me.

"That might be true, but it doesn't matter to the FBI, does it?" I ask because the anxiety I'm trying to reign in is eating me alive. "I'm a hacker, and if they're looking for a reason to accuse me of something, they could find it. Now that I'm neck-deep in this mess with Leonard and Oliver, all they need is an excuse to take me in. They could easily build a case, even if there's nothing there."

Silver leans forward, reaching across the coffee table to squeeze my hand. "Roxanne, listen. You've got Leonard and Raphael. Do you honestly think either of them would let the FBI come after you? They both have too much power and influence to let that happen. And Raphael didn't choose Agent Harris by accident. He trusts him."

I shake my head, releasing a shaky sigh. "I know

they'd try to protect me, but you don't understand. If the FBI decides to dig deeper, they have all the authority they need to do it. Even if Harris is on our side, they could still decide to seize me for questioning. The minute they start looking into my past, it could be over. They can twist anything I did to sound criminal."

Silver's eyes soften, her grip on my hand firm. "Roxanne, you're safe. I know that you don't believe me, but I trust Raphael when he says that Harris will keep your name out of it. They arrested Oliver a week ago and your name never came up, even though you worked with Leonard to get him behind bars. Not even to praise you for the outstanding job you did. Do you think that's a coincidence? That somehow *everyone* overlooked your part in it? And let's be honest, Leonard would never let that happen. You've seen how much he cares about you. Don't you think he'd do anything to keep you out of harm's way?"

A faint smile tugs at my lips despite the weight in my chest. She's right. Leonard has proven that he cares, that he's willing to go above and beyond to keep me safe, to shield me from the worst of this mess. He's stood up for me in ways I never expected—even when he has every right to be completely devastated by the turn of events. He's always thinking about me and my wellbeing.

"He's done so much for me," I murmur. "Even when

his life is crumbling, and his situation is worse than mine."

Silver's lips curve into a smile. "Of course he does. I don't know if you've noticed, but that man looks at you like you're the only person in the room. He'd walk through fire for you."

Her words hit me like a punch, and I'm overwhelmed by the implications. I know Leonard cares, but hearing it out loud from someone else makes me realize just how strong his feelings are. It's easy to forget, sometimes, in the craziness of these days. But Silver is right; Leonard has shown his protectiveness, his attempt to keep the worst away from me. The realization grounds me, bringing a sense of calm I haven't felt in days.

"You really think so?" I ask to have some sort of confirmation.

She raises an eyebrow. "I'm sure of it. He hasn't taken his eyes off you since all this started. And Raphael? He may be this big shot in politics, but he's just as protective of you. You've got two powerful men who won't let the FBI lay a finger on you, not without putting up a hell of a fight."

I sigh, sinking back into the couch, letting her words wrap my heart like a comforting blanket. "I want to believe that. But you know me by now. I can't just sit here and let other people protect me. I'm not used to other people fighting my battles."

Silver laughs softly, shaking her head. "That's the problem with you, Roxanne. You're so fiercely independent, but sometimes, it's okay to accept help. Leonard and Raphael—they're not just random people. They're people who care about you. And to be honest, they're a lot scarier to go up against than you are."

A laugh slips out before I can stop it, a little burst of relief breaking through the tension. "That's probably true," I admit. "Raphael can be terrifying when he's protecting someone he cares about. And Leonard…well, he's ruthless when he needs to be. And my pink hair doesn't help."

Silver nods, her gaze softening. "They wouldn't just protect you out of duty. They're doing it because you mean something to them. Especially to Leonard."

A warmth rises on my cheeks. I'm not blind to Leonard's feelings, or at least to the way he looks at me sometimes, like he's seeing past every wall I've built around myself. And I can't deny that I feel the same too, something I haven't felt for anyone else before. But I'm scared the timing is wrong—with all this betrayal, secrets, and danger.

But maybe I can trust him with this, let him guide me for once. It's scary but, at the same time, reassuring. I've always felt alone, battling the entire world, but now, for the first time in my life, I can trust other people.

"How did you do it?" I ask, struggling to put my

thoughts into words. "How did you trust Raphael so completely with your life? Weren't you scared?"

Silver gives me a small smile. "I was terrified, but I had no other choice. I tried to push him away, to run far from him, but he gave me every reason to stay. He showed me I was safe with him. And looking back now, I can see that I was safer with him than all by myself."

I nod, and a smile tugs at my lips. "Is this one of those moments where I look back and realize that it was all in my head and I should have been calm and collected?"

Silver leans back, watching me with a bit of amusement in her eyes. "Well, it's normal to feel scared. I would worry if you weren't, but you have to trust people who tell you everything will be fine. Because they can see the situation from the outside and think logically without fear interfering with their thoughts."

I take a deep breath, letting her words sink in. She's right. Leonard has shown that he's willing to fight for me and protect me even when it means putting himself at risk. These are not empty words; he actually kept my name out of this situation. And maybe I can allow myself to rely on him. I'm not facing this alone after all.

"So," Silver continues, her tone brightening, "are you going to keep denying you two are a couple? Because I don't believe it's just casual."

The question hangs in the air for a moment, but in the end, everything seems so clear. How didn't I notice this before? Am I so blinded by what is happening that I can't see past my nose?

"I think," I say slowly, meeting her gaze, "we are definitely a couple. I can see myself in it for the long run with this one." I've never felt so confident in my entire life.

Silver's smile widens. "I'm so happy for you two. I can't wait to plan the wedding!"

I bark out a laugh. "Well, now, don't rush things. I said I'm in it for the long run, not the white dress."

"It doesn't have to be white!" She winks at me, and I smile.

I can see the happiness in her eyes, and I don't want to ruin it for her. She had a rough life; I can let her dream for a bit if it makes her happy. I never thought I would get married, but I also never thought I would fall in love. In the last few months, I've discovered that I misjudged a lot of things in my life—and a lot of people too. I had a one-track mind, convinced I knew everything, that I already had everything figured out. I was wrong. I was so, so wrong. But the important thing is to learn from your mistakes and I think I'm on the right track for that.

I smile, feeling the last of my fears slowly start to fade. For the first time since this nightmare began, I feel like I can breathe again, like I can face whatever is coming with a little less fear and a little more faith. Because I'm not alone.

33

LEONARD

I sit across the cold, metal table in the prison's visiting room, my hands resting in front of me. The sterile, gray walls feel suffocating, as though they're watching and accusing everyone in this room. Oliver sits across from me with that same scowl I've seen on him lately. Unfortunately, now it's even deeper than before, and there's a disturbing coldness in his eyes. His cuffs clink as he shifts in his seat, shooting me a look dripping with anger and resentment.

Beside me, my lawyer is silent, watching Oliver with the detachment his job demands, as if he's just one more case he is dealing with. And across from him sits Oliver's lawyer, who leans back in an unimpressed manner, probably just studying the situation and trying to avoid getting involved in whatever's about to happen between us. I came here for one reason—to hear from Oliver himself why he betrayed me, throwing everything we built together into the garbage. But now that I'm face-to-face with him, I wonder if I'm ready for whatever version of the truth he's about to dump on me.

"Why?" I finally ask, my voice steady, my eyes fixed on his. I want him to see that he can't avoid confrontation this time. "Why'd you do it, Oliver?"

He scoffs, shaking his head. "Why?" he repeats, his voice full of bitterness. "You really don't know, do you?"

"No," I reply, keeping my tone calm, almost cold. "I don't. We had it all. Built it from nothing together. Did you want more?"

Oliver leans forward. His eyes harden as he studies me with something that looks like disdain. "That's exactly the problem, Leonard. We built something special. Something for the purpose of helping people, remember? We were going to protect innocents. We created this company to keep people safe, for those who can't do it on their own."

"I remember," I say slowly. "That's why I'm here, why the company exists. I haven't forgotten, Oliver."

He scoffs again, his expression twisting into something ugly. "You're so full of bullshit. You are so caught up in your empire that you've lost sight of everything we stood for. You started chasing money, prestige, power—

all these shiny distractions. You've turned what we built into just another corporate machine."

"That's not true," I reply, feeling the spark of frustration inside my chest. I snuff it out, trying to stay calm. "I expanded, yes. I started new ventures because I wanted challenges, to push my boundaries. I wanted to know what I was capable of, but I never stopped caring about what we do. My focus has always been on our first company...on protecting people."

Oliver's laugh fills the room. It's a loud and angry sound surrounding us with a chilling feeling of madness. "Protecting people? Really? Do you think that's what you're still doing? You're living in your own bubble, launching new companies, piling up cash, while the people who need help are left in the dust. How is that protection?"

"Just because I started new businesses doesn't mean I abandoned our original mission," I say, struggling to keep my composure. "I'm still fully invested in the cybersecurity company, still working to protect our clients, just as we always planned."

Oliver shakes his head, his expression full of scorn. "You're lying to yourself. You don't care anymore. You just want to be the king of everything, don't you? King of your own little empire."

The accusation stings, but I refuse to let it show. "Is that what you think?" I ask, my voice calm but also challenging. "That I'm some kind of power-hungry monster? You've known me for years, Oliver. You know what drives me, what my principles are. You're the one that completely lost contact with reality."

He narrows his eyes, and his mouth curls in disgust. "I thought I did. But somewhere along the way, you lost sight of what really mattered. While you were busy playing CEO, I was left to actually keep the business running, to fight for our clients, to keep the mission alive. Meanwhile, you were strutting to board meetings and going to that club with your billionaire buddies like that's all that mattered."

I feel the anger burn inside me like lava ready to explode, but I keep it contained. "I trusted you to run things because I knew you were the best person to do it. You didn't want any other responsibility; you just wanted to work on the products. I tried to give you the same opportunities that I had, and you refused to even consider them. Just because I expanded into other projects doesn't mean I abandoned our mission. I believed in you."

He leans back, arms crossed, his expression shifting to something colder, more calculating. "You can't see it, can you? You can't see how blind you are. You used to care about the people we were helping, but now you only care about building one company after another. A long time ago, you knew our clients by name; now, you don't even know our employees' names. That's what I couldn't stand. That's why I did it. I couldn't watch you destroy what we created."

His words sink in, and for a moment, I study his face, looking for the friend I once knew, the partner who stood by my side, who shared my dream. But all I see is a man consumed by resentment, someone who's twisted our past into something unrecognizable.

"I never lost sight of what we created. I just created something bigger. To help more people, to research new technologies, so we could lower our prices to reach more people in need," I say, feeling a sense of finality and realization filling my chest. "I expanded because I wanted to make an impact, to use our success to reach more people, to protect even more than just our clients. I kept my focus, but I wanted to do more. You're the one who lost sight. You're the one accumulating billions in offshore accounts, putting the clients you're so fond of at risk."

He lets out a bitter laugh, his gaze unyielding. "You think adding more zeroes to your bank account counts as making an impact? You think building an empire was the answer?"

I shake my head, feeling a calm settle into my bones. "No, but with all those zeroes, I helped a lot of people across many fields; I made a difference in the community we live in. I measure 'my empire' by the people I've helped and the lives I've made easier and safer. That's always been what mattered to me. What did you do with your money except spread it into other countries where the people that really need it can't reach it?"

He laughs bitterly, dismissing my words with a wave of his hand. "I was saving my family. I tried to ensure a future for the people I love. Don't judge me for where I decided to put the money."

For a moment, I feel a pang of guilt, wondering if there's truth in his reasoning. Maybe he needs that money for his family. I lost track of his personal life a long time ago. But from what I heard about his marriage, he's the one who destroyed it. Not me, not his wife. *Him.*

"Which family, Oliver?" I ask in a quiet tone. "The one that abandoned you? Your wife and your kids don't even want to talk to you because they're ashamed of what you did. They didn't even want to look me in the eyes when they told me they didn't know you were stabbing me in the back. The family that *I* put on a private plane to escape this hell before being torn apart by what *you* did? How do you think they're dealing with the fallout? Don't tell me you did it for your family because you know that's a massive pile of bullshit."

He looks away, his jaw clenched, and for a moment, there's a flash of something in his eyes—regret, maybe, or doubt. But it vanishes as quickly as it appears, replaced by a hardened mask of anger.

"I did what I had to," he says, his tone defiant.

"Someone had to put a stop to this madness. Someone had to make you see you've lost your way."

I stare at him, realizing there's nothing left to say. He's trapped in his own version of events, convinced he's the hero of his own story and that his betrayal was somehow justified. And in this moment, I feel a sudden, unexpected sense of closure fill my chest.

I came here hoping for answers, hoping that maybe there was a way to understand why he did it. But now I see that Oliver is lost, consumed by his own anger and resentment. He's chosen his path, and there's nothing I can do to change that.

"I didn't lose my way, Oliver," I say, rising to my feet. "I just kept going. And if you couldn't keep up, that's on you."

He glares at me, his expression twisted with fury and bitterness. "You think you're better than me? You think you're some kind of saint?"

"No," I say quietly, looking him straight in the eyes. "I just know who I am. And I know I didn't betray everything we worked for."

I turn away, feeling the weight of his betrayal lift from my chest. It's over. Whatever friendship we once shared is gone now, and it's not my fault. I came here to try to save something, anything at all, but there is nothing left for me to save.

As I step out of the visitor's room, my lawyer follows

silently, and I feel a strange sense of peace. I finally have clarity. There was nothing I could have done to save Oliver from himself.

It hurts to realize that the person I once trusted more than anyone else is gone, replaced by someone I don't recognize, someone who's chosen to view me as the enemy. But as painful as that realization is, it also brings relief and closure.

Walking out of the prison, I take a deep breath, letting the cool air fill my lungs. I'm leaving Oliver behind, leaving the betrayal and the anger and the bitterness in that cold, gray room. It's time to move forward, to focus on what I can still protect, what I can still save.

As I get into the car, I catch a glimpse of myself in the rearview mirror, and for the first time in a long time, I see someone who's certain of his path, someone who knows where he's going and why.

It's a long road, but it doesn't scare me.

34

ROXANNE

I sit on Leonard's couch, curled up beside him, both of us staring at the TV. The news blares in front of us, one headline after another scrolling across the screen, each one announcing a new name, a new arrest. The scope of the FBI's operation is jaw-dropping, spreading across cities and companies all over the country. It originated with Oliver's case, but the reach is far beyond anything I expected. Inside trading, stolen industry secrets, shady deals—all of it coming to light because of what Oliver had stashed on his computer. He's such a narcissist, he didn't think he could be caught so he kept everything in his possession.

We watch as the news anchor explains the latest updates, each name bigger than the last. A graph of Leonard's companies appears, the stock price going up and down because of the unpredictability of this situation. Leonard's hand is resting on the arm of the couch, his fingers drumming in a slow, steady rhythm, and through his calm expression, I can see the veil of worry behind his eyes. I place a hand on his arm, hoping it'll reassure him and remind him he's not alone in this.

He glances over at me with a small smile, though it's tainted with a worry he doesn't often show. "I know it's just a waiting game now," he says softly, his voice barely audible over the TV. "But it's strange. Even though I did the right thing, helped them bring him in, I can't shake this...uncertainty."

I nod, understanding completely. "This kind of thing never has a clear outcome. People will believe what they want to believe, even if you're on the right side. But the people who really matter—they know you're not tied to any of this. You helped the FBI because you have nothing to hide."

He shifts, turning his gaze back to the TV. The anchor has moved on to discuss market reactions, the stock prices fluctuating as more companies are implicated in the scandal. "I hope you're right," he murmurs, almost to himself. "But people are quick to doubt. They'll see my name with his, and some of them will wonder. I'm just a billionaire wanting more money, in their eyes."

I squeeze his arm. "They might wonder, but you've

built something that's more than just a name on the sign outside your building. People know you, they know your reputation. It's not so fragile that it'll just fall apart because of Oliver's mistakes. Also, every honest person in your circle, every mogul not dealing in shady business practices, will respect you for this. You put your company on the line to do the right thing. That counts for something."

He takes a deep breath, looking thoughtful, like he's trying to weigh my words. There's a hint of relief in his eyes, but the worry is still there. "Maybe," he says finally. "But it's hard to predict. The market, the board, the clients…all I can do is brace myself and deal with whatever comes next. Fix what I can, if there's anything left to fix."

Leonard's always been like this: calculated, prepared with a solution. But I know that no matter how much he prepares, he feels the weight of what he's built. Seeing it crumble would make anyone doubt the light at the end of the tunnel. Even someone as unshakable as him.

I rest my head on his shoulder, and he shifts, wrapping an arm around me. The news moves to a different story, but it doesn't matter. The atmosphere in the room remains thick with the heaviness of it all. Leonard's body is warm beside me, steady in a way that reassures me, even if I'm feeling some of that weight too.

"You'll figure it out," I say, my voice soft but certain.

"Whatever comes of this, however the market reacts, you'll handle it. You always do."

He lets out a quiet chuckle, the corners of his mouth lifting just a little. "I wish I had your confidence in me."

"Leonard," I say, pulling back slightly to look him in the eyes. "You've gone through difficult times before and survived. Because you are a capable person. You think just anyone could build an empire like you have? Plus, you're not alone this time; you have me, Raphael, and all your friends that have reached out in these few days. That's not nothing."

He nods, taking that in. "I know. It's just…Oliver and I built this together. There was a time I trusted him more than anyone. And now that he's gone, it feels like I'm watching pieces of the past crumble and disappear, things I thought would always be there."

I sigh, understanding that feeling all too well. Losing someone you once depended on makes you feel like the ground is going to disappear under your feet any moment. "You'll fill those holes with something new," I tell him, lacing my fingers with his. "Something that's just yours that you won't have to see crumble again. You've already proven you can start from scratch and become anything you want. It's the same now, only you just have to rebuild rather than starting from zero."

He looks down at our hands, his thumb brushing over my knuckles in slow circles. "You're right," he says quietly, almost to himself. "This isn't the end. It's just one more challenge. One more project to focus on."

"That's exactly it," I say, giving his hand a gentle squeeze. "A challenge. And challenges don't break you, Leonard. If anything, they make you stronger."

He chuckles again, a little lighter this time. "How do you know exactly what I need to hear?"

"Well," I say, leaning into him, "it helps that I believe every word. I admire you—for everything you have achieved *and* for the heart you hide behind those suits."

He smiles at me and raises an eyebrow. "Even when you thought I was a heartless asshole?"

I look up into his eyes, and I hope he believes every single word I want to say. "I was blind. I was so convinced I was right about everything that I didn't give you the benefit of the doubt. You're right when you say I was just a kid at my sister's wedding. I wasn't mature enough to understand the person right in front of me. I believed the gossip about you without spending one minute to check if it was true. I spent my days justifying my distrust in you instead of comprehending your reasons. I was wrong."

He smiles and kisses my head. "I'm happy you came to your senses," he whispers

"It was a long road, but I made it." I chuckle.

We're quiet for a long moment, letting my confession sink in. This is the first time I've ever admitted that I was wrong to someone else. I need to process this moment too.

"I'll figure it out," he says after a while as if trying to make sense of the thought in his mind. "If there's fallout, if there's anything to fix, I'll do it. I won't let his actions define what we've built."

"That's the spirit," I say, smiling up at him. "This *doesn't* define you. And no one who truly knows you would ever think otherwise."

He nods, the tension in his shoulders easing just a bit, and I feel a sense of relief settle over me too. It's strange, sitting here with him, watching his world all over the screen and Oliver's betrayal casting shadows over everything he built. But even with the weight of it all, I know he'll come through. He's too strong, too smart, too determined to let this bury him.

We sit in silence for a while, just listening to the news, letting the storm of this day settle around us. He leans down, pressing a soft kiss to my forehead, and for a moment, I close my eyes, letting myself just breathe him in. In the quiet of his home, it dawns on me how this event will disrupt my life too. I won't be the same, and I can't go back to my past life either. I've discovered a new world, and I confess that I like it more than the one I was in before. Even with its challenges, even if there isn't a straight road ahead, I want to see where this path will take me.

When I open my eyes, I see him watching me, his gaze full of gratitude and something else, something unspoken but heavy with meaning. And in that moment, I know that no matter what comes next, we'll face it together.

The news continues to buzz in the background, but it feels distant, belonging to another world. Right here, in this small bubble of peace and warmth, it's just the two of us.

35

LEONARD

'm deep into a document, staring at the projections for the next quarter, when the door to my office swings open. I look up, surprised, to see Roxanne standing there, a determined look on her face and an energy in her that I don't quite recognize. Usually, she'd call or knock, especially given how focused she knows I get during work. But today, she's here, unannounced, and I already feel my mood lifting just at the sight of her.

"Roxanne," I say, a hint of a smile pulling at my mouth. "Didn't expect to see you here. Did you miss me?"

She steps inside, closing the door behind her, and I can tell immediately that she has something on her mind. Her gaze is full of those big dreams she carries in her heart. She's not here for the advice I promised about how to build her own company, nor to check in on the aftermath of the Oliver case. No, this is something more. I push my laptop aside, giving her my full attention.

"I came here to talk," she says, her voice low but firm, "because I've been thinking about everything—about the company, what we've gone through, and where I fit into it all."

"Okay," I say, gesturing to the chair in front of my desk, but she shakes her head, choosing to remain standing. Her eyes are steady on mine, and I can feel the conviction in her even before she starts to speak.

"I don't want to have my own company," she says, and the words surprise me. "I mean, I thought I did. I thought that was my path, what I'd been working toward all this time. But these past months…everything we've been through together…it's shown me something I didn't expect." She pauses, taking a breath, and her expression softens just a bit. "I want to work with you, Leonard. Not alongside you, not as a competitor, or even just as a partner. I want to be part of what you're building here because I see now that we share the same ideals and the same morals. And together, I think we could do great things."

Her words hang in the air, and for a moment, I just look at her, letting them sink in. Roxanne isn't someone who makes decisions lightly. She's calculated and thoughtful, and for her to come to me like this, to tell me that she wants to be part of what we're doing here—it's massive. More than that, it's humbling.

I lean back in my chair, taking her in, trying to gauge her thoughts. But there's no doubt in her eyes, no hesitation. She's thought this through.

"Roxanne," I begin, choosing my words carefully, "you know the company's going to feel the aftershocks of this trial for a while. Clients, the board, the media—everyone's watching us closely. We're not in the clear yet, and things are going to get difficult. This path isn't exactly a safe one right now."

She nods, taking a step closer, and I can see the determination on her face. "I know. I'm not here because I want an easy path. I'm here because I believe in what you're doing and because I believe in you." Her voice softens, but the conviction remains. "I've seen the way you handle this company, the way you handle the challenges, even when it would be easier to just walk away or let someone else take over. You haven't. And that tells me that your heart is still in the right place, no matter what's happened with Oliver."

She takes a breath, her gaze never leaving mine. "You care about people, Leonard. And you built this company to protect them, to make a difference. That's why I'm here. Because I want to do that too. And if you'll let me, I want to do it with you."

For a second, I'm stunned. This isn't what I expected when she walked in here. We've never talked about this outside the office, maybe because we're taking more time to enjoy life instead of drowning in work, but she's had time to think about it. A lot of time, when she was at home alone. To hear that she wants to stay, to stand by me, is more than I could have asked for.

"Roxanne," I say, and there's a heaviness in my voice I didn't mean to reveal, a vulnerability I don't often let surface. "I can't promise this road will be smooth. There's a lot of trust that needs to be rebuilt, and there will be days when it feels like everything's at risk. I'm honored you'd want to be a part of this, but I need you to understand that it won't be easy, and I don't want this to interfere with our personal relationship." This is what I fear the most, that it will split us apart.

She gives me a small smile, both gentle and firm. "I'm not worried about that, Leonard. I'm not worried about whether or not this will be easy. I'm not here for an easy job—I'm here because I believe in the work, and I believe in you. More than that, I *trust* you. I've thought a lot about our personal relationship, how we are moving toward something that will last for a long time, and I'm sure the reason why this isn't just a fling is because we share something deeper than physical attraction. We share the same heart and values, and until we're both on the same path with that, there's nothing that can shake our personal life."

Her words hold a weight that leaves me breathless. They are powerful and honest. She *trusts* me. After everything we've been through, after watching a close friend betray me, after seeing the cracks that Oliver left —she's telling me she trusts me. Knowing she has faith in me, in what we're doing, feels like a weight I hadn't even realized I was carrying suddenly lifting.

I stand, walking around the desk to stand in front of her. For a moment, we just look at each other, the silence stretching, filled with something that I can only describe as excitement. Then I reach out, taking her hands in mine and dragging her to my chest.

"I don't know what I did to deserve this kind of loyalty from you, but I won't take it for granted. I can promise you that. If you're serious about this, if you're ready to be part of this, then I want you by my side. I can't think of anyone better to help me rebuild and take this company forward," I say, my voice steady.

Her eyes brighten, and she squeezes me in a warm hug, a look of relief and satisfaction spreading across her face. "Then let's do it. Let's take this on together, whatever comes our way."

I release her but keep my gaze steady on her. "I can't promise it'll be smooth sailing," I say with a slight grin, feeling a weight lift as I realize how serious we both are about this. "But with you here, I feel like we might actually have a shot."

She laughs, a genuine, warm sound, and it fills the room with an energy that feels like a new beginning. "I don't need smooth sailing," she says. "I need a cause worth fighting for. And I know this is it."

"Plus, this means I get to see you every day. A perk I can't resist." I wink at her.

"Are you telling me you'll finally bend me over this desk and fuck me silly?" she purrs in my ear.

I let out a low growl as I grab her by her waist and turn to sit her on the desk. She squeals and chuckles at the same time while I slip between her legs. I crush my lips on her and deepen the kiss as her hands tighten around my neck and her body presses against mine.

I don't know what I did to deserve her, but I'm sure of one thing. I will never let her go.

EPILOGUE
ROXANNE

The sun is setting, casting a golden glow across the city skyline, and I watch it from the window of Leonard's office, where we've stood side by side through some of our hardest days. It's hard to believe that so much time has passed since those turbulent times, yet here we are, stronger and more in sync than ever. I smile, feeling a sense of peace settle over me, a peace we've fought hard for.

Leonard steps up beside me, wrapping an arm around my waist. "What's on your mind?" he asks, his voice low and warm.

"Just thinking about how far we've come," I say, leaning into him. "Everything we've built together."

He presses a soft kiss to my temple, and I feel the familiar surge of warmth that comes whenever he's close. We've been through hell and back and faced scrutiny from every corner of the world, but we never lost sight of each other—or our shared vision. Even in the worst moments, when the world seemed determined to break us, Leonard was a constant, just as he is now.

Rebuilding his reputation after Oliver's betrayal wasn't easy. We lost clients, faced endless media speculation, and sometimes wondered if we'd ever fully recover. But Leonard never faltered. His belief in what we were doing, his commitment to helping people, was unshakable. And with every step, he proved to the world —and to me—that he was exactly the man I'd thought he was.

Now, looking around at his office, filled with the signs of his accomplishments and our shared achievements, I feel a fierce pride in everything we've done. Not just in the empire we've rebuilt but in the love we've nurtured, in the partnership we've forged.

"I never thought I'd find this," I admit, my voice barely more than a whisper.

He pulls back slightly, studying my face. "Find what?"

"This…" I gesture around us. "This life. This love. A place where I belong, where we create something meaningful every day."

Leonard's smile softens, and he lifts a hand to tuck a strand of hair behind my ear. "You belong here,

Roxanne. And you've made this place what it is, just as much as I have."

It still feels surreal, sometimes, to hear him say things like that. I never wanted to find love. If anything, I'd been determined to follow my own path. But meeting Leonard, working with him, seeing his passion, his vision—somewhere along the way, I stopped seeing him as just a partner. He became my anchor, my safe harbor, and together, we created something even more powerful than I could have imagined.

"We're doing it, aren't we?" I ask, my gaze drifting back to the city lights. "We're making a real difference."

"We are," he says, pride evident in his voice. "And it's only the beginning. I've been thinking about expanding the safety surveillance program we started last year, maybe bringing it to a few more cities."

I turn to him, excitement sparking. "Really? That could be huge." I pressed for that—a public surveillance system to make the streets safer, especially for women.

He nods, his eyes bright with the same fire I saw in him from the start. "It could be. And with you by my side, I know it's possible. I think we've shown people that we're serious about this, that we're here for more than just profit."

We've spent years proving ourselves, not just to the public, but to each other. The fallout from Oliver's betrayal had cast a shadow over everything, and there were days when I wondered if it would ever truly clear. But Leonard never gave up, and that unwavering strength gave me the courage to stay focused, even when things seemed bleakest.

"Do you ever wonder," I ask, my voice soft, "what he would think? About where we are now?"

Leonard's face darkens slightly, and he lets out a sigh. "Sometimes. But then I remind myself that Oliver made his choices. He lost his way. And in the end, we had to move on."

I nod, understanding. There are still days when I feel sad, remembering the friend Leonard lost and the dreams they once shared. But we've found our peace, and I know that where he is now, he no longer holds power over us. We've reclaimed our lives, rebuilt from the ashes, and turned our shared vision into something even more beautiful.

"Hey," Leonard says, drawing me back to the present. "No more looking back, okay? No more sad faces."

I smile, nodding. "You're right. We've come too far to waste time sulking."

He takes my hand, intertwining our fingers, and we stand there in comfortable silence, watching the last light of the day fade. It's a simple moment, yet it feels like everything. It's our special ritual, the one we've shared every night since we started working together years ago.

We stand here, tall and proud of what we overcame and basking in the strength of our relationship that helped us withstand the storm. Without that, we wouldn't be here right now.

The sound of his phone buzzing breaks the quiet, and he gives me an apologetic look. "Probably another press inquiry."

I laugh, shaking my head. "You know, for someone who's cleared his name completely, you still seem to be the media's favorite topic."

He chuckles, rolling his eyes. "Guess I'm just irresistible."

I raise an eyebrow, pretending to consider. "You might have a point."

He squeezes my hand, and I feel a rush of warmth that's as familiar as it is thrilling. Every day with Leonard feels like a new adventure, a new chance to deepen the life we're building together. We've gone through more than most couples ever do, yet somehow, we're still here, stronger than ever.

"Let's get out of here," he says suddenly, his eyes alight with mischief. "It's been a long day, and I think we deserve a night off."

I raise an eyebrow, playing along. "Oh? And what do you have in mind, Mr. Walton?"

He leans in, his voice dropping to a low murmur. "You'll have to trust me."

And I do. More than anyone else in my life, I trust him. So I let him lead me out of the office, feeling a sense of exhilaration building as we step into the elevator together, hand in hand, ready to embrace whatever the night holds.

As the doors close, I catch one last glimpse of the city lights. I know there will be more challenges ahead, more moments when we'll have to fight to hold onto everything we've worked for. But standing here, next to Leonard, I feel ready for anything. We've already faced the worst—and we came out the other side stronger, together.

Whatever the future holds, I know one thing for certain: as long as we're together, there's nothing we can't overcome.

ACKNOWLEDGMENTS

And so, dear readers, we've reached the end of the Los Angeles Billionaires series. Leonard Walton, with all his brooding billionaire charm and surprisingly soft heart, marks the final chapter in this rollercoaster ride of love, drama, and scandal. But don't worry—I'll be back with new stories soon! You can't get rid of me that easily.

First, to my husband, Dario—thank you for putting up with my endless brainstorming sessions and for pretending to care about fictional billionaires and hackers while I muttered dialogue over dinner. You are truly the MVP (Most Valuable Partner) of this journey.

To my editor, Staci, who knows how to wield a red pen like a samurai wields a katana—thank you for making sense of my madness and ensuring Leonard didn't come across as a grump in a fancy suit (unless, of course, he needed to).

To Annalisa, my Italian editor, for helping me bring Leonard to life in another language. You've turned "grumpy hacker banter" into poetic prose. Grazie mille for your talent and patience!

And finally, to my readers: you've stuck with me through sexy billionaires, enemies-to-lovers drama, and all the swoony, spicy goodness in between. Thank you for every comment, review, and message—it's your love for these stories that keeps me writing. You are the real stars of this series, and I promise to bring you more swoon-worthy adventures in the future.

So, until the next book, dear readers, I raise a virtual glass to you. Here's to new beginnings, unforgettable characters, and (always) happy endings.

With love and a heart full of gratitude,

Erika

ABOUT THE AUTHOR

Erika Vanzin is the Italian Amazon bestselling author of the rock star romance Roadies Series.

After traveling around the world with her husband, she settled down in Seattle, enjoying the marvelous Pacific Northwest. She brought from Italy a couple of suitcases, fifteen boxes full of books, and her most successful novels translated into English.

While she is not writing, she enjoys reading books, watching the Kraken hockey games, and working on DIY projects.

Keep in touch with Erika via the web:

f facebook.com/erikavanzinauthor

○ instagram.com/clumsyeki

♪ tiktok.com/@authorerikavanzin

⑫ pinterest.com/ErikaVanzin

ⓐ amazon.com/author/erikavanzin

BB bookbub.com/authors/erika-vanzin

g goodreads.com/erika_vanzin

ALSO BY ERIKA VANZIN

Los Angeles Billionaires Series (Complete Billionaires Romance)

The Producer: Aaron

The Senator: Raphael

The Actor: Harrison

The Broker: Elijah (Novella)

The Mogul: Leonard

Roadies series (Complete Rock Star Romance):

Backstage

Paparazzi

Faith

Showtime

Betrayal